FALSE
FLAG

Also by M.G. Harris

The Joshua Files series

Invisible City

Ice Shock

Zero Moment

Dark Parallel

Apocalypse Moon

The Descendant Code

The Mind Game: Volume One

The Mind Game

FALSE
FLAG

M. G. HARRIS

DARKWATER

First published in 2025 by Darkwater Books
An imprint of Harris Oxford Limited.
41 Cornmarket Street, Oxford, OX1 3HA

ISBN 978-1-909072-62-6

TheMGHarris.com

'The Mind Game' logo design copyright Gareth Stranks

For Amber, my beautiful first grandchild.

Bug Out Plan

Something about his eyes gave it away. We have instincts for subtle warning signs, that's a fact. I'm learning to pay attention to any sketchy feelings I might get about a person. Then again, I'm probably more aware than most of what expressions a taxi driver sends my way. I'm obsessive like that, I watch the driver. In a taxi, I'm vigilant. You should be, too.

Well, I was in trouble. A forty percent chance of trouble, at least, and that's too high. If you were in a car that you knew had a forty percent chance of blowing up, would you get in? You wouldn't, right?

Luckily, I was in the best seat in the house. In case you don't know which one that is, it's in the back of the car, diagonally opposite the driver. When you sit directly behind, he can't reach back to grab you, that's true. But when you sit behind the driver you can't see where the taxi is going. On the diagonal you get to keep one eye on the taxi driver and one eye on where they're taking you. If he reaches behind to grab you or even with a knife, he still must have one hand on the wheel, one eye on the road ahead if he doesn't want to crash. So, he's going to be flailing. In that situation, your job is to have *your* left hand ready to grab *his* right hand and push it forward, while you keep staring ahead, eyes on the road.

Ideally, you checked *before* you took the ride that the door was not on child lock. Only a naïve idiot gets into a taxi without checking that the passenger door actually opens from the inside. Don't get offended; that's not such a huge confession, I was a naïve idiot myself only a few weeks ago. In fact, I'm pretty sure I didn't check the taxi on the way back from the airport, after Marc Mackenzie, a.k.a 'Kenzie' and I returned from Havana.

Anyhow, I was in the primo seat, when this particular driver began to veer wildly from the route I'd requested. That's another tip – always follow the route he takes, on your phone. How else will you know if your ride might be taking you where you don't want to go?

The driver did a swift check in the rear window, the instant before he took that left turn. I made the mistake of blanking him. You're supposed to make sure the driver knows *you* are fully aware of everything that's happening. You're not supposed to look like an innocent lamb being steered toward the barbecue.

One second too late, I remembered that I hadn't set out to become a lamb chop. I sidled closer to the rear passenger door, my right hand on the handle ready to open it, when the car slowed down. As we approached the traffic light, I put on my best innocent-lamb expression. The instant the car went into a crawl, I yanked the door open, leapt out and sprinted in the opposite direction.

Okay, I'll admit that the driver sounded genuinely shocked and dismayed at my rapid exit. It's *just* possible he wasn't trying to abduct me. But better to run than to sit in the back of a car, wondering whether you're going to end up with a bag over your head in some damp basement at the end of your ride. I've tried the bag-over-head option – cannot recommend it.

It took me almost two hours to walk back to the cabin; two hours through zero cell service, which of course made Zara and Bobbie almost desperate with anxiety. When I told them I'd used their training to almost certainly escape an abduction, they were significantly relieved. The calm lasted through dinner, but only the main course. By the time we got to dessert they'd already begun to question why I'd been identified by a taxi driver. Maybe we weren't as safe as they supposed?

Kenzie had said almost nothing so far, but he barked out a sardonic laugh at that. "Nobody is safe, anywhere. Not from Chekists."

Frankly, it was good to know he actually cared. We'd been hiding out in a cabin somewhere in the Shenandoah National Park, but other than allowing his moms to debrief the two of us after our trip to Mexico and Cuba, Kenzie had become entirely preoccupied with some new secret project, a project that entirely excluded me.

I don't know whether having his moms on board made our joint secret less exciting for him. For me it was a giant relief to have their support. Kenzie appeared indifferent. He retreated into his cyber world. Within a few days he'd begun talking about his new buddies online. When he talked at all, that is, when he wasn't glued to a screen.

Back when I started telling my story, we agreed to put a pin in the whole mystery of exactly what it was that had so absorbed Kenzie, back before my podcast about Maxim Santiago and everything that ensued. Well, the time has come to delve into all of that. Because bit by little bit, Kenzie was starting to spill the tea.

Zara and Bobbie had been our firm allies, from the minute we'd returned from Dulles International airport. They'd already packed bags and loaded up the car with groceries and toiletries. They gave us a few minutes to grab any last-minute items from the house in Falls Church, then made us get into the back of the SUV. Less than twenty minutes later, we were heading for the hideout.

That's right, I said 'hideout.' In the three days since we'd departed for Mexico and Cuba, Kenzie's moms had acquired a legit 'bug out location' – the place you run to when the world is ending. Or in our case, when Chekists are after you, whichever comes first.

I'm still surprised at how versatile his moms turned out to be. I would bet fifty dollars that most parents could not plan a bug out on two days' notice. Bobbie is pretty handy, and Zara has a natural level of paranoia that turns out to be ideal for when you actually *are* being chased by a foreign government, in our case Chekists, foreign intelligence agents of the Third Russian Empire.

Zara became hyper-vigilant from the moment we called from Mexico City airport to confess that we'd run away to find Maxim Santiago. She'd watch from the upstairs window until Bobbie replaced her with a webcam. After analyzing hours of webcam footage, they concluded that someone was driving the same blue Volvo past the house, every couple of hours. And that was enough for them to launch some almost-forgotten plan they'd made years ago, after Bobbie's furious ex, Nadine, tried to steal toddler-Kenzie. Their plan entailed running away to a cabin that belonged to one of Zara's friends.

Or at least that's what they told us – at first. The truth was more complicated. Isn't it always? But we'll get to all that.

We were having lunch in the garden behind the cabin, a small grass rectangle surrounded by dense, high hedges. Whoever had built this cabin took privacy extremely seriously. When Bobbie and Zara went back into the cabin to fetch dessert, Kenzie turned to me.

"That's some bullshit, right? The taxi driver story, you made that up, right? If the guy left the child lock unlocked, then it's highly doubtful he expected to abduct you."

"I didn't make it up," I told him.

Kenzie laughed briefly. Then he fixed me with a steady gaze, now serious. "I think we're good, Padi. Nobody's going to find us here. If they were, they would have done it by now."

"Oh yeah? What about 'No one is safe from Chekists?'"

He gave me a mischievous wink. "So maybe I embellished a little. If there's anywhere that's safe from Ilyin's goons, it's got to be the Great State of Virginia. Also, I like it here. Lake right on our doorstep, cool woodland trails. It beats Falls Church in summer. My moms can work from home, so it's not like we're seriously inconveniencing them. Just very chill. I'm getting time to think. Learn about new things."

This wasn't entirely news to me, given the screen-time he'd racked up, but he'd been guarded until now. "Anything in particular?"

Kenzie huffed out a sigh. "You could just ask me what I'm working on."

"I've asked you a bunch of times."

"Nah. You haven't. Oh sure, you tiptoe around the subject, but you don't ask. What do you think I'm doing? I'd love to know what's making you so suspicious."

"I assumed you were learning some new hacking techniques. And I figured the less I know, the less I can say when I have to testify."

"You're wrong." He seemed smugly satisfied at having misled me.

I sighed. "Fine, then what?

Kenzie's grin became glassy, forced. And he said nothing.

"Oh. I get it." (I didn't.)

"It's not hacking," he said eventually. "But it's not entirely legal either. So, if that's why you haven't been asking me directly, maybe it's a good tactic."

I hesitated. "Is this something important?"

He nodded.

"Then I support you. Anything I can do to help?

He thought for a moment. "Not right now. But I appreciate the offer." He gave me a warm smile.

"For what it's worth," I said, suddenly realizing that I had to speak up on this, "I do think that taxi driver was sus. I get your point about the child locks, but I'm pretty sure the guy could have turned on the child locks the moment he realized I was getting suspicious. I honestly don't think he realized I was on to him. Not until it was too late."

His eyes widened in something like admiration. "Nice going, Padi. No wonder my moms seem so happy. They'll be stoked to know their training paid off."

I wasn't so sure. Until now, the bug-out plan had felt like a game. Something about that taxi driver had stirred fears within me. However isolated this cabin was, it was still vulnerable. If anything happened to us out here, no one would know about it, maybe for months.

Olga's Note

In the depths of Virginia's mountains, our cabin was hidden, a secret refuge, secluded, mysterious. Foliage enveloped the house and its garden, intertwined greens in emerald, moss and jade. Nature's brush strokes even made an impression on me, who isn't usually distracted by pretty surroundings. At least, not when I'm figuring out how to stay out of reach of the Czar's secret agents.

I'm not entirely sure who owned the cabin. Maybe Olga, maybe Olga's employer, the United Nations Office of Counter-Terrorism? Certainly not Zara's buddy, as Kenzie's moms had initially claimed, back when they were still trying to normalize the whole 'bug out' situation.

Inside the cabin I increasingly got a feeling that escape was the main purpose for whoever stayed there. Solitude, nature's pulse. That's how it was for us, at least until my incident with the taxi.

When Bobbie and Zara returned with the blueberry pie Bobbie had made, it was obvious that they'd had some private discussion and come to a decision. Bobbie sliced into the pie and its thick blue filling oozed out. She slid a generous slice onto my plate and handed me the bowl of whipped cream. For a few minutes I forgot about everything but the pie.

With a crackling cough, Zara cleared her throat. "Marc, Roni – we thought you should know a few things about why we came here."

Kenzie seemed bewildered. "Why now?"

"Well, the taxi incident," Zara said, frowning.

"That's all? You heard Padi. Nothing really happened."

Bobbie chipped in. "Whatever. It's enough." She appeared to be unfazed. "You said it yourself Marc; there's no hiding from the Cheka."

"I was joking," he blurted. "So let me just get on top of this. You think whoever is after us managed to track us down to within a few miles?"

Firmly, Bobbie nodded. "It was only a matter of time. After you two disappeared into the Cuban forest, or wherever you ended up going, we followed Olga's last instructions."

Very prepared as it turned out, my legal guardian. Two days after her death, her attorney had delivered in person a handwritten envelope to the Mackenzie home in Falls Church, Virginia. Inside were two notes: one to me and one to Zara and Bobbie.

Zara continued the story, which I'd heard a few times since we'd arrived at the cabin. I swear, this was probably the most exciting thing that had ever happened to them, at least you'd think so, from the way they enjoyed telling it. "Olga warned us not to wait, she left us a key to a safety deposit box. That's where we found her letter to us, and the map to this safe house."

Kenzie had just that instant wandered into the kitchen and pulled off his headphones. There was a new detail in this latest version of their account, something neither Zara nor Bobbie had mentioned before. "Wait," he said, frowning. "Now it's a 'safe house'? You told us it was your buddy's hunting lodge!"

I wasn't imagining it, Kenzie seemed genuinely upset to have been kept in the dark for almost three weeks. Understandable, but not surprising to me. Zara was a vault, but Bobbie's emotions usually simmered away somewhere close to the surface. It'd been obvious to me that she'd been wound tighter than a conga drum, ever since we returned from Cuba. Were we about to find out why?

In a conciliatory tone Zara said, "We couldn't tell you very much. Olga advised us to say nothing until we're in the clear. We were going to tell you everything, and soon. But then the taxi thing. You must admit, that is kind of a red flag."

Bobbie added, "Frankly, we'd agreed between ourselves that if anything strange were to happen, we'd tell you at once."

This was becoming frustrating. "So, what now?" I blurted. "You already told us half of it. Just tell us the rest!"

Bobbie breathed in slowly before replying, as if she were trying to stabilize her mood. "Olga told us we'd have to watch you carefully if you had any contact with the Krylov Foundation children. Three weeks at least, she told us. Gave us a list of things to watch out for."

"What things?" I said, interrupting. "And when *exactly* did Olga tell you all this? Because she didn't say *word one* to me about it."

Olga had kept back quite a bit, as I'd learned from my conversations with Maxim Santiago, who turned out to be her literal nephew. Like him and Masha, her sister and Maxim's mother, Olga was a two-way telepath, a 'two-dub.' I don't know how she managed to escape the clutches of a 'controller,' the term for the people and organizations that purchased telepaths from General Krylov.

In fact, her past was something of a mystery. Yet for some reason, my parents had trusted her enough to make her my legal guardian, something she had apparently taken more seriously than I'd noticed when Olga was still alive.

Zara ignored my last comment. "What she told us to watch for? Certain behaviors," she admitted, with a shrug. "Things that might suggest you'd been put under some kind of psychic influence."

I reeled. "And you believe that?"

"Why wouldn't we?" asked Bobbie.

"Because it's crankery."

"Also, you didn't answer her question, Ma," Kenzie said. "Like, *when* did Olga tell you all this?"

"We'll come to that," Bobbie said, directing a brief, placating murmur at her wife. Then she turned her attention to calmly dividing up the rest of the blueberry pie. After a moment she began to speak again. "It is, as you say, pretty far out. But what you told us about Maxim and the others… I mean obviously with that in the mix…" She looked straight at me. "Roni, at least *admit* it's a possibility?"

Kenzie butted in. "Hey, if you won't answer our question, can you at least tell us: what did Olga's letter say?"

"Read it for yourself," replied Zara. She disappeared back into the cabin and emerged a moment later, unfolding a sheet of paper. In the meantime, Kenzie took a moment to spoon some whipped cream onto his pie. When Zara returned, he scootched up to me so that we could both read the handwritten note.

Dear Bobbie and Zara,

Thank you for everything you've done for Veronica. I occasionally visit and also talk to her mother in prison. Both parents are so grateful that you have given her the home that by their actions they denied her.

However, you must know that there is one significant loose end in Veronica's past. It is possible that someone from her childhood will one day return. I have carried the responsibility of monitoring for any sign that this might happen. Because if it does, she might be in danger. I cannot say more, I wish I could, but even this letter might prove incriminating one day.

Zara, Bobbie, if you are reading this then, I'm sorry. It means that I am no longer able to protect you. Now you must take over security arrangements, in the event that this individual might return to Veronica's life.

In this envelope you'll find a key to a safety deposit box at the Wells Fargo in Dumbarton. Please use its contents to keep yourselves, Marc and Veronica safe for as long as necessary.

I'll leave it up to you to decide how much of this you share with Veronica. My letter to her is simply a personal message of affection.

Warmest regards,

Olga Garcia

P.S. Don't under any circumstances go to the FBI!

In silence, we read the letter a couple of times, then Kenzie pushed the sheet back towards Zara. "She means Maxim," he said.

"I wonder why she talks about him as a threat to me, instead of both of us," I mused.

Kenzie pulled back the letter, which Zara had left untouched in the middle of the table. He pointed to the single mention of his name.

"What d'you mean? She did. *Please use its contents to keep yourselves, Marc and Veronica safe for as long as necessary.*"

"But also – *Because if it does, she might be in danger.*" I turned to Zara. "What else was in the safety deposit box?"

"Like we said already, a map to the cabin and its key. Plus, an audio recording on a memory stick. Olga's attorney left instructions at the bank, too. They were to leave us alone in the safety deposit room. We were to listen to the recording as many times as we needed. Then we were to hand the attorney the memory stick. He dropped it into acid, in front of us."

Kenzie chuckled, impressed. "Acid, really? And what was on the audio?"

Bobbie and Zara exchanged swift, corroborating looks. "Among other things, the answer to your question, before; '*when exactly did she tell you all this.*' In

13

that audio, Olga told us about Maxim Santiago's history at the Krylov Foundation."

For a few seconds we were silent. This felt huge.

"That explains a lot," I admitted. "On the flights back from our trip we were kind of worried you'd think we made it all up."

Bobbie snorted. "Probably would have done just that, if not for Olga's letter."

In a calmer, soothing voice Zara said, "You have to admit, it sounded ludicrous – flying to Cuba on a private plane owned by a narco, stealing an ex-Soviet military helicopter, breaking into a secret camp full of telepathic kids."

Sardonically Kenzie said, "Oh, *that* you found 'ludicrous,' but the idea that we'd been put under 'psychic influence', that was fine?"

I'd spotted that the letter was dated just one month *after* my parents began their prison sentence. "Olga was planning this from the moment she became my legal guardian. Maybe even longer."

Kenzie asked, "Do you think she talked to your folks about the possibility that Maxim would come back? I wonder why she didn't tell my moms?"

"Maxim and his little brother Sacha both escaped from the Krylov Foundation at the same time. Olga must have known. She told me she'd been searching for Maxim for years. She didn't go so far as to tell me that she knew about the Krylov, but now we know she did."

Kenzie gave a short, thoughtful nod. "She was *one hundred percent* still searching for Maxim. I'm guessing she'd only do that if she knew he wasn't still at the K-Foundation."

"When she spoke to you about Maxim, did Olga happen to mention his psychic powers?" asked Bobbie.

I shook my head. "She basically told me nothing concrete about him. Kept me guessing."

"She was probably going to tell you, though. On the trip you guys were supposed to take," Kenzie reminded me.

I shrugged my shoulders. "Maybe. Who knows?"

"Well, as I said, she told us a few other things in that audio," concluded Bobbie, as though that made Olga's previous silence acceptable.

The sunlight bathed the cabin in a warm glow as on the worn-out wooden table Kenzie and I piled up the blueberry-and-cream-streaked plates now emptied of pie. I noticed that his moms shared a guarded look, which piqued my curiosity.

"All right," Zara began. She sounded serious yet her voice was tinged with a touch of mischief. "What do you make of Olga telling us *not* to go to the FBI?"

I raised an eyebrow. "Aren't the FBI the go-to guys for this kind of stuff?"

Bobbie nodded, her face a mix of concern and uncertainty. "Yes, we thought the same thing. I'm sure Olga had her reasons. But I have no clue what they were."

"That's all we've got?" Kenzie crossed his arms. "Olga drops her bombshell, we bug out into the wilderness, but she's left us in the dark? That's just great."

Zara raked a hand through her hair. "It's frustrating, I know. Olga was a smart woman, though. There will be a good reason for this."

Bobbie became thoughtful for a moment, then began to speak, slowly. "You told us that Maxim Santiago and the other telepaths in Cuba were originally descended from Russians. You said that Kremlin agents were after you in Mexico. Maybe Olga was worried the FBI might have been infiltrated by Russians?"

A mix of confusion and worry bubbled within me. "But if we can't trust the FBI, then who can we trust?"

Bobbie leaned back in her chair. "I agree, it's a mess. Until your taxi incident, I'd begun to wonder if Olga was simply paranoid. But now, I don't know." She lifted her head, eyes slowly taking in the outline of the cabin, and then back to the garden. When she spoke again, there was an edge to her voice. "Could be we're not safe here anymore."

"Maybe Olga has other contacts," I suggested. "Like that Tobias guy, her valet, or butler or whatnot. We could try reaching out, see if he or any other contacts have any insights."

Intrigue sparkled in Kenzie's eyes. "Yeah, like a secret underground network or something. That'd be cool."

"Yeah, it wouldn't hurt to dig a little deeper, maybe figure out what Olga was really onto."

Zara nodded. "Exactly. We owe it to Olga to find out why she was murdered. If she doubted the FBI, then we can't trust them to do it."

I wasn't sure how you could owe something to a dead person, but I was relieved to know that Zara feeling this way had turned her into an ally. "Yes, definitely. Bobbie, Zara, I get what you're saying about staying here. But until we understand more, I don't feel safe to go home, either."

My last statement landed like a load of damp laundry, squashing Kenzie's excitement. Even though it'd waned, he seemed eager enough to get behind an

Olga-memorial mission. "You're right, Ma. There could be more to find out; things she didn't think to tell us."

He had a point. A little grudgingly, I said, "Olga did what she could to watch out for us, even in the event of her own death or disappearance. So maybe we do owe her."

As we huddled together in the cabin, surrounded by uncertainty and unanswered questions, one thing now gave me a feeling of warmth. It was a base of trust so rock solid, it reminded me – just a little – of the trust it'd taken for Maxim to 'incline' me to fly a helicopter with zero training. Kenzie, me and his moms, at least we had each other.

THREE

PEGASUS

Kenzie's bedroom was sparsely furnished with worn hard wood floors underfoot. A single, metal-framed cot was pushed against the internal wall and draped in a faded blue, handmade comforter. Beside the window stood a small pinewood desk at which sat Kenzie, poring over his laptop amidst copious paper clutter. Two black-and-white photographs of the Blue Ridge Mountains hung askew on the wall facing the bed.

Through the single window, I glimpsed the world outside awakening to a new day. The view stretched across a sea of towering pines, their branches lazily swaying. From the front yard, a narrow dirt path snaked across a meadow and disappeared into the forest beyond. A distant humming broke the silence. A moment later the source of the noise floated into view, a biplane, little more than a speck against the vast expanse. It was the first airplane I'd seen since we arrived, other than the passenger jets whose contrails scored the sky.

Kenzie looked up from his computer screen. Here at the cabin, he was usually up before me and always on his laptop, engrossed.

"Biplane," I said, pointing through the window.

"Oh, really?" He tapped the keyboard for a few seconds. "Let's check that boy out on the flight tracker. Uh-huh, biplane it is. No airfield anywhere close. Wonder where it's from?"

I leaned on the window ledge, watching as the airplane arced into a turn. "No clue. But it's coming this way."

He closed his laptop. "Gimme your phone."

A little bewildered, I did as he asked. He switched it off. We both watched the plane approach on a direct path for the cabin. It dipped slightly, but not so low as to seem threatening. When it flew past, it did so around fifty yards to the south, not overhead. Kenzie took a photo on his phone. When the plane was gone, he handed me back mine.

"What was all that about?"

"Spyware," he said, simply. "If the plane had gotten close, they'd be able to put something on your phone. Like Pegasus."

"What? This, again? Olga told me she found spyware on my phone. Not Pegasus; something else. In any case, she removed it."

He sniffed. "She told you that? Then Olga was wrong. Your phone has Pegasus."

"Huh? You said the same thing as Olga, after you ran a check."

"No, no." He gave a slow shake of his head, worryingly solemn. "I said I couldn't *find* Pegasus, using the tool I downloaded. But Padi, I didn't totally rule out that it could be there. I *specifically* said that I hadn't been able to run a full check. So yeah, Olga found spyware and yes, whatever she told you, it almost certainly *was* Pegasus. My guess? That's why she couldn't remove it. I didn't know at first, but now I'm sure."

I sat back on the bed, scowling. "Come on. First it isn't Pegasus and now it is?"

"Oh," he said, loftily. "Then you know how this works, do you?"

I tossed a pillow at his head. "Obviously not, dumbass. So why don't you explain, since apparently, I'm such a doofus?"

He took a breath. "It took me a while to figure it out. I checked your phone last night. Spotted some strange behaviors. It was overheating. Battery drained faster than it should, it was acting sluggish."

"Yeah, but… how does the spyware work, exactly? Break it down, like I'm eight years old. And easily bored."

Eyerolling, he said, "Like I already told you, Pegasus is a type of spyware. It was developed by some guys known for creating surveillance tools for governments."

"Yeah, yeah, that much, I know."

"Oh really? Stop me if you get bored."

I growled, baring my teeth, until he laughed.

"It's designed to infiltrate a phone without you even knowing. Once it's installed, it can access all your data. It can read your messages, calls, emails, it can even turn on your camera and mic."

"Jeez, for real?"

He nodded, very serious. "Oh yeah. Pegasus turns your phone into a souped-up surveillance device. That's why it was so important to throw out your old SIM, once we knew it was compromised. It takes all your phone's data, and it starts exporting it to a server. Like how your photos and your text messages upload to the Cloud."

"Okay, explain like I'm twelve, then. Because I'm pretty sure you already told me all this, the night before we left for Mexico. Although not the part about turning on the camera – that is *twisted*. What I don't understand is *how* it gets installed on your phone in the first place?"

"Yep, relevant. There's a thing called a 'zero-click' attack. The software exploits vulnerabilities in apps like WhatsApp. When you receive a maliciously crafted message, it triggers the installation process. Doesn't even need any interaction from you. It's pretty sneaky."

"Is there any way we can figure out how much the spyware gave away about me?"

He considered the question for a moment. "Well, that's what I started trying to do, but I wasn't able to complete the check before we went to Mexico."

"Can you do it now?"

"For sure. We should probably start by searching for any suspicious apps or unfamiliar processes running in the background. Also, we need to scan for any network connections that shouldn't be there."

This felt like a lot. "Is there a simpler way to check?"

"Yeah, we can use antivirus software that's specifically designed to detect and remove spyware. Scan your phone, identify any malicious programs or processes."

"That'll work, will it?"

Kenzie gave a noncommittal shrug. "It should give us a pretty good overview of the damage."

"And after that, any way to get rid of the spyware?"

"There's always a factory reset. Just as a last resort."

I huffed in exasperation. "That's all? Why didn't we do that ages ago?"

"You'd lose a lot of data… But yeah, probably should have," he agreed. There was no hint of guilt or even regret.

I placed my phone on the desk. "Guess it's all my fault, then," I commented, sourly.

"You didn't know. And I guess I've had other things on my mind."

There was a brief silence and then awkwardly, he grinned. When I didn't respond, the quiet stretched into a flat minute. Eventually I broke it. "Yeah. We noticed that." From the reluctant look in his eyes, I could tell that I didn't have to articulate my question: *What's on your mind?*

"I'll tell you all about it. Soon. When I'm done researching."

I leaned back against the bed frame. "Whoa. That sounds serious. Maybe you should tell me, at least? For insurance."

Kenzie considered this. "Can we wait? Just until I'm ready." His tone had softened to include a note of pleading. "First, we need to deal with your phone. Then we should talk to my moms about leaving this place, going someplace else."

With huge reluctance, I had to agree. Now it wasn't just my thing with the taxi driver yesterday, but also some random old-timey airplane buzzing this isolated cabin, apparently out of the blue. "Feels kind of dramatic," I said. "But yeah, I have to admit, something feels hinky."

I rose, weary and on edge. Printouts of Kenzie's research lay scattered about, a mirror of my jumbled thoughts. He watched in silence for a few seconds before joining me in tidying up. Our anxiety hung thick in the air. A daunting conversation with his parents lay ahead. No one enjoys hearing that they're in danger.

Kenzie's eyes met mine. Determination mixed with unease, banter was absent, our silence punctuated by rustling paper. Time to confront Bobbie and Zara.

I had a sense of what was coming – after all, this wasn't our first rodeo. Mingled scents of yeast, caramelized sugar and cinnamon floated up from the kitchen, quite the distraction from our tricky situation.

Kenzie sniffed the air, like a puppy. "Bobbie's famous cinnamon rolls. Two bakes in two days? Sounds like shit got real."

I grinned. "You think she's trying to dull the pain?"

He held the door open. "Bobbie likes to bake in a crisis. Gives her headspace for thinking, making a plan. Laugh it up, but we should definitely check out those rolls."

"Sugar and spice, the answer to everything."

"Slugs and snails, baby."

Quietly, we padded across the cabin's worn floors, the scent of cinnamon lingering in the air. As we passed the kitchen, I noticed the rolls on the counter – golden swirls, glazed to perfection. To avoid any temptation, we headed for the garden, where Bobbie and Zara sat on a bench.

They were deep in conversation. Urgency hung in the air. Bobbie caught my eye and gave us a tired smile. "Oh, there you are. We were about to call you. Rolls are almost ready to eat."

Kenzie and I took the two remaining chairs from the deck.

His moms glanced at each other. Zara let out a sigh. "You tell them, my love."

"We need to change our security protocol," Bobbie's concern was palpable. "If our fears about Roni's taxi incident are justified – and they well might be – then our trail might have already led Chekists – if that's who is after us – to the nearby town. We need to keep our phones off within a five-mile radius."

Kenzie consulted me, wordlessly, before responding. When I shrugged and gave him the 'go-ahead' eyebrow-raise, he continued. "It's worse than that, Mom. I found signs of infiltration on Padi's phone, more than just tracking. We need to ramp up our security."

Anxiety flashed across Bobbie's face, but within a few seconds she'd managed to replace, or at least cover her initial response, with an expression of determination. "You're right, Kenzie. No more gaps."

Zara nodded in agreement. "We'll start from scratch, redo everything. New identities, new location."

"New identities?" I asked, taken aback. "How? You got the number of a forger or something?"

Zara gave a shy, almost embarrassed shrug. "Something like that?"

I looked from Bobbie to Zara. "And you're okay with that?" I found their lack of alarm to be pretty astonishing. Obviously, I'd underestimated how prepared Kenzie's moms were for an eventuality like this.

"Olga explained everything, in the audio. There's more than one safe house," Zara offered, sounding cautiously hopeful.

My eyes narrowed briefly, then I smoothed out my features and hoped neither woman had noticed my momentary suspicion.

They're not telling us everything. Why?

Silence settled; the weight of our decision heavy in the air. The peace of the garden was a stark contrast to the urgency of our conversation.

Bobbie's eyes met ours once more, her firm resolve shining through. "Then you both agree?"

Warily, Kenzie nodded. "Obviously. We should move."

"After we try those cinnamon rolls," I said. "I mean, it's getting tense and all. But there's no need to completely lose our minds."

PANDEMONIUM

We headed upstairs to pack our things, footsteps muffled by the carpeted floor. Our rooms awaited, filled with three weeks of memories and a gnawing sense of paranoia, which it turned out was justified. There was a hint of weariness in Kenzie's eyes.

"Time to play Tetris with our belongings," I said, wryly.

"You don't always have to lighten the mood, Padi."

I opened the closet on the landing and handed him a suitcase. "Oh yeah, I do."

In rooms on opposite sides of the landing, we got on with the miserable task. I pulled out shirts, jeans, and socks, the fabrics cool to the touch as I folded them into the suitcase. Through the open doors I could see Kenzie doing the same, his hands deftly packing his essentials in the style he'd learned from an online video that ended with all your stuff in rolls as tight as cigars. No thanks, not for me.

Every so often, we paused in our task to munch on the cinnamon rolls we'd rescued from the kitchen. The first bite released a burst of warm syrup. Straight-up heaven, and you always make time for heaven.

As we packed, Kenzie's attention diverted briefly. His focus shifted to my phone, which he'd connected to his laptop, while he ran another set of tools. After ten minutes, he resumed whatever he was doing to remove the spyware he'd discovered. I watched, a mix of anxiety and gratitude coursing through me.

"Playing detective and tech wizard, all at the same time," I commented. "Nice."

"Glad you think so. Maybe I'll add 'multi-tasking superhero' to my resume, just for you."

Almost an hour after we'd gone up to pack, Zara popped her head around my door. My progress must have met with her approval because she did nothing other than grin and give me a thumbs up before turning to Kenzie.

"What's going on here?" she asked, dismayed as she looked the room over.

"Checking on our packing prowess, Ma?" Kenzie said. "Is there a grade for efficiency?"

"You'd be failing if there were," Zara snapped back. "Are you still playing on your computer? We need to clear out, remove all traces that we were ever here."

Kenzie's fingers paused over the keyboard. He looked around, connecting with Zara. "What d'you think I'm working on? *Digital* traces."

"Glad to hear it. Can you be ready to leave in thirty minutes?"

"I'm almost done with Padi's phone. No more snoopers."

Zara exuded pride as much as relief. "Oh, I'm glad, Kenzie. We need to be thorough."

"On it."

We left our secluded safe house in the direction opposite the one we usually took. From what Kenzie had discovered, someone had been snooping on me via the phone. We figured that the nearest town, where we usually bought supplies and gas and where I'd been picked up by the suspicious taxi driver, had to be out of bounds, as of right now.

The drive to our new destination, yet another small rural Virginian town, passed by with an eerie tranquility. Our SUV glided along the winding road, engine purring. The scenery passed by in a blur – rolling hills, sprawling fields and the occasional glimpse of an old farmhouse nestled in the distance. As the SUV approached a gas station on the outskirts of town, a sense of foreboding settled over me. Its derelict state felt like a rude reminder of the fragile nature of what we'd believed to be a sanctuary. Despite this, hopefully, we pulled up to the pumps. On closer examination, however, they looked like they went back to the 1970s, at best. They appeared ready to crumble into rust powder. Basically, a depressing mirage.

"Gas availability might be a problem," Bobbie admitted. It was rare to hear her sound this nervous.

I asked, "How much do we have?"

Eyes fixed on the road ahead, she replied tersely, "Hopefully, enough."

From the corner of my eye, I caught a glimpse of movement. A metallic brown sedan lurched into view. It overtook us with a calculated sluggishness, crawling to a stop even before the traffic lights turned red. *Unsettling* was the word.

Between gritted teeth, Bobbie hissed, "What the hell's he trying to do?"

"Mom, be careful…"

"He might be trying to trap us," I added.

"It has D.C. plates," noted Kenzie.

Bobbie nodded once, then swerved out from behind the brown sedan, maneuvering until our SUV had sidled up alongside, both cars waiting for the lights to turn.

Nervously, I checked out the driver of the brown car, which I now saw was some kind of Chevrolet. He was a white man in his thirties or forties. In one swift motion, he pulled a ski mask over his face. I felt like I'd taken a shot of adrenaline straight into my thigh muscles, felt them tense, ready to sprint.

"Drive, Bobbie!" I urged, my voice tight.

Bobbie evidently grasped the gravity of the situation. The lights turned green, she slammed her foot down and the SUV leapt forward, accelerating as we overtook the metallic brown Chevy. A small, rural town came into view as we raced through its main street, landmarks blurring past. The old clock tower seemed to be frozen in time, also a local diner, its red neon 'Harmbuger' (yes, really) 'Happy Hour 5-6pm' sign flickered as if celebrating the typos.

Panic seeped into the air we breathed. Kenzie and I pleaded with Bobbie to take an off-road route. I felt sure that our four-wheel-drive vehicle had the advantage in the woods, where narrow trails and thick foliage could deter our pursuer. With grim determination, his mom veered off the main road at the first hiking trail. Our tires gripped the rough terrain well, but occasionally went into barely controlled skids. The forest swallowed us, branches of some rotten trees reaching out like gnarled fingers. Our SUV was sturdier than I'd have guessed and pressed on, navigating the treacherous path with unwavering resolve.

The sedan was now in relentless pursuit. Its driver matched our every move. The engine's roar echoed through the forest, a constant reminder of the danger that trailed closely behind us. As the chase intensified, our surroundings transformed into a blur of lush greenery and fleeting glimpses of sunlight. If the two cars turned out to be evenly matched on the terrain, the lush foliage was an advantage, shielding us from prying eyes.

Tremors coursed through my veins as the SUV surged ahead, its engine growling as we hurtled through the dense forest. Our midnight blue Ford Explorer tore through the underbrush, leaving the pursuit in our wake. Behind us, the brown Chevy with a masked driver carved its own path through tall grass and unruly weeds, following us like a phantom. The tension ratcheted up with every passing second.

Kenzie and I avoided looking at each other but I was sure he wanted the same things as me; to urge Bobbie to push harder, to outrun this relentless – and to be honest, scary – masked man.

Bobbie gripped the wheel, cursing under her breath each time the car banked, and we gasped for air, seatbelts clamping tight. Zara, steadfast in the passenger seat, held on tight, her knuckles white against the dark leather. In the backseat, Kenzie and I were tossed about like pillows in a fight. I bit my lower lip trying to stop myself from yelling, "Bobbie, faster!" which, I'm guessing, would have achieved nothing.

The sedan roared behind us, the noise reverberated through the forest. Obstacles appeared in our path, and we winced loudly at every swerve and shimmy. Fallen logs and scattered rocks rattled around us, while each jolt shot through us like an electric charge.

Then suddenly I realized that I could no longer hear the car behind us. Clutching the handle on the side of the car, I turned to peer through the rear window and into the trees. No sign of the Chevy. In the pandemonium of the chase it was a brief respite, a lull in the storm. I held my breath, straining to hear any sign of danger. And then, cutting through the silence, a distant hum pierced the air.

"What the heck…?" muttered Bobbie. We all stared through the sunroof, but there was nothing above us but the forest canopy.

I turned my head, my senses on high alert, and focused on a few chinks that led straight to the sky above. And there it was: a helicopter emerging on the horizon. Its menacing silhouette grew larger with each passing second. The thump-thump-thump of its rotor blades pulsed through the forest until our car seemed to shudder along with its rhythm.

The helicopter closed in, flew lower, skids grazing the canopy above. The forest quivered beneath its weight and more than one of us instinctively threw arms up to protect our heads.

Bent double in the back of the SUV, Kenzie and I finally looked directly at each other. He whispered, "We're screwed."

FIVE

INCEPTION

Briefly, all four of us peered through the sunroof at the helicopter as it swooped, directly above us. Then, with barely any hint of a pause, as though they hadn't noticed us, it flew over, retracing our path.

I exhaled, slowly. "Could it be, they're not searching for us?"

We continued to watch through the foliage, catching an occasional glimpse of the blurred rotor blades. Kenzie turned to me. "They're going after Brown Chevy."

Bobbie started the engine. "Good, in which case it's none of our business."

"Wait a bit," I objected. "We can't *know* that. Don't you think we should stick around?"

Kenzie agreed. "We should find out why they're after this dude."

But Bobbie was clearly uninterested. Zara turned to face me and Kenzie in the rear seats. "Remember what Olga told us? *No FBI.*"

Instinctively, I turned my head, scanning for the helicopter. The noise of it had receded to a raucous hum, yet it was nowhere to be seen. "You really think that was the Feds?"

Bobbie gave a noncommittal shrug. "Don't particularly fancy waiting around to find out."

Kenzie and I sank back into our seats, sharing a muted sigh of frustration. It was fine when Bobbie and Zara made sensible decisions I agreed with, but right now, running did not make sense. We had no idea what we were running from. What if we were running from someone who could help us?

I found myself longing for the freedom we'd had in Mexico and Cuba. "Kay. Where now?"

Bobbie said, "I have no clue."

Her tone was clipped, dismissive. She didn't enjoy being the captain of this venture, or maybe it was just that she didn't appreciate my interventions. The hiking trail we were following became gradually wider and after another ten minutes we could see a sunlit meadow ahead. When we reached it, Bobbie parked the car in the shade of a huge ash tree.

The meadow was impressively rustic, nestled within a ring of towering trees. Rays of sunlight filtered through the canopy and cast a warm glow. A scent of pine mixed with earthy notes of damp soil and fresh foliage. Sprinkled throughout the meadow were wildflowers in cheerful hues: purple lupines, goldenrod and orange butterfly weed.

"Nice," I concluded. "Pretty."

"'Nice,'" echoed Kenzie. "'Pretty.' That how the script for your next podcast is going to begin? I like it. Minimalist!"

"Why would I *ever* podcast this?"

He clicked open his seatbelt and grinned. "Got to keep making that content."

Zara announced, brightly, "Snacks in the trunk."

Kenzie and I climbed out of the SUV, popped the trunk and picked out a giant packet of cheese Doritos.

"Is it cool if we take a stroll?" I asked. Zara nodded. Her attention was elsewhere, watching Bobbie unfold a huge map of the Shenandoah National Park and then smoothing it down onto a bed of low grass.

Kenzie watched them for a few seconds and then set off after me. When he caught up, I offered him some tortilla chips. "It sucks that your moms won't tell us the plan. Makes me feel like I'm about twelve."

"Not all that surprising," he observed, through audible crunches. "It's not like they *don't* have reason to believe we'd take off without them."

Briefly, it occurred to me that he was joking. But no. Kenzie accepted blithely his parents' wildest conspiracy theories about us.

"What's with you?" I blurted. "Not only is that a mean thing to say, it's also stupid. We would never."

Calmly, he blinked. "Wouldn't we? My moms know we ran off to Cuba with a guy we hadn't seen since we were twelve, that we stole an ex-Soviet military helicopter. What's the big deal about taking a car, after that?"

"It's different," I said, grunting with exasperation. "Maxim came up with that plan, it's not like he gave us a lot of choice."

"Right. And your Auntie Olga warned my moms that we might somehow be under Maxim's telepathic influence. So, y'know, in their heads, one thing leads to the other."

I'd been about to say that Maxim's powers couldn't reach me here, but any objection I came up with died on the tip of my tongue. The truth was, I couldn't be one hundred percent certain their theory wasn't on point. We didn't know the range of his powers and we didn't know his current location. Olga, I had to admit to myself, had been wise to include that possibility.

"Do you think Olga had psi powers?" Kenzie wondered, plucking a few chips between three fingers.

As he fed one after the other into his mouth, I considered my response. "Yeah, course."

"You *do*? How come?" He sounded startled, as if his question hadn't been serious.

"Maxim told us."

"When was this? I don't remember him saying anything like that."

Kenzie's manner had changed instantly, from casual to suspicious. It threw me enough to make me want to backtrack from the whole scope of what I'd figured out.

"You don't remember? That first evening, in the hacienda. When he was telling all his backstory. I'm pretty sure he told us that Olga was his mom's sister, that she was a 'unicorn,' too. A two-dub. So, she obviously had powers."

"Well… if you say so. If you're sure you've remembered that right," Kenzie admitted, doubtfully. "Because there was a lot going on that day. And if that's right, if she did have powers, how come Olga ended up working for the United Nations? Maxim told us that Krylov only sold two-dubs to enemies of the West. And remember that Vault 7 document we found? The only intelligence agencies listed as potential buyers of 'unicorns' were enemies of the West. And Israel."

"I think Maxim said she defected?" I replied, wrinkling my nose. Kenzie was right, a lot had happened that day. But I was reasonably sure that Maxim believed Olga had powers. "Whatever. Let's not get sidetracked. I'm saying that if Olga was Masha's

35

sister and Masha was born in the Krylov camp, then how could Olga not also be born there?"

My question was a red herring. I knew that the Krylov Foundation kids often had surrogate mothers, which meant there were two mothers through whom Olga might be Masha's sister – the egg mother and the surrogate. One of those routes involved zero inheritance of telepathic powers. Maxim's birth mother had been a young woman from Santiago, hence his name. In the breeding program that created all the Krylov kids, aged fourteen years old Masha had donated – under dubious consent at best – the egg that made him. In theory, Olga could have been Masha's half-sister through a non-telepathic, surrogate mother.

Given what I remembered Maxim telling me, I was pretty sure this wasn't true. There was a good chance Olga had telepathic powers, whether she grew up in the Krylov camp ot not. More than a good chance, based on the evidence of my own.

I cast my thoughts back to the few days we'd spent with Maxim and before that, the whirlwind of what now seemed somehow semi-deranged behavior, as we'd searched for clues to his whereabouts. A dim memory sparked inside me.

It wasn't quite true that I'd simply 'tagged along' with Olga's mission. At Maxim's side, it'd been difficult to admit specifically *what* drew me to search for him. Even when he'd prompted me to examine the question more closely, I'd shied away from confronting it. Over the past weeks, however, I'd come to accept the real reason; a deep-seated crush on Maxim, one I wasn't about to confess to Kenzie.

'Why did you come here, Padi?' Maxim had asked. *'Were you looking forward to going to Mexico with Olga? What*

*about it felt exciting? What happened? You hung out with Olga;
she persuaded you to go to Mexico. Olga dropped you off, she went
to her hotel, it got late, you fell asleep. By the morning Olga was
dead. Your trip should have been off, surely? Yet later that day
you decided to go to Mexico anyway. Is that what you remember?'*

It had felt like being put in checkmate. Maxim's
surgical logic had peeled back the layers of bluff I'd
used to conceal my true motivation, even from myself: *a
dream*, the night before I'd left for Mexico. Later, in the
small hours of the morning, Olga had been murdered in
her hotel room. At the time I had the dream that
persuaded me to go to Mexico, she'd still been alive.

If the K-Foundation two-dubs could 'incline'
people to do things, if they could cloud minds and in
other ways mess with people's thoughts and emotions,
maybe they could also do something like in that movie,
'Inception,' – maybe they could plant a cleverly-crafted
dream?

My dream that night had been weird, each detail
quite memorable, way more than in regular dreams.
Even now, I could close my eyes and experience myself
back in that Mexican market, where me and Dream-
Olga discover Dream-Maxim amongst heaps of
brightly-colored and scented fruit, heavy warm air,
Chichi Peralta's *Procura* playing on a stereo somewhere,
while Olga triumphantly grins and tells me, *Ya chamaca,
ya lo encontramos* – Girl, we've already found him.

Over the past weeks all these details got
smooshed together and in a flash of insight, I saw it.
Maxim had *intended* for me to understand that I had
been 'incepted' by Olga. He'd led me there. I just hadn't
wanted to see.

With hindsight, I could see how she might have
done it – she'd waited in her car outside Kenzie's house

after she dropped me off, patient and quiet until I fell asleep. She'd worked her psychic powers and then driven to her hotel, confident that by morning I'd be bursting with enthusiasm for our trip to Mexico.

Which of course, I was. Even though by then, Olga was dead.

"We can be ninety-nine percent sure that Olga had telepathic powers," I told Kenzie. Still couldn't bring myself to say what had led me to this conclusion. How could I admit to my brother-slash-best-friend that any romantic feelings he might have for me were wasted, because five years ago I'd stupidly given my heart to stupid Maxim?

"All right, finally," he said, sounding relieved. "Then we can agree – Olga had plenty reason to warn my parents."

"I guess so," I grumbled. We'd ventured deeper into the woods, our steps in sync with the crackle of leaves. I stopped. "We should turn back. See what Bobbie and Zara have come up with."

Kenzie nodded and snatched the bag of Doritos. "You've had way more than me," he objected when I tried to hold on.

"Fine. What do you think of your mom's theory?

"You mean about Mister Helicopter being FBI? Figures, if they were chasing Brown Chevy and not us."

"But that's strange. *We* ought to be way more interesting to the FBI. So either they don't know who we are… Or they *do* know and they're protecting us."

Vigorously, he nodded. "Hell yeah, if they knew what went down in Cuba, the Feds would be *very* intrigued by us. A whole heap of government agencies would find us *super* interesting, if they knew any of that."

We fell silent. The sky had quietened, other than birdsong and the rustle of wind through the trees, as though nothing had recently shattered the gentle sounds and occasional stillness of the wilderness. Ahead, I could just begin to make out the low voices of Kenzie's moms.

Kenzie and I were on the same page about Olga, even if he wasn't totally up to speed on what I had now concluded about her own brand of telepathic powers. It was fine, I told myself, to keep this one thing from my best friend-almost-brother. The idea that I'd been 'incepted' so that I'd agree to go to Mexico in search of Maxim, was just a crazy hypothesis. Might not be true at all.

And a crazy hypothesis, I told myself, is one you should probably keep to yourself.

SIX

Book Code

Olga had left instructions for how to access her various safe houses. The first was the place we had just left. On her list of safe houses, presumably that cozy cabin-in-the-woods was the nearest to Falls Church. The initial message from Olga had led to its key and a folding Virginia road map, on which was marked the address.

The location for the next safe house in the series, however, had to be figured out, like some sort of treasure hunt. Kenzie's moms had only the address to another safety deposit box, as well as a string of numbers. Kenzie's guess? The number was a combination lock. But Bobbie had a different theory, inspired by some scribbled writing on the edge of the map itself, the title of a book; *A Mortal Stretch* by E.L. Lewin.

"The number itself is not a combination. It might lead to one, but this string of numbers? It looks like a book code," announced Bobbie.

I had no clue what she was talking about but was relieved that she seemed so confident.

"There's no other reason for a book title to be written on the map. *A Mortal Stretch* is a very popular book. We should be able to find it in any passably good library." She ran her finger across the map, searching for a nearby town that might have such a library.

Seemed like the kind of thing Kenzie would know. I sent a quizzical look in his direction, but he wasn't even listening. To judge from his furrowed brow and the intensity with which he focused on the ground, his mind was miles away. Normally, he'd be eager to be the first to point something like this out, but not this time. Maybe because we'd dumped his combination lock theory? Even so, it struck me as unusual behavior for Kenzie.

So, I asked Bobbie, "Um, what's a book code?"

"It's a very basic way to communicate in code," she said. "Both people have a copy of the same book. This number refers to a location in the book. Now I'm guessing that in this case it's something like chapter, line, word. For example – one-zero-five-six would be chapter ten, line five, word six."

"How do you know it's not page, line, word?"

She considered. "Because this book is so popular. It's gone through lots of editions, all with slightly different pagination. The only way to locate a word in a book like that is chapter, line, word."

I counted the numbers in the string scribbled onto the note they'd found in the safety deposit box. If you examined it closely, there were two sets of three numbers and one set of four, each separated by a space. "And you are sure that there's more than one safe house? Did Olga actually say that in the audio?"

"She 'actually' did," Zara confirmed. "There are, in fact, three. Let's hope the next one turns out to be safe."

Kenzie held a twig in his hand, flicking it against a nearby tree trunk in what felt to me like increasing irritation. After a moment he blurted, "Why should it be safe? For all we know, they've put Pegasus software on mom's phone. Or yours, ma. Then no matter where we go, they'd track us."

Zara side-eyed him, eyebrows raised. "In that case, dear Marc, I think you'd better check and see if any of that is true. Why don't I make a picnic for us, while you do that?"

Given that Kenzie's tech wizardry was the only thing giving us a fighting chance to stay ahead of our pursuers, I was a little surprised he wasn't happier to offer his services. But lately this was becoming normal for him. It was as though he had something more interesting going on, something compared to which the pesky reality of what we were going through was some huge annoyance.

As Kenzie pulled his laptop from a backpack, quietly I muttered, "You cool, Kenz?"

Scowling he replied, "Sure. Whatever."

I followed him as he went to fetch his moms' phones from the car. "Hey, stop. I can tell something's wrong." I caught up, touched his arm, but he wouldn't face me.

"Nothing's wrong."

"Oh yeah. It is." I reached across to the opposite seat in the SUV, picked up one of the phones and handed it to him. "Is there something else you'd rather be doing?"

He flashed me a sharp look. "Such as?"

"Not a clue. That's why I'm asking." There was a tense silence. "Don't brush it off though. Don't…" I broke off. How could I ask Kenzie for the whole truth when I was holding something back, too?

Kenzie seemed to notice my flash of anxiety because his tone became warmer. "It's no biggie. Nothing to do with any of this. It's just that I have other plans, projects. And that should be all right! You have your podcast, I have my…" He broke off abruptly.

"You have your… what?"

He sighed. "My climate activism," he replied, eventually.

I waited for him to say more but when he didn't, I unintentionally let out a chuckle. "You? A climate activist? Since when?"

He was quiet for too long, and a flush of pink bloomed in his cheeks. "Long time."

I thought back to before Mexico. "I thought it was some cyber project. Climate activism, really? When did it begin."

"I used to go on those school climate strikes, remember?"

"That's right, you did. Is that what you'd rather be doing now? Climate activism?"

With a slow, almost ambivalent shrug he said, "It'd be more useful than any of this, anyhow. Face it, we're *hiding*, Padi. No more school, our future on hold. I can *use* this time. It doesn't have to be wasted." He hesitated for a moment, as if wondering if he dared to go further. "Don't you sometimes wish you'd never gone searching for Maxim Santiago? Look at the trouble it's gotten us into. We had a nice life. Now all four of us are on the run. And why? For what?"

"Well… We did manage to stop a dictator from kidnapping a bunch of telepathic kids to weaponize in his genocidal war."

Kenzie took a deep breath and nodded a few times. "Yeah, yeah. Barely. It could easily have gone differently. And if we hadn't shown up, I'm pretty sure Maxim would have found someone else he could 'incline.'"

That stung. I could barely get out a dry-mouthed response. "Maybe."

I longed to tell Kenzie that he was absolutely wrong. That the only reason the inclining had worked at such a distance was because Maxim and I had such a deep connection, one that went back to our childhood. Where else would he find a 'latent' like me, a normie that could receive telepathic signals?

No point, though. I sensed a belligerent mood under his veneer of nonchalance. There'd be a better time for this conversation. Right now, Kenzie needed to prioritize checking whether his moms' phones had been compromised, like mine.

He connected one of the phones to his laptop and tapped the keyboard in a series of lightning-fast keystrokes. Then he stopped. "Forget this. I need Internet access. We'll have to wait until we get to the library."

Internet access, I had to admit, was our best bet for researching any contacts of Olga's who we might reach via Tobias. Another great reason to head for a library and solve the book code, if Olga's cryptic reference to *A Mortal Stretch* was indeed a message for us.

Overhearing us, Zara paused on the way to a small clearing, where they'd laid out a rug and four cans of soda. In her hands were three Tupperwares of cold roast chicken, chopped carrots and cubed cheese. "Then you'd better eat quickly," she chipped in. "And we'll head straight there."

Kenzie snapped shut his laptop. "All right. But you'd better expect that whoever is searching for us will probably be waiting for us there."

Zara froze. "Why… how would they know?"

He waved the phone in her face. "Spyware. Phone tracking. I've been trying to tell you, but Mom was too busy driving like a maniac. They might be listening even now. They have a pretty good idea we're here, even if they've stopped following us."

She ignored his undisguised scorn and mulled this over. "*If* there's spyware."

"Obviously, 'if.'"

Zara smiled, widely. "Then we'll pick another town. And this time, we won't breathe a word." She raised a finger to her lips and whispered, "Shh."

Kenzie shook his head. He turned to me, scowling. "It's almost like they're enjoying this."

I grinned and flicked his upper arm hard enough that he winced. "It's a good strategy. Get a clue, K."

We eased into a silence that I suspected was more likely the four of us enacting a sullen drama. By pointing to the map and in ad hoc, improvised sign language, we agreed on another town's library to search. We began to pack away the picnic. When we were done, Kenzie wiped his hands on his jeans and hooked his thumb in the direction of the woods. "Pee break."

"Good shout. Me too."

On the way, I tried once again to get him to open up about his climate activism. But he was reluctant to share anything at all, until we were on the way back. In a tone that was thoroughly conspiratorial, he said, "I'll tell you, if you promise not to tell my moms."

"Ooh sounds ominous. What have you got planned? Blowing up a pipeline, or something?" I laughed for a couple of seconds and then stopped when I noticed his stunned expression.

"You can't say anything to them," he whispered fiercely.

I lowered my voice. "Tell me it's 'or something.'"

He gave a solemn shake of his head and said, very softly, "But it's not."

"Dude! You're not serious."

"I am one hundred percent serious."

And in his eyes, I saw the truth of it.

SEVEN

DAISYBANK

While his moms refilled the gas tank, Kenzie and I wandered into the library. He headed for one of the more secluded desks, slapped on his headphones and flipped open his laptop. Meantime I looked around, expecting to be greeted by a small town's attempt at architectural sophistication. You know, those tiny buildings that look like someone accidentally sneezed on a dollhouse? But to my surprise, the library seemed like it belonged in a city, with its grand columns and elegant façade. Clearly, someone had raised the bar in this one-horse town.

Inside, the place was even more impressive. It had high ceilings that made me feel like a hobbit in a giant's world. A central, octagonal chamber was lined with high shelves against which leaned a ladder on rails and in the center, two battered old Chesterfield leather couches, where a couple of readers leaned back in lazy enjoyment of their hardback volumes. Natural light poured in through large windows, illuminating the neatly arranged desks and bookshelves. In sweatpants and a scrunchie, I felt a little underdressed; a place like this deserved my Sunday best.

I made my way to the children's section and there it was, like a shining beacon of literary magic; *A Mortal*

Stretch by E.L. Lewin. I snatched it off the shelf. It was the only copy: not a chance I was leaving it for some snotty-nosed ten-year-old. As I turned the pages searching for the page indicated by the book code, I couldn't help but appreciate the irony. In this grand library, surrounded by towering bookshelves and the knowledge of ages, here I was, using this famous novel like the yellow pages.

I turned to the chapter indicated by the first of three sets of numbers and began counting lines, then counting across the line to the word indicated, which was 'rain.' Then I deciphered the rest of the code. *Rain, morning, tree.* It didn't make much sense. I double-checked. Same result. I took out my phone and was about to type the words in, when I remembered that our phones weren't yet secure.

I headed around to the alcove in which Kenzie had buried himself and tapped lightly on his left headphone. Waiting for him to reply, I studied his laptop screen. It was open on the website of what appeared to be an engineering project named 'Daisybank.' No sign of any daisies on that page, only images of oil drilling equipment.

My heart sank. Was Kenzie thinking of going through with the madness of trying to blow up a real-life pipeline? What he was contemplating was exponentially more difficult than what we'd done in Cuba. And crime on American soil would have consequences far worse.

He raised both headphones and gave me a relaxed grin. Now that he was back on his pet project, his mood seemed to have lifted. I showed him the deciphered text. For a second, he looked puzzled and then brightly he said, "Rain, morning, tree? Three random words? Oh, that is brilliant."

Still mystified, I watched him bring up a website: Three Word Location. "Every location has been described by three random words. Genius!" He typed in three words and watched as some GPS coordinates were revealed. From his messenger bag he took a notebook, ripped out a page, and scribbled down the address and GPS coordinates.

"Olga was one smart cookie," he murmured. "Or maybe it was just her training."

I narrowed my eyes. "And that's it, that's the location of the next safe house?"

Kenzie broke off, already closing the Three Word Location window as he drifted back to the world of Daisybank. He pointed to my phone on the desk, next to Zara's and Bobbie's which were plugged into his laptop. "I'm done with your phone, bee-tee-dubs." He put on his headphones.

I picked up my phone and switched it on. Nothing seemed different. "My phone all good?"

He snickered. "Oh, it was a hot mess. But it's clean now. I'm running the checks on my moms' phones now." Then with a waft of his hand he dismissed me. "Go find them, they went to the general store. Tell them I need another couple hours. Get some coffee or whatever."

I lifted his right earphone. "Stop shouting," I murmured. "Fine. I'll do what you said."

He'd already stopped listening. I made my way to the general store to hunt down his parents, unable to shake the feeling of disquiet I'd gotten from seeing Kenzie so absorbed in the Daisybank website. Something told me this wasn't just a side-project that he was using as stress relief, while we were on the lam. How long had it been going on?

Once inside the store, my eyes scanned shelves lined with random knick-knacks and strange paraphernalia. As I came up behind Bobbie and Zara, I guessed they were examining some jeans or shirts or even beef jerky. But no. They were leaning over and peering into a glass cabinet. On the wall directly in front of them hung at least ten varieties of rifle and inside the cabinet, dozens of handguns.

"Whoa. What's going on?"

Bobbie and Zara were huddled together, their eyes fixed on the display of handguns and hunting knives. It was as bad as it looked. In low voices they were evidently quite seriously contemplating buying at least one weapon.

I approached them cautiously, my voice laced with a mix of disbelief and concern. "Um, guys, what's going on?"

Bobbie flashed a mischievous smile. "You never know when you might need to defend yourself. Plus, Zara has some serious hidden talents that just might come useful."

I turned to Zara, my eyes widening. "Hidden talents? Oh please, say more about *that*."

Zara chuckled. "Bobbie's exaggerating. You see, back in Chile, I had an unexpected encounter with some rather... let's just say, intriguing situations. You might say that I gained some expertise in using a pistol."

"You had a secret life as some kind of outlaw? Serious?"

With an enigmatic lift of one eyebrow, Zara turned back to the gun case. "Very serious."

"Oh, I'm gonna need details."

"Well, you're not getting any," Bobbie said, suddenly protective of her wife. Her attention returned swiftly to the gun cabinet, and she called over the salesman to unlock the cabinet so that she could sample the goods. She picked up a compact pistol in her right hand and turned it over. I couldn't tell if she was pretending to know what she was doing or whether she actually did. "Glock nineteen," she said. "Fits nicely in my hand, reliable and packs enough punch to rock anyone's world."

Zara merely crossed her arms and observed us, skeptically. "Are you sure we need anything like this, darling? Is there any chance we are just imagining the Chekist? Remember that time when I thought I saw your father at the bank?"

At this mention of her father, Bobbie's easy smile vanished. But a second later she recovered. Between gritted teeth she said, "That's a great point. Even if there are no Chekists, there *is* my dad."

Listening in, the salesman grinned in slow realization. "You're being chased by a Chekist? Awesome!"

I said nothing. It seemed like something we shouldn't be mentioning in public.

Bobbie turned to him. "Let's say we are. Got any advice?"

The salesman pondered a moment. "Those guys almost always carry SIG-Sauers."

"Do they?" I asked, wide-eyed. Then I fixed him with a calculating stare. "How'd you know?"

He dropped the grin. He selected one from the tray. "Give it a try? We got a shooting range in the back."

A crafty grin spread across Bobbie's face. I saw that she was all in on getting the gun. The unease I'd begun to feel swelled up and I wondered; were we really in so much danger that a firearm could be a solution to our problems? It wasn't ideal. I'd been looking forward to eating a hamburger but now I was contemplating the existential question of self-defense.

Raising both hands in mock dismay, I said, "Hey, you ladies are on your own with this! I'll be at the diner."

I'd taken about ten steps outside the general store, when I heard the door opening again, then heard footsteps catching up to me. Warily, I checked over my shoulder.

An African American woman, maybe forty years old or thereabouts, was headed straight for me. She had on a navy pants suit with a pale blue blouse and the kind of shoes that don't make for good foot chases – high and noisy. I waited for her with a non-committal smile on my face. It seemed like the decent thing to do.

But I should have run.

EIGHT

MARGO DANIELS

"Thank you for waiting, sugar!"

From her jacket pocket the woman pulled out a clean white pocket square and used it to dab her brow. She drew a couple of deep, refreshing breaths and then beamed at me. "Long time since I tried to run in heels." She nodded in the direction of the diner that was a little further down the road. "You want to get coffee? I'd sure love to chat some."

I observed her a little longer, listening for any hint of a foreign accent in her speech. In fact, it was a pretty authentic-sounding Carolinas accent. Don't ask me which one, north or south, because my ear is not that good, but we've holidayed in North Carolina, and it sounded like what I'd heard there.

Not bothering to hide my suspicion I said, "You want to talk to *me*?"

A smile quirked at the edges of her mouth. She had a pleasant, friendly face, sparkly honey-brown eyes, brown skin and the kind of cheek dimples you'd like to see on the face of a beloved *gringa* auntie. The navy suit and blouse didn't seem to fit with her face or her bouncy, shoulder-length chestnut waves. But one look at her shoulders and bust told me that the entire outfit had been tailor-made for her slightly stocky figure: no sign of tightness anywhere, a perfect fit.

"Well, honey? Are we going to eat some pie together, or what?"

"Pie? Why would we? You can't seriously expect me to sit down with somebody I never met before, who just now accosted me in the street."

"Oh, sure." She flashed me what I guessed was meant to be a reassuring grin, reached into her inside jacket pocket and took out a badge. I'd expected a police badge but when I saw the words 'Central Intelligence Agency,' I froze. My cynical smirk fell away. Our eyes met and I saw that her smile had turned sly and knowing, as if to say *I got you good*. Printed directly beneath her rank – 'Targeting Officer' – was her name: Margo Daniels.

A bunch of theories ran through my head, while in front of me I could see CIA Targeting Officer Margo Daniels quietly and with some amusement, watching my eyes widen. "Good to meet you, Veronica Padilla."

"How…" I managed to sputter, after a moment. "And why? Why are you chasing us? We thought it was the FBI, or even Chekists."

"Chekists? Nope. Leastways, I don't think so."

"The guy in the brown Chevy who chased us. That was your people?"

She grinned brightly. "Yup. That'd be Dashiell. None too bright, but he's loyal."

"And the helicopter? That *wasn't the CIA*?"

"No, the chopper was FBI. They've been protecting you. Sometimes we tread on each other's toes. But not to worry. We figured it out."

My lower jaw slackened. Kenzie's mom's theory was right! "Then we haven't been off the grid at all?"

"Oh, sure. I mean, a little bit, anyhow. To the Chekist, maybe. Just not to us or the Feds."

I paused. "Is there any point in us going to the next safe house?"

Daniels didn't reply at first, just pursed her lips and gestured towards the diner. "Better go inside. They got air conditioning. I don't know about you, but chasin' y'all and these shenanigans, they're kind of wearing me out." She let out a merry chuckle, like bells being rung by an altar boy.

I turned back in the direction of the general store. Following my gaze, Daniels said, "Marc and his parents are going nowhere without you, Veronica."

"It's Roni."

She held open the diner's door. "You got it, hon."

Inside the diner we sat at one of the powder blue and pink booths. The decorative theme was, apparently, bubble-gum. The instant we sat down a server appeared with two menus.

"Have anything you like," offered Daniels. "It's on me. Least I can do."

I put down the menu. "In that case, I'll have a cheeseburger followed by a slice of Atlantic Beach pie, a slice of chocolate chiffon pie and a vanilla milkshake."

Margo Daniels grinned widely. "Great choices. I'll have the same."

When the server had taken our order and was out of earshot, the officer leaned across the table and in a low voice said, "We've been observing you for long enough to know what you and Marc did in Cuba."

The alarm I felt must have registered in my eyes, because she immediately tried to walk it back. "Hey, hey. Relax. You're not in trouble. We know what those 'unicorns' are capable of. They made you do it, honey. Isn't that right?"

I didn't answer and her sly grin told me that she didn't expect me to.

Our suspicions had been on the money, from the start. *Pegasus!* It wasn't Cheka who'd hacked my phone, but the CIA. Kenzie must have gotten to our phones too late. I didn't know what to make of this. My thoughts were blurring, my tongue felt slow and thick in my mouth as I struggled to figure out everything that we might have said in the vicinity of the cell phones.

Daniels glanced swiftly over both shoulders, checking that we were still in our small bubble of isolation. Then she turned back to face me. "Now, I gather y'all have been doing some code cracking. You wanna give me the low down, the de-brief?"

I hesitated.

She rolled her eyes. "We're tracking you, honey. FBI, too. We're gonna find out, eventually. Now, given what you just asked me about the safe house, I'm guessing that y'all are still huntin' for your next hidey-hole. Am I right?"

Reluctantly, I nodded. I don't know why it was so difficult to lie. Probably because I couldn't come up with another explanation on the spot.

Daniels held out her hand. "Lemme see."

I handed her Olga's map, on which I'd written the deciphered code – *rain, morning, tree*. She examined it for a moment, a smile hovering about her lips. "Nice," she commented. "Very nice. We can work with that. She tapped on her phone for a few seconds, took out a Sharpie pen and scored thick black lines over the decrypted words. "Tell Marc that you made a mistake. Then you did it over and got the right answer. *Fork, mountain, apple.*"

I read what she'd written, then what she'd scrubbed out with the Sharpie and finally, I looked back at her. "What the…?"

"Fork, mountain, apple," she repeated patiently, as though I were a distracted nine-year old. Utterly self-assured, she added, "Trust me. The next location you got planned? That's a hard nope from me. Lookit, any Chekist worth her salt will know by now that you've gone country. They won't expect you to go back to the city. No, no, better that we put you in one of our places in the city, Bethesda. It'll take the FBI more time to catch up to you, too. And you don't want the FBI following you, am I right?" She winked, like this was an inside joke.

I was silent, thinking fast. What would Kenzie say, when I told his moms a different three-word location than the one I'd originally told him? There was no way I could keep this encounter with Targeting Officer Daniels a secret, not from him.

Then I focused on what she'd said about the FBI. "So… you think we *don't* want the FBI to know where we are?"

She shrugged. "Either way, they're gonna find out. Eventually."

Her answer sounded evasive. I peered at her, curiously. "Would it be a problem if they found out, like, pretty soon?"

Olga's note had said not to trust the FBI. Was this CIA officer in some roundabout way confirming that advice?

Daniels cleared her throat, then sidestepped the issue. "I'll cut to the chase, Roni. I need *your* help. We need you to arrange a meeting between us and Alexander Montecristo."

At the sheer silliness of this, I relaxed and began to laugh. "Wow. You really have been wasting your time. I *don't know* anyone called Alexander Montecristo."

A look somewhere between irritation and befuddlement crossed her face.

"Maybe you know him as 'Sacha'? I *know* you know his brother, Maxim Santiago. Come on, Roni. No games, not with me. You know the deal; we just know too much about you. Like how you met up with Maxim Santiago in Tapachula. Like how something serious went down in Cuba. Oh yeah, we know all about that, we got SIGINT tells us you stole a chopper."

"'SIGINT'?"

"Signals intelligence," she replied, with forced patience. "Information gathered from communications, signals and whatnot. Now we just need you to help broker a deal with his brother. We're pretty sure…"

She broke off as the server approached with a tray. When he'd finished setting down the two cheeseburgers and all four servings of pie as well as two milkshakes, Margo Daniels handed me a spoon. "Dig in."

I put it down, and picked up the cheeseburger in two hands, mouth already watering. "I can't help you. I have never even spoken to Maxim's brother. No idea where he is, or even what he looks like."

Daniels ate two spoonfuls of chocolate chiffon pie before switching to her burger, and then took a long slurp of vanilla milkshake. "Sweet Jebus. Delicious! Can you imagine being gluten and lactose intolerant? That would suck so bad. I'd miss out on my favorite foods."

"I'm pretty sure there are good alternatives," I muttered. "Thanks for the food and all, but are we done here?"

She smiled until both dimples showed. "Oh, I don't think so, sugar. You think I chased you halfway around the state of Virginia just to end up eating burgers and pie with y'all?"

I spooned some Atlantic Beach pie into my mouth and savored its lemony sweetness before replying. "Well, 'Targeting Officer' Daniels, I don't know what to tell you."

She put down her spoon of pie, sighing with growing impatience. "We have reliable information that the Atlas Group has been in touch with you. You may know them as telepaths, originally out of Russia, now based in North America. Alexander Montecristo is their newest recruit, he escaped from the camp in Cuba, a little over two years ago. Escaped with his older brother, matter of fact, but for one reason and another, Maxim didn't make it off the island until a year later."

I stalled, uneasy as I reviewed what she'd told me. It was true that Maxim had a younger brother, Sacha, he'd told me this himself. It was also true that Sacha most likely belonged to the Atlas Group. In fact, Maxim had straight-up accused Atlas of sending me the anonymous message that kicked off my search for him in the first place, basically using me as their unknowing proxy to uncover his location.

Okay, so maybe Margo Daniels did seem to have at least *some* genuine information about Maxim's brother. Yet I couldn't know for sure whether this 'officer' was an undercover Chekist or a genuine CIA operative.

She pushed aside her plate, leaned forward on both elbows, and rested her chin on folded hands, looking deep into my eyes. "What's on your mind, sugar? What can I do to ease the way?"

I took a slow breath. "Anyone can make a badge. What even is a CIA 'Targeting Officer'?"

"Oh, that's simple." She quirked a smile and delicately sipped her milkshake. "I find people who have the skills, aptitude and connections that could make them useful to the Agency."

"Well, you're way off, with me. I've only just graduated high school. In fact, thanks to all the drama since we got back from Cuba, we didn't even get to go to our own graduation ceremony."

"That's too bad." Her eyes were large with what felt like genuine sympathy. "But I promise you, there'll be other graduations, bigger and better ones. The type for the very special individuals who serve their country in a way that very few ever can."

Despite all my efforts to resist getting drawn in by this scenario, the picture she painted was compelling. Grudgingly, I said, "Maybe I could believe that you belong to some kind of intelligence agency. But really, how can I know for sure, which side you're on?"

Daniels eyed me with a *soupçon* of skepticism. Then she gathered back the plate containing her cheeseburger and took a couple minutes to finish it before replying, unfazed at the prospect of letting me observe her mulling it over.

"Lookit, *Roni*. Your buddy Maxim Santiago may have managed to fly under the radar. But his brother and the rest of the Atlas Group? That's a horse of a different color. Now, if I up and ask them for a meeting directly, what do you think will happen? Those tricky Atlas Group types just gonna burrow a little further into whatever rabbit warren they got going on. But I'm betting that if *you* ask for the meeting, a whole different story."

"Why? I'm nobody to them. And Maxim's not in contact with his brother."

"Well now, I'd have to take your word about Maxim. And you're anything but 'nobody.' In fact, Roni, I happen to know that the Atlas Group has taken an interest in you." The corners of her eyes crinkled in appreciation as she watched my mouth form a circle of surprise. "You didn't know? Well. Bless your heart. Then I'm guessing that this is going to be somethin' of a surprise."

NINE

SET-UP

In the shade of a cottonwood that stood outside the library, Kenzie kicked up both feet and rested them on the wooden bench so that the soles of his sneakers pressed against my thigh.

"A CIA officer followed us out here," he began, skeptically. "She bought you dinner, gave you a new three-word location, and told you not to mention the change in plans? Sounds *super* normal. Padi, are you sure you didn't imagine her?"

I lifted his feet up by the ankles and unceremoniously dropped them back onto the ground. He didn't resist, just sniggered. This was the kind of man-spreading silliness he'd often done when we were kids, but more recently had dropped, until just now. I couldn't tell whether he was intentionally negging me or had genuinely reverted to some thirteen-year-old version of himself.

"Of course I didn't imagine her. I'm almost sick from eating burgers and pie. You know me, I'm a social dessert eater. I would never pig out like that alone."

He made a big deal of nodding ponderously, eyes half-closed as if in deep thought.

"Let me see if I follow. Not only are we going to live in a different safe house than the one Olga picked for us, a CIA safe house in Bethesda, but also this 'CIA

Targeting Officer' wants you to set up a meeting with the Atlas Group. Atlas Group being something connected with the Elena Atlas House in Siberia and the Atlas Studios in Georgetown, and allegedly involved in helping 'unicorns' escape from the Krylov camp. Do I have that right?"

I nodded. "I know how it sounds. But she showed me her badge. And all that stuff about Atlas Group? We confirmed a lot of that, and Maxim confirmed the rest. So, y'know, it's probably true."

"She *showed you her badge*," he repeated, as if trying to parse an unknown language. "And told you to lie about where we should stay next."

"I believe her," I said, forcefully. "Obviously I asked the same questions as you."

"Well hey, good to know. Why'd you think she's CIA – apart the badge?"

"She knew so much about us."

"Could be Cheka."

I shook my head, feeling a surge of helpless anger rearing inside my chest. "We know that Brown Chevy was chasing us, Margo Daniels herself said they were CIA. And the chopper that chased them was FBI."

"Oh-ho, following us in a Chevy Cruze and then getting chased away by the FBI that doesn't sound like Chekists at all!" he said, dripping with sarcasm.

"No," I objected. "She spoke with a perfect accent. No hint of Russian. She… She's American. From one of the Carolinas, I think. In fact, yeah, I'm sure of it."

"Maxim also sounds American," he pointed out. "But he's Russian Cuban – at least assuming he told us the truth."

I shut my eyes, forcing out all the doubt he'd introduced. "Sometimes you have to trust your gut. Margo Daniels was telling me the truth."

"Alright," he conceded. "Even taking her at her word, why does CIA want to meet with Atlas?"

I shook my head. "I don't know why. She didn't say."

Kenzie pressed his lips together firmly, as if silencing himself. After a while he said, "You have to admit it, the Chekists probably want to track down their lost two-dubs. Czar Ilyin believes all those Krylov kids belong to him. He's not cool with any of them escaping. Atlas Group helps them escape. Makes sense it's a priority to catch 'em all."

"They're not Pokémon," I snapped.

But he made a good point. On paper, there was a chance the woman I'd met in the diner was an undercover agent of the Cheka. The difference was that I'd met her, talked to her, shared dessert with her. If she was one of theirs, her cover was flawless. I refused to accept that any imposter could be so convincing.

"I believe her," I repeated. "You know what else? She strongly implied that Maxim's brother Sacha and Atlas have been onto us from the start."

"How so?"

"She told me the Atlas Group knows that you and I went to the Atlas Studios in Georgetown. And the fact that she knows we went there, by the way, is another thing that makes me think she's telling the truth about being CIA. Remember? You said from the beginning it was the CIA that put spyware on my phone."

"Good memory." Kenzie gave a low whistle. "That is an excellent point."

"By the way," I said, frowning at myself for having forgotten what Kenzie had been doing in the library. "Did you get the chance to run the full check on our phones?"

"Uh-huh," he said, offhandedly. "Yes."

"And??"

"Oh, they had us. Like, almost total surveillance. Zara's and Bobbie's phones were hacked since the day Olga was found dead. Your phone still had some junk files, but it'd stopped broadcasting data once you took out the SIM card."

"Omigod. What about yours?"

He chuckled and gave a modest smile. "Clean. But then I take precautions with security. A *lot* of precautions."

"Too bad you didn't think of extending that to the rest of us," I said. I hadn't intended to provoke but I could see he took it badly at first, pouting for a few seconds until it seemed to occur to him that I maybe had a point.

"Possibly," he said, grudgingly. "It's a learning curve, 'kay? A very steep one."

I placed a hand on his arm and squeezed. "Wherever you are on that curve, you're a long way ahead of the rest of us. It's the CIA, they have all the cards."

He nodded, a distant look in his eyes for a long moment. A tiny furrow in his brow appeared, then deepened, as though something else was troubling him. I was about to ask what it was, when abruptly he asked, "You think 'Abby', our anonymous benefactor, was the Atlas Group, that they sent that message *Remember the Forgotten Village?* And not Maxim, after all?"

"Maxim's always denied sending it," I told him. "He even told us he thinks Atlas sent it, remember? And also – it makes sense of what Daniels told me. It also means that I could try to contact the Atlas Group the same way they contacted me – through my podcast."

With lips pressed firmly together, he nodded. "Figures. If everyone who's searching for Maxim went ahead and set up a search alert for his name, it'd lead to your podcast. That would include your guardian Olga, Chekists, CIA and maybe the Atlas Group, too. When you published the trailer for your podcast, Maxim's name would have come up in the program notes. Someone who knew him very well sent that first message to you. Only Maxim or someone real close to him could have known about the jazz piece we played together when we were all kids. It could have been his brother."

"My thoughts exactly. I'm guessing that now they're watching for any new comments on my podcast."

"If they're any good they are," he acknowledged. "So, are you going to help the CIA, if this Daniels person really is CIA?"

"I'm not sure I can refuse. She made it pretty clear that the CIA knew enough about what we did in Cuba to get us in a lot of trouble. But also, I think it might be good for us? For closure, I mean. We got into this because of 'Abby' posting that message on my podcast, after all. And it's not like we've been too far off track with our hunches, even if they weren't always on the money. Like, we'd guessed that the CIA listened to the pod. Before Olga had me fake-kidnapped, we even wondered if somehow the CIA posted that

'Forgotten Village' message, remember? Then, I thought it was her, but now I *know* Olga wasn't our anonymous benefactor. Maxim said he wasn't, either. It'd be good to finally get to the bottom of that, to find out who did post it."

At the other end of the bench, Kenzie crossed his legs and placed his hands on his knees like he was doing yoga. "Huge if true," he agreed. "It'd mean that all along, we've had not just Chekists and apparently also CIA on our six, but also Maxim's younger, cooler bro."

"Define 'cooler'?"

He threw back his head and groaned. "Oh man, it's so obvious. The way Maxim talks about his brother. Dude was what – twelve? Three years younger than Maxim, when they escaped from the Krylov camp. Made it all the way to Havana. Unlike Max, baby brother actually made it off the island. And now Sacha, ay-kay-ay 'Alexander Montecristo,' is part of some free-world, telepath underground railroad? Meanwhile Maxim is still stuck in Cuba. Yeah, I know which of those two boys I'd rather be."

I couldn't speak, feeling anger rising within me. It took me by surprise and for a few seconds I sat in silence, shaken at my own resentment. What was making me feel so instinctively defensive of Maxim? It was clear, when we parted ways, that the boy we'd known in elementary school had grown into a powerful and dangerous telepath. Despite the misgivings that had filled me on that last day in Cuba, I could sense the revival of whatever had drawn me to him in the first place and sent me chasing after him, when Olga told me she'd found Maxim Santiago.

For a few more seconds, I struggled with my conflicted feelings and eventually managed to say,

"Okay, good to know. Sounds like you agree that I should try to contact Atlas somehow, see if there's any way they'd agree to a meeting?"

"I didn't say that. But if you do, I should go with you."

With a helpless laugh, I said, "Assuming they agree to the meet and I'd in any way be invited? Sure, why not? Unless you're too busy with your pipeline-blowing project?"

I was teasing him, but in his expression, I spotted a brief flare of anger, which Kenzie instantly buried. "Watch what you say in front of that CIA officer, would you? And my moms. Could get me in trouble."

Smirking, I quipped, "Ya think?"

I got to my feet, and we made our way back to the car, where Bobbie and Zara were carefully repacking the trunk. We'd left the last house in such a rush that Zara's usual meticulous packing hadn't been achievable, now they were correcting that.

"I love your moms" I said fondly as we approached. We paused a little way back, out of earshot of his two parents, absorbed as they were by the task of playing Tetris with our bags. "No matter what the situation, they maintain their high standards."

"I wonder how they'll react to the news."

"You mean, that it turned out to be the CIA chasing us, not Chekists? We don't have to tell them. Daniels seemed pretty sure that no one else is tailing us, now they've shaken the FBI. We're on the lam to stay away from Chekists, right? That's what Olga told your parents. So we should just stick to that plan."

"What if there's a mole at the FBI or CIA? Isn't that exactly what Olga warned against?"

"The Feds are off our trail, so hopefully they can't give us away now. Which was Olga's main concern, FBI not CIA. As to the latter, not a lot we can do about them. For now, I think we have to trust Margo Daniels, go to the CIA safe house, not Olga's."

"Trust Daniels," he pointed out, "a person that we haven't met,"

"I've met her."

Kenzie rolled his eyes in exasperation. His shoulders heaved up and down a few times. He seemed to be wrestling with his conscience. After another irritable sigh, he spoke again. "Fine. I trust *you*. I guess that is all that really counts for me. Not sure it'll be that way for Bobbie and Zara."

I hesitated, replying to Zara's quizzical smile with a small wave. "Then we don't tell them. They don't need to know about any meeting with the Atlas Group. The most important thing for them is to keep us safe."

He sucked in a long, shaky breath and gave me a searching look. "Damn. This Margo Daniels must really be something. Takes a lot to make you lie to people who trust you, yet one cheeseburger dinner and this lady's got you eating out of her hands, ready to swerve right off course, switch lanes and start taking orders from the CIA."

I gave his chest a playful shove and pushed past him, heading for the car and his moms. Now wasn't the time to mention the not-so-subtle threats of consequences for what we'd done in Cuba, which underlay Margo Daniels's request.

TEN

RECON

I tried talking more to Kenzie in the back of the car, but at first, he seemed vague, his responses mostly monosyllabic, like his mind was mostly elsewhere. In the front, Zara and Bobbie were deep in a discussion about one of their friends and whether she and her partner should go ahead with a divorce or try one more time to make things work.

Eventually, Kenzie engaged with me, but only to bring it back to his quibbles. "Go to a *different* safe house," he mused. "But don't mention it's not actually the one your *tia* picked. Set up the meeting with Atlas, go to the meeting, but don't tell Eminem about the meeting. That's your plan?"

Eminem was our secret name for his moms, a code for 'Mom' and 'Ma' – 'M' and 'M.'

I gave an uncomfortable nod, moved a little closer to him and lowered my voice another notch. "It sounds bad, when you put it like that. But if we *do* set up the meeting, we can't tell them about it. No way Eminem let us go, if we do that. I don't think you're aware how rattled they were by us taking off to Mexico and then finding out everything we did in Cuba."

"Oh, I'm aware. Don't blame me!" Vigorously, he shook his head. "You're the one who insisted on telling them."

"Yes," I hissed, digging a finger into his ribs until he let out a suppressed wince. "Because we need them to trust us. We'll go to this new safe house. Once we start to venture out for supplies, we'll find someplace suitable, a place we could suggest for a meeting with Maxim's brother. Then one day we'll do a bit more than fetch the supplies. And that's all. No need to lie."

"Other than about the safe house."

He had me there. I tried to shrug it off. "The other one isn't safe, if we've been compromised. So technically there's only one safe house – and we're going there."

He observed me for a couple of seconds and then burst into peals of laughter. "Oh, wow. You actually believe that will work!"

"Seriously? Mister 'I'm gonna blow up an oil pipeline' is lecturing me about being frank with his parents?"

Kenzie frowned. "You're making me wish I'd kept my mouth shut."

"Why didn't you?"

"Because we're in it together. Whatever 'it' is. Because I need someone I can trust. And if that's not you then…"

He stopped talking. I'm pretty sure I heard a crack in his voice. I reached out a hand and took his in mine. "You can trust me. I promise. Doesn't mean I'm not going to tell you what I think about your plans, though. I don't want to have to visit you in prison."

He leaned his head on my shoulder, and I felt his muscles gradually relax. After a moment he began to talk again, half to himself, as though he was using me as a sounding board. "It won't come to that. Firstly, who knows if this will ever happen. So far, it's just me and some other folks chatting and what-if-ing. Secondly, there are lawyers who are putting together a pretty solid defense for this kind of activism. These fossil fuel companies are trashing the future of everyone on this planet. Some communities will be affected worse and more quickly. People from those communities have a right to defend themselves. And if the only way is to break the company, then that is a legitimate action of self-defense."

It sounded kind of marginal to me. "Has anybody gotten off the charges by using this kind of defense, yet?

He tensed briefly, then sat up straight, withdrawing so that we were no longer touching. "There's a group," he began, still speaking quietly, squinting at Bobbie through the car's internal mirror. "Five people. Two were minors – just. They knew they'd get the least sentence, so they arranged to take the blame. They're in prison now. And one of them used the defense I'm talking about. Got a reduced sentence. Five years instead of ten."

"Jeez! They were what, seventeen? And now this boy's in prison until he's twenty-two?"

"What are you two talking about back there," called Bobbie. She sounded medium-suspicious and had spotted Kenzie monitoring her via the mirror.

"About this guy we heard about who's in prison for cyber-fraud," I said, probably not very convincingly.

Zara turned around, eyes wide with curiosity. "What did he do?" She faced me, intense expectation written on her face.

"Boosted some crypto," Kenzie broke in, coming to my rescue. "And would have done no time at all, but that would have meant giving up the other three."

"There were others?" Zara asked, her eyes narrowing. She probably smelled chicanery but couldn't be sure.

"There were," he confirmed. Then he turned to me and said something that would have confused Zara no end. "Worth it. When you think of what we have to lose, it's totally worth it."

I was reeling. *He's actually thinking about this pipeline thing.*

"What happened to the others?" Zara asked, now apparently invested enough in the story to know how it ended.

"Well, that girl, she got serious jail time. It wasn't her first offense. She did two months in juvie and now she's in some prison colony. The others…"

Zara frowned, b-s- detector probably in the red zone and interrupted, "Roni said 'guy.'"

I decided to double down. "Yeah, I thought it was a guy."

"No," Kenzie insisted, shooting me a glare. "A girl… Charly. With what some might think sounds like a guy's name, y'know, like 'Bobbie' or 'Roni.'"

"Is that Charlie with two 'e's? A 'y'? Or eye-ee?" asked Zara, winking and poking Bobbie in the arm. Bobbie said nothing, focused on driving, but I could tell she was listening attentively and periodically glancing at us sharply in the car's internal mirror.

"Charly with a 'y'" gritted Kenzie.

I folded both arms across my chest, enjoying watching his coded performance. "So, what's 'Charly' doing now?"

"The heck would I know?" he scowled, to Zara's laughter. But the instant his mom finally turned away to face forward he leaned in close, whispering to me, "And Charly is the one running this op."

I mouthed back, "From prison?"

"She gets messages out. There are ways." He ducked down into the footwell, to avoid yet more chary scrutiny, this time from Zara. "Darn, my laces."

As he bent to tie them, I took a few seconds to compose myself, relieved that he and Zara had both been too distracted to notice the shock that had surely registered on my face as he'd spoken about the climate activists. Frankly, I wasn't sure that Zara bought his crypto-heist cover story, but Kenzie had chosen well. In that car, only one person had the first clue about crypto, and it wasn't her. He'd thrown his moms off the track, anyhow.

Meantime, it had taken a minute for my somewhat distracted brain to comprehend the gravity of his new project. But finally, I got it. And the size of it was almost too much for me to handle without gasping aloud, or something worse.

I recognized that fire in his voice – I'd last heard it when he had demanded to join me on the quest for Maxim Santiago. At the time, I'd believed it was a one-off. I'd never really thought of Kenzie as a risk taker. I'd seen him more as an adorable dork with a penchant for researching cybercrime, although not actually committing it – so far. Yet I knew deep down, the boy who'd helped break into the Krylov camp in Cuba was something different, something more.

Kenzie had flown secretly to Cuba with me, on a narco-plane. He'd helped liberate a camp that had imprisoned around twenty telepathic kids and teenagers, who'd faced being sold as slaves to the secret services of the planet's worst authoritarian regimes. He was an outlier, a person who'd go the extra several miles to save someone's life.

Why had I ever believed he'd limit himself to mere research, once we returned from Cuba? I had to face it. Between the two of us, it felt to me that Kenzie was the wild one.

We arrived tired and hungry from the long drive and already missing our rural idyll in the Shenandoah National Park. The CIA safe house was in Bethesda, on the north side of the Potomac, same as Washington DC, roughly the same distance from the Capitol as where we lived in Falls Church. It has similar houses in the residential district, and we wound up in a place a little smaller than Zara and Bobbie's home, and a lot less nicely decorated. Downstairs it wasn't too bad; they'd taken some effort to make it look like a regular living room with couches and a TV and a normal kitchen. Upstairs however, the pretense had been dropped. Nothing but cot beds with worn bed linen and the bare minimum of towels.

"How long do we have to stay here?" Zara asked in evident dismay.

Bobbie sighed. Neither woman was happy at the CIA officer's intervention in our living situation – and that was without even knowing about it. "Olga's letter didn't say. So presumably, indefinitely."

"Do you think anyone would mind if we made it more homely?"

"What? No. Overkill," Kenzie said. "It's government property. Our taxes already paid for what's here."

Zara's voice sounded heavy with sadness. "Homeliness isn't the real problem though, is it? We're still cut off from our lives. And we don't even know for how long."

I cleared my throat, urging myself not to dwell on what Zara had said. "We're gonna head out and explore the neighborhood. Maybe we can pick up a few things for the house."

Then I grabbed Kenzie's hand and led him out of there, before either parent could object.

ELEVEN

RETURN TO ATLAS STUDIOS

Kenzie was happy enough to escape that rather melancholy, empty place, but when he realized we were waiting for a bus rather than shopping locally for trinkets, he demanded answers.

"I want to go back to Atlas Studios. It's open until seven in the evening – I checked."

He looked startled. "What? But we're banned from Georgetown. Still gotta worry about Chekists."

"We're banned from school and anywhere near it. But the Chekists weren't following us before Mexico – that was the CIA. Therefore, Cheka probably doesn't know we went to the Atlas Studios. It's not one of our regular hangouts," I said, trying to be optimistic. "Maybe it's safe."

He said nothing but the surprise didn't leave his face for almost a minute. When eventually it did, a deeply pensive expression took its place.

There'd been a time when we'd suspected Chekists might have followed us to the Atlas Studios but now that we knew it was the CIA who'd put spyware on my phone, I wasn't so sure. Someone had left a message for me to find in the restroom – FIND UNICORNS – written by finger and revealed only when steam from the hot water faucet condensed on polished stone that functioned as a mirror.

This much was certain: whoever left FIND UNICORNS knew we were at the Atlas Studios. There was a chance we'd been followed and that someone had sneaked into the restroom just before me, to leave the message. But I hadn't noticed anyone leaving the restroom as I went in, nor had there been anyone in the room with me. Something weird happened to me in there, I knew it. Minutes had passed, minutes I hadn't noticed, as if I'd been in some kind of trance. They'd even had to bang on the door to get my attention.

Now that I knew it was possible to be 'inclined' by a two-dub, I had a theory about what had probably happened. I'd been inclined to finger-write FIND UNICORNS on the mirror for myself to find. A message from a two-dub, via my subconscious mind.

The question was – *which* telepath? They had to be physically near enough to me, although not necessarily with a line of sight. Maxim had managed to incline me from miles away, but he and I had an emotional bond that reached deep into our childhood, which made a psi link between us that much easier. He hadn't told me enough about how the ability worked, what were its limits or range. So, I had to hypothesize.

What if a two-dub that was a stranger could incline a person, but they had to be in a line of sight? Or at least, a line of sight within sometime of being inclined? In that case, they might need to be physically much closer. Maybe a two-dub who didn't know me would have to be in the same building, or just outside?

What if the person actually worked at Atlas Studios? It wasn't unreasonable to suggest that members of the Atlas Group might hang out in a museum funded by an organization with a similar name, an organization with roots in Russia, just like the Atlas Group itself.

I didn't feel like talking Kenzie through every step of this reasoning, maybe because I wasn't certain if it made sense. All I knew was that I needed to understand what happened to me, or if something even *had* happened. It was one thing to know that Maxim Santiago was able to 'incline' me. But the idea that a nameless, faceless person might walk past me in the street and interfere with my mind, even worse, incline me to actually do something, that was an idea that I found scarier by the day.

I needed to know if another two-dub like Maxim had inclined me to write FIND UNICORNS in the mirror that day. If they had, I needed to look whoever did it in the eye and ideally, stay away from them for the rest of my life. I knew instinctively that once Margo Daniels knew we were wandering around the city she'd force Kenzie's moms to rein us in. If there was a time to return to Atlas Studios, it was today.

Kenzie surprised me, however. I didn't need to explain anything to him, because on the bus to Georgetown he turned to me, cupped a hand over my ear and whispered, "I think I've figured out why we're going to the Atlas Studios. Don't talk about it though, cos I think Daniels might have put spyware on your phone, again. At the diner."

Appalled, I turned to him. Solemnly, with his lips pressed together tightly, he gave a couple of emphatic nods of his head. Leaning in, I spoke into his ear. "If you're right, you think she'll be tracking us through my phone?"

Gently, Kenzie pushed me away and took another turn speaking into my ear. "Yes. Which is why next stop,

I'm getting off the bus with your phone. I'll lead them on some wild goose chase for an hour or so. You head for the Atlas Studios. We'll catch up later."

It was a while before I managed to take my eyes off his departing figure. I'd talked myself into worrying that he'd moved on from our mission to find Maxim Santiago, that he was more interested in his climate activist pals and their reckless plan to blow up an oil pipeline. I was wrong. When it came to the Maxim mission, Kenzie was one step ahead of me; he'd figured out that if the CIA had been onto us from the start, using us as unwitting assets to do recon for them, then despite his efforts to scrub my phone, they might have found a way to keep tracking us.

Inwardly I groaned, remembering how Daniels had picked up on my ploy to distract her with desserts at the diner, and turned it back against me, made me believe she was this charming Southern auntie with a sweet tooth, not a shark working for the government, while she sneaked spyware onto my phone.

I'm an idiot. Everyone knows you can't con a con.

Anyway, thank goodness for Kenzie. He'd given me a way to spend an hour or so investigating the Atlas Studios. At the thought of some rando strutting around DC and fooling with my mind, my guts stirred into a cold froth, like snakes sliding over ice. One way or another, I had to know. Because if that was a thing, I could get fully on board with helping the CIA. I'd arrange the *heck* out of a meeting with the Atlas Group, if it could help me put a face to my psychic stalker.

Just like the last time, it was pretty quiet at the Atlas Studios. The same woman as before was there, the one I'd nicknamed 'Boujee,' although her appearance was so different that at first glance, I didn't recognize her. Last time she'd rocked a sulky, borderline eating disorder, photographic model vibe. Today her long hair tumbled loose and wavy over her shoulders, she wore wire-rimmed glasses and gave off more of a willowy life-model-with-her clothes-on situation, with a floaty muslin shift dress that seemed to have been casually thrown on top of beige linen dungarees with nothing underneath. The biggest betrayal was her nails. Last time I'd admired the scuffed, end-of-the-month look, but this time they were salon-perfect.

Boujee was working reception again, leaning against the counter and using brightly colored pencils on a mandala-themed coloring book. I thought I glimpsed a flicker of recognition, when I emerged from the rotating glass door, and made a point of looking her straight in the eye. She masked any recognition pretty well, if so and gave me a faux-friendly smile.

"Hi, welcome to the Atlas Studios. Would you like to stay for a free workshop? It starts in twenty minutes. Germaine will be showing us how to sculpt a block of blue ice into a crumbling glacier."

I shook my head. "I wanted to check if I left my keychain here. I lost it about three weeks ago. I've checked everywhere else; this is my last hope."

Boujee drummed pearly fingernails against the counter and thought for a moment, narrowing her eyes as if trying hard to recollect.

"I got locked in the restroom," I added, helpfully.

She eyed me with unmistakable skepticism. Oh, this girl *for sure* recognized me. She knew I wasn't here for some lost keys. "We did have a keychain handed in. But that was last week. Not, y'know, 'about three weeks ago.'"

I decided politely to insist. "May I please check the restroom? Perhaps my keys fell behind the cistern?"

Boujee pulled a very obviously fake and mirthless grin. "Sure. I mean, the cistern is built into the wall, so probably not... But feel free to take a look." She reached under the counter for the restroom key and slid it across to me.

I replied with a stony glare. Boujee was in on it, whatever 'it' was. "By the way," I quipped, trying to sound casual. "Any chance that Alexander Montecristo was here three weeks ago, when I visited and maybe lost my keychain?"

For a brief moment she was unable to mask her surprise at hearing me name Maxim's brother. Confusion followed. She looked down at the counter, her beautiful, long fingers intertwined in what seemed to be an attempt to control any fidgeting. When she raised her eyes to me again, it was from beneath her lashes, as if vulnerable and a little afraid.

I recoiled. *Are you kidding me with the Bambi eyes?* Pressing her, I said, "So, was he?"

"I don't know who you're talking about," she said, coyly.

I'd never seen anyone so obviously fake. I turned and hurried to the restroom. By the time I'd gotten inside, I had to lean against the cool stone wall to stop myself from shaking.

Alexander Montecristo *had* been at the Atlas Studios that day. Boujee, with her pathetic attempt to hide the truth, had all but confirmed it. It didn't matter that I hadn't noticed him – there had been enough opportunity for someone to stay out of sight, especially an innocuous teenager. I was sure of it: Maxim's brother 'Sacha' had been in the building at the same time as me.

He'd inclined me to write FIND UNICORNS on the mirror. Alexander Montecristo had tampered with my brain, used me like a puppet, long before I even knew such a thing was possible.

Goddamn right, I wanted to meet him. Margo Daniels might be a government stooge, but this time it would be *me* using the CIA.

TWELVE

LABYRINTH

Well, I was back in that restroom. The instant I felt the bolt lock the door; a weird sensation took hold of me. It felt kind of like the opposite of *déjà vu:* instead of a jolt of recognition as a memory was triggered, I had an odd feeling of something out of place in the memory, something *wrong*.

I'd revisited memories of this place several times over the past weeks, yet now, it was like I was seeing it for the first time. In my memory there'd been a stone mirror over a round wash basin made from distressed steel. Now I saw that the mirror was made from matt-finished, gray sheet metal, not stone, the same material as the basin. In my memory the industrial duct that ran across the ceiling was polished metal that shone. But in reality, it was just more of the same dull, distressed steel.

Over by the basin, I wrote HELLO AGAIN on the mirror, then turned the faucet. It took a full five seconds before it grew hot enough to make steam, another five seconds before any of that steam condensed on the metal sheet that functioned as a mirror, and two full minutes before there was enough steam to read the writing.

I closed the faucet. In my memory, I'd been able to read the message immediately. No wonder Kenzie had fetched Boujee to help get me out of there. I must have been lost in inclination for ages. The telepath who'd inclined me could have been upstairs, out of sight. Or maybe they'd been hovering near the restroom door, behind Boujee and Kenzie. Would Kenzie have noticed? If he'd been freaking out about me, I could see him missing a detail like that.

Taking one last look around the place, I tried to fix its true appearance in my mind. Would the memory now get rewritten with the correct details? I was curious to find out, and a little worried about what that said about how reliable any memory could ever be.

After I exited, I asked Boujee for a piece of paper and a pen, scribbled a message to Sacha Montecristo and handed it to her.

"Be a pal, give this to Sacha."

She didn't even read the message, instead batting her copper-shaded eyelids a couple times. I waited, my features arranged in my best attempt at patience, until I was persuaded, she finally understood that yes, really, I wasn't buying her nonsense.

Boujee wafted the paper in front of me, petulantly. "I don't know who that is."

I took a single breath. "Oh-kay, sure. Just leave it on the pin board in your staff room, or whatever."

I turned to leave. She called after me, half-hearted. "You're wasting your time,"

Without turning back, I waved. "Can't wait to chat to him. I have questions for the lad."

And yeah, he called me. Well, texted me. Someone did, anyway, the following morning, when I was back at the Bethesda house; texted me with a time and an address.

Watching me text a reply, Kenzie asked, "Atlas Group? It's on?"

"Hundred percent."

Truth was, it felt more like ninety. Going off a hunch and bluffing someone weren't tactics I'd dared try before. A mixture of logical reasoning and intuition had led me to revisit Atlas Studios. Whoever had texted me, they'd suggested we meet in the center of the labyrinth of the Georgetown Waterfront Park at 4pm. Kenzie and I arranged another expedition to fetch supplies and once again, he ran interference for me, while I headed for the rendezvous.

I decided not to let the CIA officer know. It would be a test of whether they'd once again hacked my phone. Each time the bus slowed at a stop, I peered outside, scanning the line for Margo Daniels. But there was no sign of her. As I rode into Georgetown, I began to regret my decision.

If you set up a secret CIA meeting, does it count if you don't tell the CIA?

As I approached the waterfront park, I stopped to read one of the noticeboards that displayed a map. The labyrinth was about seventy yards away. It was warm enough that I wore only a blue-and-pink striped T-shirt and light blue jeans, a beige, knitted cotton hoodie tied around my waist. No phone – that was with Kenzie, so I couldn't be traced. The CIA, I assumed, would have read the text about setting up the meeting. At least – they would if Margo Daniels actually had sneaked spyware onto my phone, while we ate pie.

Nearing the labyrinth, I continued to survey my surroundings. The ridiculousness and possible danger of what we'd done was only now hitting me.

Why hadn't I simply told Daniels about the meeting? What if whoever showed up from the Atlas Group decided that I was a CIA stooge and broke off contact? I could give Daniels the phone number from which they'd texted me, but it was probably a burner, soon to be chopped into pieces and dropped into a garbage can.

Would Daniels follow through with her veiled threat to expose what we'd done in Cuba?

Again, I asked myself who'd show up to the meeting. I was hoping it would be Maxim's brother but couldn't be sure. How many fifteen-year-olds were in the Atlas Group? In my mind they were a shadowy bunch of Russian Americans, plus at least one Russian-Cuban teen. Not all that Cuban, either.

Maxim, when we'd been school pals at the international school, had spoken clumsy, accented Spanish. He and his brother had been born and lived in Cuba for most of their lives. Yet, imprisoned within the Krylov Foundation camp in a forest many miles from Santiago de Cuba, they knew nothing about Cuba. For Maxim, Sacha and the other two-dubs – so-called 'unicorns' prized on the black market by intelligence and security agencies – the outside world simply didn't exist until they were sold to a 'controller.'

Twenty yards from the labyrinth, I spotted a slim teenage boy wearing a blue-and-yellow plaid shirt over a white T-shirt and faded gray jeans. He seemed to be waiting tentatively on the edge but the instant our eyes made contact, he began to stride towards the center. Aside from the two of us, only one other group was standing on the labyrinth's outline – a woman with two little girls. They were playing the game properly, beginning from the outer edge and navigating inwards according to its design.

When I reached the center, I saw that the plaid-clad teenage boy was deceptively tall. His slender frame was delicate, nothing like Maxim's. His shoulders were narrow, his face and features were those of a younger boy, not a fifteen-year-old. Maybe he'd had a recent growth spurt or something and his body had been stretched to take up three inches more than a year before. Either way, he came over as more of a tall kid of about thirteen, not like some of the fifteen-year-old football players at school. His eyes were green, and his skin was lightly tanned. His light brown hair was short on the sides and long bangs styled into up-swept spikes.

This boy's in flux, I thought. Wonder if his brother would even recognize him?

As I thought this, the boy's eyes crinkled. He smiled a fresh, honest smile. The timing was so perfect, it crossed my mind that he'd heard my thought. But that was impossible, according to what Maxim had told me. Only another telepath could broadcast their thoughts. A normie, or even a 'one-dub' like me, could not be 'read' because we couldn't 'send.'

"You shouldn't believe everything my brother says," the boy said, as if intervening in a conversation. Despite his youthful demeanor, his voice was fully broken and deeper than Maxim's. His smile became apologetic, and he rubbed the back of his head with one hand.

For several seconds, I could only gawp at him, wordlessly. My reaction seemed to freak him out a little. Hurriedly, he stuck out a hand. "I'm Sacha, Maxim's brother. It's so good to finally meet you."

I managed no more than "Omigosh."

He was reading my thoughts. *Definitely.* Maxim had sworn he couldn't do that. *You shouldn't believe everything my brother says.* I felt queasy, remembering some of the thoughts I'd had in Maxim's presence. Yet amid the wave of panic, a stern voice within me insisted that I also recall the misunderstandings we'd had, he and I. *That dude did not know your thoughts,* the voice said. *Sometimes he didn't even pay attention to what you actually told him with your words.*

Sacha reached for my hand and made contact, gently. I allowed him to slide his fingers around mine. "Follow me?" he said, eyebrows raised in hope. Then he led me away. Apart from the tiniest hesitation, I followed.

THIRTEEN

A QUESTION

Sacha lured me to a coffee truck by the river's edge. In something of a daze, I watched him order two vanilla ice cream cones and iced coffee for us both.

"You're kind of young to be drinking coffee," I observed, pointlessly. He responded with an evasive smile and for a few seconds said nothing. It was a perfect response, given he'd probably noticed I was digging about for something to say.

"Your CIA handler is over there," he announced, out of the blue. When I turned slightly towards my left, he touched my hand and locked eyes with me. "Don't turn around," he whispered, tilting his head slightly in warning. "It's what you wanted, isn't it? To bring CIA to me?"

Like Maxim, Sacha used 'CIA' without the definite article – a sign that they'd trained together, perhaps?

Anyhow, there was no point being sassy or clever, no point trying to keep my thoughts to myself or trying to outwit a person who can literally read your mind.

"How do you know all this?"

He took in a slow, considered breath before replying. When he blinked, I couldn't help but notice his long, dark eyelashes. He was a sweet-looking kid, with such a gentle presentation that I had to wonder if it was genuine. This boy had escaped Cuba when Maxim couldn't. Kenzie believed this made him the tougher kid, but watching Sacha I began to reflect that maybe something else had factored. Maybe Sacha had been rescued because he'd been the cuter, younger brother?

Eventually, he asked, "You think we have been surveilling you?"

I nodded.

"Well," he began. He spoke for a moment and sounded so strangely like his brother that I actually missed what he said.

"I'm sorry," I said, attempting a smile. "What d'you say?"

"I said – we've been watching your podcast website."

"So how would you know about any 'CIA handler'?"

He laughed out loud. "Honestly? I was joking around. I didn't know for certain, not until just now. But I know how to spot someone shadowing me. Then I guessed right, yes? You actually made a deal with the CIA?"

I was shaking my head, nodding my head, totally outside of my normal ability to deal rationally with anything. *This guy was for sure reading my mind*. How was I supposed to deal with that?

"I'm sorry," I managed to say. "I'm having kind of a hard time handling the whole mind-reading thing. Do you usually have this problem with non-telepaths? Like, do you tease us, make us think you can read minds, when you can't? Or are you trolling me, right now, and you can, in fact, totally read my mind? See, now that you're having your fun and all, do you get that

I don't know whether to trust a goddamn thing you say?"

He didn't reply. All the humor had drained from his face.

"Or is it that you don't know any normies? Is it like… Are you all in some kind of two-dub clique?"

Sacha sighed and I sensed sadness in him for the first time.

"Well…? Which is it?"

He swallowed. For just a second, anger loomed, behind his eyes. "I'm sorry," he said quietly, staring into his iced coffee. "I can't read your mind."

He raised his head and watched me for several seconds, observing my conflicted emotions playing out.

"Then why the hell did you say it, you little prick?"

Sacha flinched. "Why did I say *what?*"

"Oh, dumb games now?"

"No. I mean it. What do you think I said?"

"I don't *think* it. I *heard* you say it, not even five minutes ago. '*You shouldn't believe everything my brother says.*' You said it right when I was wondering if you could read my mind and remembering that Maxim said no, you can't."

His eyes widened. "Oh-ho. Got it. I deserve that. I wanted to find out if my brother told you he could read minds. It's the kind of thing he would do. I guess I let him influence me too much. Hence joking around with you."

I shook my head, unconvinced. "It sure seemed like you read my mind."

"I can maybe guess what you're thinking, sometimes, from context. I'm pretty good at that. But anyone can learn to do it."

Con men do that, I thought. Is that what he was – a con artist?

He gave the merest shrug of his shoulders, like shaking off a fly. "Are you saying that Maxim *did not* tell you that he could read minds?"

Still somewhat resentful, I replied, "Disappointed, much?"

"Course not, that's good, it's a good thing that he didn't lie to you about that," he said after such a long pause that I wondered if he believed it. "Maxim wasn't a very nice person, back when we were growing up. He liked to play mind games. When you're a telepath, mind games are on a whole other level. But you were his friend, weren't you? That's what you said in your podcast."

Sacha had listened to the trailer for *What Happened to the Santiagos?* It was the only episode of that series we'd ever made, although I'd written scripts for others.

When Olga had me abducted and brought to her safe house, she'd urged me not to make any further episodes. She'd warned me of the dangers of posting any more information about Maxim. By then, Kenzie and I had uncovered the link to the international trade in 'unicorns' in a leaked CIA document, although we didn't know yet that 'unicorns' meant telepathic kids trained to be secret agents. Even so, I knew just enough to believe Olga's warning.

Neither Olga nor I had accurately assessed the level of threat to us. We thought something might be approaching but we were wrong. The danger had already arrived, which is why Olga died the following day. Chekists had been surveilling her, who knows for how long. When they discovered she had a lead on long-lost property of the Krylov Foundation, the infamous

Maxim Santiago, they murdered Olga but let me go, so I could unwittingly lead them to Maxim.

I'm not sure why I told Sacha all this. It was difficult to keep secrets from so many people – Kenzie's moms, the CIA officer, Daniels, and even Kenzie. Once I'd started talking, I couldn't seem to stop. How much of what I told Sacha was news to him, I wasn't sure.

When I was done bringing him up to speed about Olga, he took a notepad and pencil from his back jeans pocket and scribbled something, turned the pad around so I could read it.

CIA are following. Can hear everything.

I read the writing, frozen in confusion. My thoughts raced, backtracking through everything I'd said since I first opened my mouth in Sacha's presence. Had I, in fact, given something important away? It'd felt like Daniels knew pretty much everything, including things I preferred she didn't. But still – it would be better to keep *some* information for a rainy day, to offer as a trade in case the CIA ever decided to act on their threats.

Sacha responded only with a barely perceptible nod, then tore away the top sheet with the scribbled note, put it aside and began writing again.

Awe-Some Burger, Tenleytown. 6.30pm.

Once he saw that I'd read and absorbed this, he tore away the page and then ripped both sheets of paper into tiny fragments, which he held in one fist.

"Buy me time?" he murmured, hopefully. Then he leapt to his feet and sprinted towards the Potomac River, leaving me blinking in bemused confusion and watching him dash like an arachnophobe who's just seen a huge spider.

That was my first surprise. One second later the second surprise came along. To the left of our table, where Sacha had identified a 'CIA handler,' but also three tables behind us, a man and woman instantly broke cover and set off in pursuit.

Hurriedly I stood up and lurched into the path of the woman as best I could. I barely managed to delay her for a second or two. She swerved in time to avoid me, using what looked like parkour skills to ricochet off a metal table instead of crashing into it.

Sacha was making a beeline for the river. When he reached it, without a second's hesitation, he made a clean dive into the water. I and a few other diners were still staring in goggle-eyed awe to see anyone swim in the Potomac, when the female officer dove in after him. She was fast but he was faster. The water seemed to be the perfect element for his long, slender frame. He cut across in less than a minute and had almost reached the opposite shore when a speedboat approached him, slowed down then two arms lifted him out of the water. The officer in pursuit became caught up in the powerful wake, when the speedboat swirled around and headed back in the direction it'd come.

More and more people were now approaching the bank to watch the drama. The male officer who'd been clocked by Sacha popped an earbud into his right ear in one smooth movement as he cleared a flower bed. I guessed he was calling for support for his colleague, who appeared to be in trouble. Someone who I had assumed was just another passer-by kicked off his shoes and jumped into the river. He swam powerfully toward the officer, who was definitely struggling against the current.

All eyes were on the water. This, I realized, was my chance to slip away. At least once, I'd seen the male officer taking note of my position, but whatever their plan for me, it seemed to have been abandoned. They probably hadn't factored in that Sacha would swim for it. Why would they even? I was still trying to wrap my head around it, seconds after the fact.

I walked backwards for a few steps until I'd melted into the gathering crowd, then I turned and sprinted without stopping, all the way to the Foggy Bottom metro station. I leapt aboard the first train and sank into the nearest corner seat, uncomfortably conscious of the sweat trickling down my back and sides, and of my heaving breaths. It took me several minutes to stabilize.

That's when it hit me: I hadn't yet asked Sacha the most important question, the thing that had piqued my curiosity from the beginning. The question that'd triggered our quest to search for Maxim Santiago and the 'unicorns.'

Had *Sacha Montecristo* posted the message *'Remember the Forgotten Village?'*

FOURTEEN

MEMORY

There was no point returning to the Bethesda safe house, if I was planning to make the 6:30pm rendezvous at Awe-Some Burger in Tenleytown. I took the metro as far as Wisconsin Avenue Northwest, then headed for the restroom at a nearby McDonald's. In the sink I rinsed my sweat-soaked shirt in the coldest water I could draw and wiped my torso, neck and forehead with the cool, damp shirt.

There were a handful of people in the restroom, but nobody bothered to look at a Sweaty Betty that for some reason liked to go running in ninety degrees of heat. After checking my watch, I took a minute to apply a little eyeliner and lip balm, my bare minimum for leaving the house.

It crossed my mind for a second that I was fixing my appearance for Maxim's younger brother. How old was the guy? Fifteen, maybe sixteen? Could be up to two years younger than me, which puts him out of any contention, at least according to my own rules. So why was I even thinking about it? I pushed that thought away and headed for the door.

It was almost six. By now I was hungry enough to eat, so I ordered on the touchscreen and waited until my McPlant, fries and vanilla milkshake were delivered. At a table facing the door, I began to eat, surprised at how hungry I was. My fingers twitched with the impulse to reach for a cell phone that I kept forgetting was now with Kenzie.

Radio silence, remember, Padilla?

The CIA clearly had other ways to track us, or maybe they'd tracked me to the waterfront park from the bus? Had they also tracked me to this McDonalds? Furtively, I scanned the area, trying to catch out anyone who might be keeping me in their sight. When a second guy locked eyes with me and began to smile as if to say *who, me?* I ditched that technique. On second thoughts, no respectable intelligence officer would get caught out with such an amateurish ploy, meantime I was putting myself in real danger of beckoning a stalker.

At 6:24pm I left and reached the nearby Awe-Some Burger by 6:29pm. Sacha was already there. He'd also taken a table facing the door and his food was already finished. I took the seat opposite.

"We both made it," he said, chuckling. His hair was still wet, slicked back from his face and giving him a scary hint of Christian Bale in *American Psycho*. There was a new awkwardness to him. His clothes were dry, I noticed. He noticed me noticing. "Yeah… They brought me spare clothes."

"So – you and your Atlas buddies planned that whole drama, the flashy speedboat getaway?"

He shrugged. "You have to plan these things. Otherwise, things get gnarly."

"That's why you picked such a public place for our meeting. So you'd see anyone following you."

"I missed one of them, actually. The one who jumped into the river after me."

"Yeah, that woman got into trouble after your ride threw a humongous wave in her path."

For a moment he seemed to consider what response would be appropriate. I really wasn't sure that he cared one way or the other about that CIA officer.

"I left my phone with Kenzie, by the way," I told him, loftily. "What with the CIA tracking me, and all."

He sounded surprised. "Oh. That's good."

"What, you assumed I'd lead them here?"

"Well sure, eventually." He shrugged. "Don't take it personally. You're new to this. CIA do it all the time. And they won't take no for an answer. We know that. I just wanted a chance to talk with you one-on-one without any intelligence officers recording us. It might be the only chance we get."

He took something from his lap and placed his hand on the table. He moved the hand away, revealing a compact, folding cell phone and an earpiece. "It's a burner," he said. "One number in the contacts – mine. Use it to talk to me. Until I tell you to break it."

"Oh," I said, too stumped for anything else. I reached for the phone and earpiece and pocketed both. "Is that all?"

"I wanted to talk to you about my brother," he said, as if it was the most obvious thing in the world. "You were friends with him, weren't you? When you were around ten or something?"

"From even younger, actually. But we were closest when we were twelve," I said nodding. "He told you about it, didn't he? About our little jazz trio."

"Maxim didn't talk about his time living outside of the camp, not until we had left. And then only one time." He fell silent for a moment, eyes glazed over, distracted, as if by a memory. Then; "Did you know we escaped?"

"I heard. What was that like? The forest around that place isn't easy. How did you manage, just the two of you?"

"There were more of us at first, but we split up after a while, to make it harder to chase us. Eventually me and Maxim got split up, too. Before that, in the camp, we didn't spend much time together. The truth is, I hardly knew him. He didn't know my stories and I didn't know his. But that one time when we were hiding out, he told me why he wanted to go back to the USA."

"Maxim wants to come back here? First I've heard."

Sacha nodded, firmly. "Back then, he did. I don't know about now. He remembered good times in that school with you and Marc Mackenzie. It was kind of incredible for me to hear that whole history, you know." He chuckled. "I couldn't imagine it. Maxim, being musical? It was just, y'know? Hard to envisage, I mean. We couldn't make music in the camp. I didn't know he could play piano. Something like that was completely out of my frame of reference, at that time. He might as well have told me that he used to be an air traffic controller, or that he played ice hockey. Things that were utterly outside our knowledge. You saw a completely different side of him. Even though you and Marc are both, y'know, not telepathic, I'm convinced that Maxim feels more kinship with the two of you than with any of us."

In his words I heard an uncomfortable undercurrent, words not precisely articulated but present just the same. Maxim and Sacha and all those other Krylov camp kids were two-dubs. Unicorns.

Differently abled from me, Kenzie, and most people on the planet. *Better* abled. That was the truth of it. Superior.

And Sacha found it astonishing that despite this, despite our mental inferiority, Maxim felt 'more kinship' with us.

"One of the first things I did," he continued, "when I finally got to safety in Florida, was listen to that song. You know the one. *The Forgotten Village*. At first, I didn't get it. I mean, it seems like a simple song, doesn't it? Ordinary. There have to be a million tunes more interesting or catchy than that one. So I kept listening to it. And finally, I understood. It's very… involving. You seem to get inside the music, like climbing inside of a giant tree and finding yourself enveloped in darkness and sound."

I caught my breath. "Wow, that's a perfect metaphor for how it feels to play that song." *Maybe he really can read minds?* "Then I guess it *was* you? Who left the message on my podcast? Remember the Forgotten Village?"

He nodded and with a smile added, "Yes, that was me. I knew only one thing about you, Roni. You can't imagine how amazed and happy I was that this small thing my brother told me, when we were hiding in the forest together, when he was actually treating me in any way like a little brother for the first time in my life, that this thing was able to connect me with you."

"Why is that so important?" I'd spoken the question aloud before I was even able to ask myself the same thing. As soon as I did, I realized that I knew *exactly* why it was so important.

To incline me in the restroom of that museum in Georgetown, the Atlas Studios, Sacha would have needed some kind of connection with me. Otherwise, I was a complete stranger. All this time, I'd wondered how he'd been able to do it. I'd assumed it was mere proximity, that he'd physically been in the same building. But it was more than that. When he'd inclined me, Maxim had relied on our deep emotional connection, something that went back into my childhood, in order to manipulate my limbs with my own brain under his direction.

Had Sacha used me the same way? Had he used inside information about me, to manipulate me?

Instinctively, I stood up and pushed back my chair so forcefully that it scraped noisily against the floor. After a brief moment, where surprise and disappointment flickered across his face, Sacha's reaction was oddly calm.

"I don't think I want to be used anymore," I heard myself saying. "Maybe you and your brother should leave me alone."

FIFTEEN

IN DENIAL

After a swift shower back at the Bethesda house, I made myself square up to Bobbie and Zara. Both moms were simmering. I'd gotten to know them a little by now, well enough to recognize that their anger – even expressed in two distinct styles – demanded a response. Problem was, I was tired, stressed and also pretty ticked off at how things had ended with Sacha. I didn't feel like talking or soothing their feelings, or whatever. I remained stony-faced, while for minutes they raged at me about their disappointment, their anxiety and all.

When they seemed to have talked themselves out, I told them sincerely, "I'm sorry."

"Good to know." Bobbie's reply was curt and predictably on point. "But we need a bit more. Don't you think you owe us an explanation?"

"Serious?" It slipped out before I managed to snap my mouth shut.

Both stared at me in total incomprehension. Incredibly, they expected me to spill the tea on what'd gone down with Sacha Montecristo. Frustrated, I cast about for a solution. I couldn't think of anything that wouldn't require me to confess that we were, in fact, staying in a CIA safehouse, that anything we said and maybe even did, was being observed by our generous benefactors.

This is why people should learn sign language.

My gaze finally landed on a pencil stub. Bobbie had taped it to the fridge next to a magnetic shopping list, because heaven forbid, we should drop our kitchen organization standards when on the lam, right? I snatched up the shopping list, flipped it and began to scribble on the back.

The CIA are watching. Listening.

They read it immediately, then glared at me for what felt like ages. Unsurprisingly, they'd grown a shade angrier. Bobbie jerked up her shoulders in an exaggerated shrug, holding out both palms as if to say, 'How come?'

I wrote: This is a CIA safehouse.

Zara refused to be silent. "What on earth are you talking about?"

I huffed out my irritation and wrote: The CIA were on to us already. They sent us here.

Coldly and now deadly serious, Zara demanded, "How do you know?"

I couldn't meet their eyes, so I bent over the paper and wrote.

I'm sorry. A CIA officer found me in the town, while you were buying the gun. She ordered me to bring us here. They're protecting us now. I had no choice.

Both stared for a long time at what I'd written, then looked up at me, finally silent.

I scribbled, So I CAN'T talk. WE can't talk.

Their disappointment was obvious, like vibrations in the air between us. Ten slow, tense seconds went by. Then Zara threw up both hands and turned on her heel. "No. Leave me out of this. I can't, anymore."

Bobbie watched Zara go and then glared at me, pointing at the pencil between my forefinger and thumb. I started writing.

The CIA officer cornered me in town with library. Said I must cooperate, or they'll get into what me and Kenzie did in Cuba. She made me change the address where Olga's code sent us, ordered us to a different safe house. THIS is a CIA HOUSE. They've been watching us through our phones. This place most probably bugged.

There was no more room on the shopping list. I passed her the completed note and watched her read it with an unchanging expression. When she faced me again, I tried to interpret her expression, but she was unmoving, inscrutable.

"You seem a little cross," I said in a low voice.

Bobbie snorted. "Cross? Oh, yes indeed." She got up, stomped across the kitchen to where two bags lay on the tiled floor, still unpacked from yesterday's shopping expedition. In one she found a thick notepad. She handed it to me. "Continue."

I pushed away the elastic band around the notepad, opened it on the first page, picked up the pencil and wrote.

Today I went out to meet someone who sent a message through my podcast. That's what led to us searching for Maxim. Message had to be from someone close to Maxim. That's who I met today — Max's younger brother, also from camp in Cuba. CIA followed me. They want to meet Max's bro.

Bobbie's eyes scanned what I'd written, then she took the pencil from me and scratched out: What do you need from us?

It wasn't clear – did she mean it angrily as in: 'What the heck do you expect?' or something? Or was Bobbie offering to help?

"You mean, to help?" I said, allowing some of the hope I felt into my voice and nervously licking my lips. I'd understand it if Bobbie and Zara wanted me out of their lives after all this. What if they'd been thinking I was as bad, as troublesome as my law-breaking parents?

Bobbie gave an impatient shake of her head. She took the pencil and wrote: You should have been open with us. "That's why I'm angry," she said, aloud but quietly.

I scribbled; Thanks for offer of help. Think it's over. Did what CIA asked.

Bobbie read this. A wry, cynical smile touched the corner of her mouth. She shook her head. "No," she whispered. "It probably isn't over. So, I have just one request." She plucked the pencil from my grasp.

Keep Marc away from THIS.

I nodded my agreement and began to trudge upstairs. The irony. Kenzie was busy with his own stuff, which for some reason his moms decided to ignore. Apparently, it didn't cross their minds that anything he was doing could be even more sketchy than sneaking out to secret meetings with a mystery Cuban boy of Russian ancestry.

I wasn't unsympathetic to this view, to be honest. Even I was surprised, when Kenzie admitted to me how he'd spent the day so far. And in terms of being clued into the fact that we were being watched, he was way ahead of me. Waiting for me beneath the pillow on my bed was a single sheet of yellow legal paper. I picked it up, saw that it was covered with Kenzie's ever-so-slightly downward slanted, expansive handwriting.

Someone is watching the house. CIA, I presume? There's a weird sound on the landline. I've seen the same car — a gray bread delivery van — circle the block every hour at 16 minutes past the hour. It slows down to a crawl when it swings by this house. Safest to assume everything we say is being recorded.

I picked up the letter and headed for Kenzie's bedroom, still reading.

It took me a while, but I managed to figure out how to bypass the router here. I've been working on that other thing I told you about. When you get back, bring this letter to my room so we can talk, k? See you soon.

Inside Kenzie's room, I closed the door behind me and waited for him to turn away from his laptop. With just the tiniest grin, he mimed a finger-pistol firing at the letter in my hand. When I grinned back at him, Kenzie handed me my phone. "The cleaning service dropped by," he whispered, blinking slowly to acknowledge my mouthed thanks. Then he waved me toward a window, pointed down at an aluminum trash can he'd placed under the window ledge. Without a word, he took the letter he'd written to me out of my hand and dropped it into the trash can. Then he picked up a lighter from his desk and lit the paper on fire.

"Burn after reading," he said in another low whisper, nervously chuckling.

"Good day?" I asked, casually. Everything we said was being heard, but if we were careful, we should be able to say a few things out loud. All the work of my true question was in my eyebrows, which I pushed as far up my forehead as possible.

He replied with a cautious nod.

"Things are…" I mimed the word 'under' by pointing at the empty space underneath the bed and then added, "…way?"

It took Kenzie a minute to catch on to the fact that we were playing charades.

"Oh. Yeah, kinda."

"Wanna go for a walk?"

"Oh no. Feels like it might rain," he said, his voice suddenly light. In the meantime, he'd reached for the yellow legal pad. He scribbled for a moment and then handed me the pad.

They have equipment that can listen to us from a distance.

He passed me the pen and I wrote, From how far?

Kenzie gave a vague shrug. "Pretty far," he said aloud.

I wrote: How did you get around the router thing?

"You really want to know?"

It struck me that maybe whoever was listening might figure out that we were talking in code and so I said something that seemed to follow from what he'd said a moment ago. "About the rain? Not really."

Catching on, Kenzie said, "It's just, like, you don't take AP physics so... Not sure if you'd follow. About the rain."

"Rain is pretty complicated," I conceded.

"Yeah. A lot of fluid dynamics. Droplet physics and all that."

When I shook my head and with my index finger, mimed a slicing line across my throat, Kenzie seemed to get the message that I'd had enough of this pantomime. "Anyhow," I said. "Good to know you've not been bored."

"Did your CIA officer woman mention how long we'll be staying here?"

I sighed. "Nope."

Kenzie became thoughtful for a second or two. Then he nodded once and turned away, back to his laptop. For the next minute or so I watched him tap-tapping onto the command line of the black screen, adding more lines of code to God-knows what program. Even though I was watching him do it, I couldn't bring myself to believe that he was actually writing code that would override a bunch of security cameras.

That's the thing about hacking. Unless you know what you're looking at, one line of software code seems a lot like another. Was Kenzie creating a new visual effect for a design tool? Or was he taking down a power grid so that someone could override the security around a gas pipeline? I couldn't tell.

So, for a little while longer, I was able to keep denying to myself that Kenzie was getting himself deep into something that was *super* illegal.

SIXTEEN

WE GOT YOUR BACKS

Within the hour, there was a knock at the door.
Bobbie called to us from downstairs, but even before I
left Kenzie's room, I knew what was up. Training
Officer Margo Daniels stood on the downstairs landing,
dressed once again in a well-fitted suit, this time a dark-
chocolate brown jacket over a pale pink blouse.

Catching my eye, she threw me a good-natured
wave. "Roni, good to see you again. I hope you're all
comfortable here?"

The CIA officer cast a beaming smile at Kenzie
and his moms. Zara waited with folded arms, seething
in silence. Bobbie had gone into a glassy, brittle yet
polite mode. In a tight voice she invited the officer to
join us around the kitchen table, where another stress-
baked berry pie was cooling.

I watched Bobbie's fake smile drop away, the
instant she turned away from the officer and toward the
coffee machine. Conscious of Daniels's eye on me, I
forced myself not to react to the scowl that replaced
Bobbie's smile, Meantime Zara busied herself with
gathering mugs for coffee and pouring glasses of water.

"No coffee for me thanks, Bobbie," I said quietly.

"Cat's finally out of the bag, I take it?" There was
a flash of white as the CIA officer bared her teeth in a
smirk. "Goose well and truly cooked? Your moms are

finally in on all the shenanigans you two young 'uns been getting up to?"

Kenzie and I nodded. "They know," I said. "You can say anything."

Margo Daniels' good humor disappeared. "Really, is that so? Marc? Can I really say *anything*?"

I saw the muscles in his throat tighten. His voice dropped to a shaky whisper. "Ye-yes."

The officer's voice became icy. "Then, you told them all about the oil pipeline, did you?"

Zara froze mid-pour. Daniels made a clicking sound with her tongue and sighed. "Guess not."

Bobbie turned back to where we were sitting, a pot of hot coffee in her hand. Her eyes were half-closed, she exuded calm. "Why don't you tell us about this *oil pipeline*, Marc?"

Kenzie appeared stricken. A genuine, rabbit-in-headlights situation. I wanted to reach out and reassure him, but I was on the edge of panic myself.

How much did he tell me and what does the CIA know? That's what kept running through my mind. That, and what could happen to me, if the CIA believed I knew something?

The only reason I'd been allowed to stay with Kenzie's family, after my parents were sentenced, was because the court was convinced I had nothing to do with their money laundering, foreign oligarch-connected shenanigans. But if it turned out I was involved in an oil pipeline bomb plot, would they still believe that I wasn't political?

"Oh no, no, you don't need to know about that, Mom." Daniels shook her head, eyes fixed on Kenzie. "Y'all are going to have to stay in the dark about it. Marc, you're a smart cookie and that's a fact. But in the

CIA, we make it our business to employ cookies who're even smarter. What happened is, you got set up. One of your little climate activist buddies is one of ours, a confidential informant. Your little, uh, your *plan*? That's a recruitment situation, is what it is."

Kenzie stuttered in disbelief. "A... Recruitment situation?"

The CIA officer nodded. "Uh huh. Think yourselves lucky. If we were FBI, y'all would be looking at prison time. Thing of it is, we went on a fishing trip, looking to hook ourselves some kids *willing* to risk their freedom to strike a blow against Big Oil 'n-Gas. And we snagged ourselves a team for an operation in which an actual pipeline gets blown up. But you're a minor, so I'm going to have to ask your moms' consent for you to get involved any further."

A stunned silence descended. Not one of us had a clue what was going on. Eventually, Zara broke it. "I'm sorry, did I hear that right? You actually *want* them to blow up an oil pipeline?"

"I want your son to help us out some, with an operation like that, yes ma'am. But only with your permission. Your boy's chance to strike the record clean, if you like. Patriotic duty and all."

Kenzie was catching on. "Then we'd still blow it up?"

Daniels considered briefly. "Yes and no. A pipeline gets blown up, you get to stick it to the fossil fuel boys, and all that jazz. Just not the pipeline y'all were planning to hit. A different one."

Bobbie filled the officer's mug with coffee. Then very calmly, staring her directly in the eye she said, "This is blackmail. Entrapment and blackmail."

Still holding Bobbie's glare, the officer picked up her coffee. She lifted it to her lips, blew on it twice then took a sip. "Tom-ay-to, tom-ah-to."

"I don't get it," I broke in. "Why would the CIA want to hire teenagers to blow up a pipeline? Wasn't the whole 'Hand of Peter' fiasco enough display of incompetence from the CIA?"

At my mention of the infamous group of assassins who'd wreaked havoc a year ago, when they'd murdered both candidates in a crucial US Senate election, Daniels put down her coffee, stiffly. Her lips briefly zipped up in a tight, straight line. After a tense moment she eventually replied, "Why? Well, that's classified. You only get to hear about your end of the deal, Roni."

Gasping, I said, "*My* end? I'm nothing to do with the pipeline thing."

"But ya'll knew about it, didn't you?" she purred at me. "Accessory after the fact. Roni, for shame! After you swore up and down you weren't a criminal, unlike your folks."

I couldn't hold back a pout. *I knew it.* The government was longing to smear me with the stain of my parents' treacherous connections, to convince the world that my parents had brainwashed me.

Kenzie was also enraged. "Padi had nothing to do with it, with any of it! We're not connected at the hip, y'know?"

Daniels clicked her tongue, soothingly. "Hey now, I'm sure it's a shock to know that you were infiltrated. But your computer security work isn't as horrible as you might be thinking right now, hon. You fooled us for a little while, stayed ahead a bit. It's just that our team catch on fast, is all." She beamed at him as her voice lowered to what I can only describe as a steely purr. "Aw. Don't pout, sugar pie. Like I said, it's not just they're as smart as you, they do this full-time. You could, too. Or you can wind up in prison." She grimaced and gave a heavy shrug. "Seems like a huge waste of potential, to me. Huge."

Not a chance I was letting this woman leave her veiled threat in the air, so I interrupted. "And what do you want from me?"

She breathed in slowly, then replied in an icily calm voice. "Just what we already agreed, Roni. Ask anyone, they'll tell you I'm the type of gal that gets all nitpicky about contracts and whatnot. All I want is for you to go back to your slippery lil' buddy, Sacha Montecristo, and *like we already agreed*, mind you, I want you to convince him to set up a meeting between me and Atlas."

"Who is 'Atlas'?" Zara asked, frowning.

Targeting Officer Daniels faced me with a broad, expectant smile. "You wanna tell her? Or should I?"

"We'll do it," Kenzie muttered.

The CIA officer gulped more coffee, then set down the mug. "A secure email will be sent to you soon, Bobbie. I need you and Zara to sign the parental consent form. There'll be some confidentiality forms, too. Then Marc, you just follow the instructions from your climate activist leader. Roni, you'll fix that meeting with Atlas." She shrugged and cracked a cheerful grin. "Wish I could tell you more but, yanno, it's classified all up the wazoo."

She turned to go, disdainfully wafting a hand in our direction. "Don't y'all trouble, I'll see myself out. Lived here a few months myself, I should know the way."

Still chuckling, she shut the front door behind her, leaving the four of us slack-jawed. Bobbie's mood shifted abruptly, became dour, determined. One by one, she pointed at me and Kenzie.

"You. And you. In the kitchen, now."

Kenzie turned to Bobbie, his jaw set in a hard line. "No. We've already explained enough. You're angry, I get it. Not a lot achieved by yelling at us, at this point."

I chipped in, "Yeah. That CIA lady seems pretty insistent."

Bobbie cocked her head on one side. "Oh, you think so? My son might have broken the law but you, Roni? You did nothing that's illegal in the USA. And if you think that we'd let you…"

It felt like she was on the verge of launching into a tirade, when Zara sauntered into the kitchen with a handgun in one hand and a notepad in the other. I was too distracted by the pistol to realize what she was silently mouthing, until finally and in evident frustration Zara said in a cajoling tone, "Guys, can you maybe help me out here?"

What with their quasi-telepathic, wifely connection, Bobbie was the first to understand. She took the notepad from Zara and read it, then showed us what her wife had written there in all caps.

WE GOT YOUR BACKS. WHAT CAN WE DO?

SEVENTEEN

SHAKING A TAIL

It was like a four-way Mexican stand-off – with glares instead of guns. We couldn't talk about anything that mattered, not with the CIA listening in. Yet, talking was what we needed to do. I saw it in Zara and Bobbie's eyes, Kenzie's too. Each one of us was desperate for clarity, and my grip on reality had become slippery. I tried mentally to grab onto anything concrete in my life.

Guess I'm basically a CIA asset now, Margo Daniels's chew toy. Me and Kenzie, both. No way he has to do this alone, that's just how it is.

It felt absurd, scary and beyond my control. I would not be able to live with myself if I abandoned Kenzie to this murky world. Someone else was calling the shots, Margo Daniels of the CIA.

If she even is 'CIA.'

"The email has arrived," Zara said quietly, showing me her phone. I snatched it out of her hand and clicked on the email titled 'NDA and parental consent.' The 'from' address appeared to be a CIA email. The sinking feeling in the pit of my belly confirmed to me that this was real, no wriggling out of it, no more clinging to desperate copes like *'if she even is CIA.'* Unless…?

"Could they have spoofed it to make it seem like it's from the CIA even if it isn't?" I asked Kenzie. "Maybe Daniels is full of it?"

"I'd have to check it on the computer to be sure. But this feels real, Padi. And when I think about it…" Kenzie sighed. "I think I even know *which* of my group is the CIA plant. I've been so stupid. Honestly, I didn't think. Never imagined it could be a set-up. Jeez." He groaned, rolling his head from the cringe. "Now it seems kind of obvious."

This feels real, he said. Getting involved with the CIA was our new reality? Pretty much a definition of 'un-real,' is what I'd have said two days prior.

We were prepared to believe that Bobbie and Zara planned eventually on 'having our backs.' Before that, however, they demanded to know why it had ever occurred to Kenzie to get involved in a crackpot scheme to blow up an oil pipeline.

"Because it would mean that a fossil fuel pipeline is going down," he told them a little loudly, very firmly. He turned to each parent. "How else are we supposed to defend ourselves from the industry's utter contempt for my future, for everyone on the planet's? Y'know?! So, yeah, good enough for me."

"Not for us, I'm afraid," Zara replied in a clipped voice. "Better explain yourself, *mijo*."

I stayed to hear the first part of his answer, which was delivered even more passionately and with more commitment than when I'd first asked him about the plan.

"The time for discussion is over," Kenzie told them. "Your generation has had thirty years to act on the information. But the media, the newspapers and the TV news, they all lied to us. They hid the truth. For *so* long. And now it's too late to persuade people. When anyone even tries to do that, they jump on stupid things, the journalists, the TV interviewers. Once it was 'are we sure though, don't other scientists say something different?' Now it's 'but is this the right way to go about it, scaring people?' And 'but you're just making this into a new religion and religions always have their doomsday prophets.' It's all bullshit, right? Idiotic excuses to delay any real action, because real action means too many people lose part of their fortunes. Tell me you see that! That's why it's too late for anything but direct action."

Watching the expressions on Bobbie's and Zara's faces shift from annoyance to concern and then gradually to amazement and awe, my heart swelled with pride in my best friend. This wasn't an easy conversation to have with his moms, but the time had come. Kenzie was stepping up.

Personally, I had some niggles about why the CIA wanted to blow up a pipeline. Kenzie was in it for the planet, sure. But the CIA? Since when did they care about climate change? Climate catastrophes would mean more security fears, which would mean a bigger role for the CIA. I couldn't figure out why destroying an oil pipeline was something they'd plot, but I was certain of one thing: it had nothing to do with the climate.

Also, I didn't entirely trust Margo Daniels. She'd started out by presenting herself and the Agency as saviors who were shielding us from Chekists. But her real agenda was now revealed – she wanted us to work for her. For all I knew, the Cheka had never been after us and Daniels herself had planted that idea. Maybe it'd been the CIA all along?

I slipped away with a mumbled excuse, pulled on a jacket and plugged a headset jack into the burner phone Sacha had given me. I put in the earbud and then dialed the only number in the phone book. When I heard his voice in my ear I said just one word. "Wait."

I stepped out into the street, glanced around and then headed into the shadows. Any second now, I expected someone to start following me. When I spotted a hooded figure emerging from a car parked almost opposite the house, I doubled my stride.

In my ear I heard Sacha ask, "Are you being observed?"

"Mm hmm," I hummed, trying to make my reply sound like I was singing to myself. The person following me was less than twenty yards behind. If their listening equipment could hear our conversations in the house, I had to believe they'd hear me speaking now.

"Now then, let's see if they're putting you in a box, or if it's just a second tail."

"A box?"

"Probably not," agreed Sacha. He seemed to think I'd know what he meant by 'a box.' "You're just a kid, they probably don't need a box. But watch out for a second tail, they'll at least have that." They'll probably be in front. Watch out for someone just in sight, someone who makes random stops. That's when they log your position. When that happens, try to catch at least a glimpse and capture it, like a mental photo. You have paper and pencil?"

Despite myself, a laugh escaped me. "No, no, no, no, no, n-no," I hummed, and tried to make it sound to any eavesdropper like I was ticking myself off.

Sacha sounded disappointed. "All right. Try to remember next time. Paper and pencil. Use it to jot down details of any tail you think you've spotted. If they have to double back, you'll see them again. Anyone you see twice in a small area, is probably tailing you.

I focused on the hundred yards ahead of me. There was just one person in that space, walking a little slower than me, almost out of range. I kept my eyes on them, waiting for a glimpse. But no sign of any stopping. They'd almost reached the main road. If they turned the wrong way, they'd have to double back to catch up with me. I had to note down something, anything that'd let me pick them up if I saw them again. As they passed under a lamp post I saw that they wore a black baseball cap and a short, dark-colored puffy jacket.

Sacha's voice returned to my earpiece. "Head for the loudest place you can find. Their listening equipment won't work so well, there."

When I didn't reply, Sacha continued. "There's a Don Pollo restaurant on the main road, to your left, about three hundred yards away. Go in there and head for the restroom."

As he said that, the person ahead of me was reaching the main road. They turned right. I smiled a little, felt a pleasant buzz of adrenaline. Shaking a tail was a lot more exciting when you had some agency and weren't just frantically following Maxim Santiago through a Mexican laundromat.

I doubled my pace and peeked over my shoulder as I rounded a corner. The person behind was still following, matching my pace. They were staring at what I guessed was a phone in their hands. Maybe it was the listening device, I don't know. A few minutes later I reached the Don Pollo chicken restaurant. The place was only a third full and not particularly loud, but at least there was some background music. Once inside I went straight to the restroom. Closing a stall door behind me I whispered fiercely into the mic.

"CIA officer is blackmailing me into setting up a meeting with Atlas. If I don't, we get in trouble for ripping off the helicopter in Cuba. So, I guess we need your help."

Sacha was briefly silent. "All right. I warned you they wouldn't take no for an answer. Tell them tomorrow, 10am, same place as today."

"Got it," I agreed, breathlessly.

"And, Roni, I won't make the same mistake twice. I mean it. Just you and Margo Daniels, or neither of you ever hears from us again."

The line went dead before I could ask how Sacha knew about Daniels. Just then the door opened and a young woman, mid-twenties, walked into the women's restroom. In good lighting and with the hood of her jacket down, I wouldn't have recognized her from the dark streets, but she looked at me just a split second too long and I knew. I washed my hands carefully, peering at the woman in the mirror the instant her back was turned. The more I scrutinized her size and shape, the more certain I became that this was the person who'd been behind me walking from the safe house.

"Tomorrow," I said, addressing the woman in a clear voice. She turned slowly, eyes widening even as she remained silent. That silence was all the confirmation I needed. "Tomorrow," I repeated. "Ten in the morning. In the center of the labyrinth of the Georgetown Waterfront Park. Just me and Daniels, or they walk."

With a final, curt nod at my CIA stalker, I turned and returned to the main part of the restaurant, ordered an orange soda and strolled back to the house. The guy in the puffy jacket and baseball cap was on his way in and actually held the door open for me. Somehow, I managed to pretend I hadn't noticed and other than a brief nod of thanks, barely noticed him. It just felt right to keep them thinking that while I might not be *totally* new to the concept of what Maxim had called 'dry cleaning,' and could spot a person trailing me, I wasn't quick enough to spot a second tail.

I had returned to the top of the street where the safe house was, when I noticed Kenzie striding purposefully toward me. He was about to call out, when he saw that I'd raised my left hand to cover my mouth – the universal language for STFU. Luckily, he got the message right away. I hurried to meet him and when we'd caught up to each other, I tugged at his sleeve and whispered, "Follow me."

Once we'd turned off the street we took off, me in the lead, sprinting across the driveway of a nearby house. I'd noticed it a few times as I'd walked to and from the safe house, the only home in the street without a gate to guard the backyard. We dashed into the garden, which was entirely dark. Nobody was home, so there wasn't even light coming from inside the house. I turned on my phone's torch and found a fence at the back that we could climb over.

Beside me, Kenzie murmured his appreciation. "I like it. Old school; ain't broke, don't fix."

Hey, maybe if I'd had some Jason-Bourne-level training, like Maxim and Atlanta, I'd know another way to shake off a tail, but I have to go with what I know. If the yard-leaping technique had helped us a few weeks ago to escape Kenzie's house without being seen, then maybe it could help us now.

We didn't even need to escape. All we needed was a few minutes away from our CIA handlers. If they *were*

CIA, that is. Or handlers. At that point, so far as I could tell, neither option was impossible.

EIGHTEEN

THE PLAN

"Alexander Montecristo," crooned Targeting Officer Daniels, extending her hand. "It's so good to finally meet you."

Sacha shook her hand in silence. He turned to introduce his older companion, who could have been anywhere between eighteen and early twenties, tall and athletic in appearance with light-brown skin and shoulder-length blonde afro hair in tight, bouncy coils. "This is my friend, Eva."

With increasing discomfort, I watched Daniels feast her eyes on the two of them.

"Well now, hello Eva. Isn't this something, finally meeting two of you Atlas folks?" She grinned at both in turn. It struck me as pure greed, like getting her hands on something she'd long desired.

We all sat down, and Daniels ordered coffee and water for the table. The table we'd taken was on the edge of the patio of the outdoor café. The Potomac River flowed past just beyond the lawn, enticingly close. Sacha, Eva and even Daniels exuded a diffident calm, tidy smiles never quite reaching their eyes.

It struck me then that they resented being here. How long, I wondered, had the CIA been trying to track them down? A shiver went through me, and I felt a sudden chill as another, more daunting question occurred to me.

Why had the Atlas Group risked their privacy for me?

Daniels had seen their faces. There was no going back from this for Sacha and Eva, their cover was blown. Might as well hand themselves over to the US government.

My eyes grew wider. Any need I had to talk disappeared. Something beyond my grasp was happening; I'd finally figured out just how badly out of my depth I'd wandered.

The server arrived and from a tray set down a French press filled with coffee, four small cups, a bottle of chilled water and four glass tumblers. My attention went to Daniels. Her hand shook a little as she poured the coffee. It was the first time I'd spotted any sign of vulnerability in the woman who'd oozed power and confidence in all our previous meetings.

Margo Daniels was nervous, while Sacha and Eva were not. They were calmly waiting for her proposal, nothing more.

Did they have the power to erase our memories of this meeting?

If things didn't go well, would I soon find myself back in the safe house with no clue about any of this? Maybe a far-fetched idea, but when it came to the two-dubs' psi powers, everything was pretty darned 'far-fetched', and I wasn't the person to decide what went too far. It'd certainly explain why they didn't seem worried that someone like Daniels could now identify them.

Daniels tipped a creamer into her coffee, stirred it, beginning to speak, slowly and deliberately explaining every detail. Over the next ten minutes she described the entire pipeline plan, patiently answering Sacha and Eva's occasional questions.

Finally, she turned to me. "You got all that, Roni? Think you and your boy Marc will be up to it?"

"Me?" It was the first time anyone had suggested I'd be involved in the pipeline job. "Why?"

"We need you to go undercover on the whale-watching expedition. Only minors allowed. Marc needs backup."

I was speechless. I couldn't abandon Kenzie. But this was building fast and sounding scarily real. I tried to scoff, pointing to Margo Daniels. "Why do you even trust her? What makes you so sure she's CIA?"

Eva blinked at me with wide eyes, slow and steady. She spoke smoothly and with believable sympathy. "She's CIA. We wouldn't be sitting here if we weren't certain."

"But how do you *know*?" I asked, stubbornly. For some reason, Eva's professionalism and reasonableness were getting on my nerves. My cup of coffee lay before me, untouched. I poured in some cream and a packet of sugar, buying time.

"I can't tell you that," Eva said, in a tone of gentle understanding. "I'm sorry. You're going to have to trust us."

Sacha nodded his agreement. Mentally, I flashed back for an instant to my bedroom at Bobbie and Zara's house in Falls Church, my podcast mic on the desk and a script in my hand. The smell of toast and eggs being fried in butter rising from the kitchen downstairs. Kenzie tapping on his keyboard in the room opposite. My old reality of a couple weeks ago. It already felt like a dream. Was there *really* no way out of this, no way back to our peaceful, quiet life?

"Roni, you don't have to do this," Daniels said, with as much compassion as I'd heard from her.

"But Kenzie does?" I snapped.

"Marc made his own bed," Daniels continued. "For months now, he's been involved with planning something like this. Either Marc does this for us, or he goes to juvie. Because you have to believe me, we don't let would-be terrorists off lightly."

Tears sprung to my eyes. Why hadn't I stopped Kenzie? Why hadn't I told his moms, made him see how crazy dangerous it was?

"I'm sorry," Sacha said, interrupting his friend. "It kind of does need to be her, though. Roni actually is important to the mission. I mean, it might work with someone else, but we'd rather it was her."

Our eyes locked for a moment. I understood at once. Sacha knew I could be inclined. He'd inclined me to write FIND UNICORNS on the mirror in the restroom of the Atlas Studios. Even without knowing how Maxim had inclined me to drive a car blindfold and then to fly a helicopter for a brief moment, Sacha already knew that with me on the team, the two telepaths would effectively have an extra pair of hands.

Daniels insisted, "Do you understand the mission, Roni? Gotta hear it from you, else I can't approve this."

I replied, in clipped tones, "Sure, I understand. The CIA have uncovered a covert mission of the Third Russian Empire. The Cheka are going to blow up a Russian gas pipeline and blame it on the USA. They'll call it an act of war and use it as an excuse to invade Alaska. Our mission is to prevent that."

"Good," she purred. "And just how do you hope to achieve that?"

"It's a 'false flag' operation. They'll set up a yacht – the *Cassiopeia* – so it looks like the bomb was on a remote-operated drone controlled from there. Kenzie and I will join a youth expedition to the Bering Sea to watch whales, or whatever. We won't interfere. We will be collecting video evidence of the movement of any boats. Marc will handle all digital evidence, intercept comms and stuff. Then, in the morning, after they've left the decoy yacht all ready to be found, we'll board it."

"Indeed. And what will you do on the *Cassiopeia*?"

"We'll remove fake evidence that is supposed to make it seem like US people did the bombing. Western weapons, phones, all of that. English-language magazines addressed to US-based subscribers, drivers' licenses, paperwork for the underwater drone, the remote control itself, plans of the gas compressor station, pipeline maps, basically anything on paper, things like that."

"Correct," Daniels nodded. "Like I promised Marc's parents, you won't be doing anything illegal," she reminded me. "Or even particularly dangerous. Chekists put stolen US military software on a commercial remote-operated underwater vehicle, a 'ROUV' that is commonly used by the US navy. They'll use it to implicate the US government. Marc will use a backdoor to hack the drone. Our technology, our permission."

"He'll upgrade the drone's software and plant some kind of code that'll implicate the Kremlin. Target will remain the same though – a gas compression station on an island," I continued, now eager to show how well I had understood.

"*Compress-or* station," Daniels corrected, not unkindly. She neatly side-stepped my comment about

Kenzie planting code to implicate the Kremlin, an action by him that I felt pretty sure would count as a crime. "It's where the gas is collected from the producing stations and compressed so it can be distributed along smaller pipes. This one is the first in a series. Hit this, and we completely destroy the ability to gather from fifty wells."

I nodded. "Right. And the inflow to the compressor station, that's the target. I get it, I do. Nobody will suspect a bunch of teenage whale-watchers."

Margo Daniels's lips drew very thin. "There's always *some* risk. But to put your mind at rest, we have solid HUMINT for the entire operation. Very reliable."

"Hew-mint?" I was puzzled. "Ah wait, you mean... human intelligence. You mean, like, a double agent? Your own person, on their side?"

Daniels lips managed a weak, slightly terrifying smile.

"Won't it blow their cover, when the decoy yacht gets found with none of the planted evidence?"

Her smile broadened, like a snake's head splitting. "That's not your problem. We take care of things like that."

I couldn't tell from her manner whether that meant they'd be getting their asset out of the country or shooting them. "That all sounds pretty scary," I admitted. "Like something for trained officers, not something I can help you with. Kenzie might feel differently, but..."

What I wanted right then, was for all this talk to stop, to go back to my old life.

"Everything is going to be fine, Roni, right after you do us this small favor. Don't worry, you'll get training. A chance to work with the best!"

We faced off, again. I noticed Sacha and Eva watching us, silent observers, like adjudicators at a big sports event. "What I don't understand," I said, grumbling some, "is why you need Sacha and Eva?"

The CIA officer looked pointedly at Eva. "You wanna take that?"

"The Chekists will bring at least one telepath to an operation like this. That's their policy. Always a telepath, just in case." Eva paused. "It's unlikely they'll bring two."

"Why bring any?" I understood why the CIA needed kids – the expedition that would be sailing near the pipeline was for just teenagers. So far, I'd heard nothing about the operation that would require telepathic abilities. "Normies can't be affected by telepaths, isn't that right?"

"Most latents think they're normies" Sacha said. He sounded deliberately vague. "It's how Chekists operate. The Czar knows General Krylov sold telepaths to agencies all over the world. It's defensive. The enemy might bring a telepath, so they bring one, too."

"All right, but Sacha, what's in this for you?" I said. "They've got me and Kenzie over a barrel. What have they got on you guys?"

Daniels sucked air through her teeth and made a scornful noise but said nothing. Sacha glanced at Eva as if to ask for permission to answer. When she replied with the tiniest nod of her head he turned to me.

"There's a lot going on right now. In the world, I mean."

I scowled, "Duh, obviously. Wars breaking out all over."

"Right," Eva interjected. "We've been thinking about how we can help."

"And you came up with working with the CIA, are you deranged?!"

"In this case, yes," answered Eva, with a shake of her head. Sacha watched her with an expression of such veneration that I suspected him of crushing on her, hard. "We've considered it thoroughly," she continued, speaking with evident care. "Czar Ilyin has been warning that he might invade Alaska, that he considers it part of Russia's imperial territory. We think it's worth making sure that doesn't happen."

"Right," I said, sarcastically. How could Eva say such bonkers stuff so earnestly? "And provoke a nuclear war? I don't think so."

Margo Daniels leapt in. "That's just it. Ilyin is gambling that the president won't defend Alaska. Not at the cost of starting World War Three. He believes we're weak. The USA, the West. That we're on the verge of collapse."

"That is *delusional.*" I reacted from instinct, defensive, in denial. Truth was, I had no clue whether the president would think it was worth starting a nuclear war to defend Alaska. Were the CIA afraid of that? Terrifying, if true.

"The way things are going right now, who can say?" admitted Daniels. "CIA believes it's worth making sure it doesn't get put to the test. Wouldn't you like to help avert a nuclear war, Roni? Even if there's only a tiny chance of the worst happening, don't you think that's something we should avoid?"

It wouldn't sink in, not at that time. How could it? All I could do was to stare at them, at Sacha, Eva and Margo Daniels, waiting and longing for one of them to burst out laughing and yell 'Fooled you!'

But they didn't do that, obviously, or else there'd be nothing to tell, and you wouldn't be reading this.

NINETEEN

BEVERLY BEACH

After Margo Daniels dropped me at the Bethesda safe house, I waited for her to drive off. Then I turned away from the house and began to walk in the opposite direction from the main road. After turning a couple of corners, I found myself in a small urban park. I found an empty bench and sat down. It was pretty warm, and I was sweating a little after what turned out to be a brisk walk, so I unzipped my hoodie and tied it around my waist.

Without thinking, I took out my phone to message Kenzie. He'd managed to clean it of surveillance software again, but could Daniels have slipped something on there a third time, while we met with Sacha and Eva? Very, super mean if so. I put the phone back in my pocket without touching it – safer to assume the CIA *were* monitoring it.

Last night, when we had met in the backyard of a neighbor's house, Kenzie had suggested that we both learn American Sign Language. Because – "We need a way to communicate that doesn't require us to do a 'cleaning run' every time we want to talk."

"Good idea," I'd replied, deadpan. "And I bet *no one* at the CIA knows ASL."

We both had a point, though. Kenzie and I really needed to figure out a sign language that no random observer could interpret. Last night we'd only managed to come up with signs for *Yes, No, Danger* and *Help*. Turns out it's not easy to invent a language quickly. We decided to make a list of the words we most needed and work from there, next chance we had.

It was almost noon, and the park was beginning to fill up with office workers sitting on the grass with their packed lunches and takeout from nearby eateries. Watching them smiling and relaxing with colleagues, I sensed an ominous cloud descending over my future. Plans I'd once had to become a professional podcaster or investigative journalist now seemed like a fantasy. Even if our mission succeeded, I'd be forever in the sights of the CIA. One foot wrong and the blackmail threat might rear its ugly head.

And if the mission failed…?

I couldn't bear to think about the scale of our failure somehow leading to nuclear war. Not that it'd be our fault, that'd be on Ilyin, if he really did attack Alaska. But I'd still somehow feel partly responsible, if we couldn't disrupt his plan. Families sitting in front of the TV, clueless and helpless. Office workers enjoying precious minutes away from the desk. A tiny oasis of nature in the city, gone. Everyone in the capital and the surrounding cities, vaporized. It seemed impossible that my individual effort and this mission itself could be so consequential.

I wasn't anti the mission, I just wanted someone to do it that wasn't me. Someone better.

More likely there'd be a series of such things. Weeks ago, I'd believed that if we rescued the telepaths from Cuba, the danger from Ilyin would be gone. But no. Turns out, the Czar had a bunch of schemes and plans. He didn't have to worry about running his empire for the benefit of its citizens, he could spend all his time plotting how to destroy his enemies. If the time came to order people under his rule to their deaths, they had no choice.

If we don't resist now, Ilyin's war will reach us, too.

A couple approached, obviously coveting the bench. One of them carried a paper bag bulging with Don Pollo's. I slid over to make room and then a few seconds later, rose to my feet and headed back to the house. There was a lot to do. Kenzie and I had to attend our first virtual briefing, then we had to go online shopping for sailing clothes.

When I arrived at the house, Bobbie was unloading the kitchen cupboards and the fridge and packing the groceries into two plastic boxes. I ran upstairs to find Kenzie rolling up his underpants and neatly sliding them into the last empty spaces in his suitcase.

"Hey, hurry up and pack. Where've you been? Don't you know we're leaving?"

I felt my cheeks turning red as anger grew within me. We were moving *again*? I'd only just figured out a way Kenzie and I could meet in secret, and found a park where I could get a moment of peace. "We're moving? Why?"

Zara stomped into my room carrying an armful of folded laundry. She dropped it on my bed and turned to me, a storm lurking just behind her eyes. "Your new boss at the CIA ordered it. We have a window to leave, forty minutes from now. She's worried that we've been compromised. Something about you and Marc wandering off on your own? You know anything about that?"

"Nope," was all I'd say. Then I began to pack. There was no point doing anything else.

Zara said nothing else, either. There was a lot more she might have unloaded on me; how it was all my fault in the first place for searching for Maxim Santiago, getting my legal guardian Olga killed, sneaking off illegally to Cuba and then very extremely illegally stealing an ex-Soviet helicopter and using it to break into the private property of General Anatoly Petrovich Krylov and liberate his personal slaves. All of that was why the four of us were no longer safe, why the Czar's Chekist foreign agents were chasing us and why the CIA kept having to move us.

No; Zara mentioned *none* of that. Having our backs was turning out to be a huge pain in the butt, yet I have to admit it – she and Bobbie stuck by their promise.

Forty minutes later we were back in the loaded car and driving to yet another safe house. Bobbie put on some ambient chillout music, and I sank back into the seat, watching cars whooshing past as we got onto the 495 and headed west. So, back to the countryside. I turned to talk with Kenzie, but his headphones were in place and his eyes were closed. His moms weren't in a chatty mood, either. Their patience had worn so thin, you could see through it. I wasn't going to risk making things worse.

An hour later we reached the seaside village of Beverly Beach, drove down one of its orderly streets, past neat lawns and pale weatherboard houses with gray tiled roofs and white fretwork porches. In almost every house, the Stars and Stripes hung from a prominently displayed flagpole. The water's edge was just two houses away when Bobbie turned the car into the drive of one of the smaller homes, a light-gray bungalow with a trimmed lawn, a neat border of lime-green shrubs and pink hollyhocks, a porch swing and the waving flag.

Kenzie woke the instant the car stopped. He checked his phone, then turned to me. "The video call starts in ten. I'll go set up the computer and camera." He followed Zara to the front door, waited for her to unlock it, then disappeared inside.

I picked up one of the grocery boxes and followed. The air smelt good, a tang of the sea. When I went into the house in the kitchen/living room I found Kenzie sitting at the large, oak table. Opposite sat Sacha and next to him sat someone I thought I would never see again.

Atlanta.

Utterly unsure what to say, I set down the box I was carrying, removed the lid and began to unpack groceries. Atlanta was on their feet in a second, paced over to me and beaming, hugged me tight. Obviously, I reciprocated.

They'd changed their look a bit, now wore their hair in a buzzcut with the letter 'A' shaved into the nape of the neck. They had on a bottle green 'NYU' hoodie over a pair of pale blue skinny jeans and orange-colored Adidas sneakers.

Flustered, I asked, "What are you doing here?"

"I'm joining your operation." Atlanta grinned, evidently happy to see me again.

I was confused. Last time I'd seen Atlanta was in Cuba with Maxim and the kids we'd liberated from the Krylov camp. What had changed, why wasn't Atlanta with Maxim any longer?

"Oh…" I managed to say. "I thought it'd be Eva."

Sacha broke in, "Eva's twenty-one, too old. And you've worked with Atlanta before."

But I'd stalled, couldn't get past the mystery of why Atlanta was here. Sacha had mentioned that he and Maxim escaped with others from the camp. Although Sacha hadn't named anyone specific, I remembered Maxim implying Atlanta was one of that group.

Had they been friends before the escape? Did Sacha trust Atlanta? Or could they be spying for Maxim? I was pleased at how stoked Atlanta seemed to be about meeting me again, but I had to know why they were *here* with me, Kenzie and Sacha, instead of with Maxim.

This, however, was not the time for such a question. Kenzie and Atlanta had evidently already had their reunion, while I'd been helping to unload the car. Now Sacha was formally introducing himself to Kenzie and asking probing questions about the mission. If there was to be any more explanation about Atlanta, I probably shouldn't expect it right now.

"You ever hacked a US military weapon before?" Sacha asked, semi-seriously.

"Ha, ha, no. I'd be in jail, obviously. They're gonna basically *give* me the hack. I just have to execute their code. Easy. A twelve-year-old could do the job. In fact, that's why they want us, apparently, for the kiddie whale cruise. We can get close without rousing much suspicion."

Watching Sacha and Atlanta with Kenzie I began to understand why they were such a good match for the mission; all four of us were minors. To be frank, Kenzie and I got carded everywhere, we were never taken for adults, but it *could* happen, theoretically. Being with Sacha and Atlanta, who looked younger, would help us to blend in with teens. Yet despite being two years younger than us, our telepathic partners seemed perfectly relaxed with the idea of going on what could be a dangerous mission.

Yeah – I didn't trust Daniels with her 'hardly dangerous at all' schtick.

It made me wonder about the Atlas Group. They were the end of an 'underground railroad' for escaped two-dubs from the Krylov camp, yet from what I'd heard, few kids ever made it all the way. How many child telepaths could they possibly have? Were they trained? It seemed likely that some Chekists would be two-dubs, too. They wouldn't be kids, not if they were sold by Krylov, when they were eighteen. They might be young, just the same. I hoped that we could at least trust the other teenagers on the expedition.

All things considered – and I *tried* to consider all things – I was actually pretty optimistic, something that was normal for me. I could never tolerate dread for very long, I'd always bounce back. Even when those instincts turned out to be mistaken.

TWENTY

CUCKOOS

While Kenzie set up the tech for our video call to Margo Daniels, Sacha helped me to rifle through the groceries for snacks. We came up with a box of Entenmann's donuts and a bag of cheese balls and put the opened packets on the table. I heard the CIA officer's voice through the computer speaker, and we quickly assembled in front of the camera.

"There y'all are, my 'A' Team," she said, beaming. "First the good news – we identified a car that's been tailing you and blew your cover. Pretty sure they're Cheka. Last seen in Bethesda following our own decoy, a false trail. Meantime, y'all got out of there. Hopefully their trail went cold but just in case – be on the lookout for a navy Chrysler Grand Voyager with DC license plate JL8735. Bad news, however, is that you're only here for the night. Tomorrow morning y'all be up bright and early at seven, cause we're picking you up by boat. Just walk to the end of the street."

She didn't give us an opportunity to ask questions but made sure to remind us that Kenzie's moms had to sign the legal documents within the hour.

Over in the kitchen I watched Bobbie leaning against the sideboard with hands crossed over her chest, observing us without expression. I knew her well enough to recognize that she was worried. I felt a brief stab of sympathy – it probably didn't feel great to realize you had no control over your teenage son's decision to do something potentially dangerous and consequential. Not that he had much choice – the CIA officer had basically blackmailed us into it.

Even with that being so, from the moment I saw Atlanta, I felt suddenly up to the task. Being around them again reminded me that we'd done something even more difficult in Cuba. With two telepaths in our team, we could surely manage a little bit of spying. Uneasily, I recalled how afraid I'd been, the night before we left for Cuba. Just like now, the idea of a daredevil mission had been sprung on us with almost zero notice. Then, we'd had no training, no backing. Just Maxim and his supreme confidence. This time, however, the CIA would be preparing us and providing backup.

We'd be fine. Right?

Wrong. It was pure cope on my part, just me trying to stave off the jitters.

Whilst Atlanta, Sacha and Kenzie were awake and we were animated and energized discussing the mission, there was no anxiety. But, when I woke a few hours later and lay listening to Atlanta softly snoring in the neighboring bed, I couldn't shake a sense of impending doom. And – senses of impending doom, that is *not* like me.

I slid from underneath the quilt and slipped through the door. In the otherwise deserted kitchen I found Kenzie, tap-tapping on his laptop.

"You should be resting," I scolded.

He didn't take his eyes off the screen. "Pot, kettle, black."

I opened the fridge, took out a pot of blueberry yoghurt and ate it standing over Kenzie, reading his computer screen.

"Just sweeping through the code they sent for the hack," he murmured. "Making sure I understand."

"I feel like they haven't briefed us very much," I said, trying to lead the conversation. When he didn't reply, I continued. "Presumably they'll do that tomorrow?"

He finally turned to me, pointing at the yoghurt I was eating. "Any more of those?"

I fetched him the other pot and handed it to him with a spoon. "Are you worried?"

He didn't answer right away and even seemed a little irked at the question. But eventually he spoke. "I keep thinking about when we were in Hacienda Narcojunior. Remember? When Maxim asked me to build the EMP generator."

I frowned. "You were fine with it."

He gave a gentle, almost sad smile. "I wasn't. Told everyone I would figure it out, but the truth was, I had no clue. It's just that, y'know, it was Maxim. We always said yes to his ideas, didn't we? We knew that if *he* thought we could do it…"

"…then we could," I finished. "Is that how you feel, now?"

Kenzie thought for a moment and then shrugged. "No. Maybe? I think I was trying to impress Maxim."

I nodded in sympathy. When had we ever *not* wanted to impress Maxim? "But he's not here."

"Right. And Sacha… I don't know. And Atlanta being here, that's cool. It's just not the same, though."

"We don't know Sacha," I agreed. "What do you think of him?" I watched closely as he replied.

"Seems like a good kid. Has an impressive resume, for sure, escaping Cuba when Maxim couldn't. If that's what really happened."

"What d'you mean?"

Kenzie exhaled, slowly. "Not sure. Just something feels off. Like we're not being given the whole story. For example, why did Atlanta leave Maxim?"

"I kept meaning to ask that."

"Me too."

"Every time I mentioned Maxim, Atlanta changed the subject," I said.

"Same."

I pressed my lips together. "We need to ask that question. Tomorrow?"

"For sure. We should also ask Sacha why he escaped and not Maxim."

"Ask us now," said a voice. We both turned to see Sacha on the lower part of the staircase. Atlanta appeared behind him, a second later.

I asked, "How long have you been there?"

Sacha descended the stairs and padded over in bare feet to join us at the table. Atlanta followed. "Long enough to hear you wondering if you trust us." He placed both palms on the table and looked impassively from me to Kenzie.

"That's not it," I began to object but Sacha interrupted. It was disconcerting to witness such commanding confidence in a boy two years younger than me. I was getting serious Maxim-flashback. Was it their telepathy, or just them, a family thing?

"Let's not waste time – it is. You want to know why I got away and not Maxim. But are you sure you want to know?"

Bewildered, I replied, "Why wouldn't we?"

"Because you seem to have a certain view of Jaguar. You both admire him. Maybe even love him. So it's going to be difficult for you to hear the reason."

I turned to Kenzie, then Sacha. "Go ahead."

After a pause, Sacha said, abruptly, "Jaguar didn't want to leave. He had different ideas about what he wanted to do with his life."

Atlanta nodded in silent agreement.

Urgently I said, "What ideas?"

"For one, Jaguar wanted to go back to the camp, rescue all the kids, get his revenge on a couple of the sentinels."

"Well, he did that," I acknowledged. "Apart from the revenge part, I don't know anything about that."

"He managed some of that," said Atlanta, quietly. "Anton, the one he really wanted to punish, had been sold by the time we broke into the camp, though."

"You knew 'Maxim,'" Sacha said, carefully. "But we knew *Jaguar*. When we were escaping, he did things that I think even he regretted."

Kenzie had become very still, his expression stony.

"What 'things'?" I insisted. "If he was such a horrible person, why did Atlanta go to him in Mexico?"

"Atlas sent me," Atlanta said, softly. "They trained me a little bit, then sent me to Tapachula."

"Atlanta is with *us*," said Sacha. The air in the room seemed suddenly cold and my fingers felt stiff. "Always has been. The only two-dub ever to escape the Krylov camp and not join Atlas is Jaguar. *He* rejected *us*, not the other way around. Even after what he did, they would have accepted him."

"But why wouldn't he join you?" I pleaded.

Sacha gazed at me with sorrow and empathy. "He wants power," he said, simply. "Power and wealth. That's not what the Atlas Group is about. When Jaguar understood that he refused to join us."

My voice became shaky. "What did he do that was so bad? Tell me!"

Shaking his head, Sacha replied, "He was angry, he was hurt. He may even regret it now."

Breaking his silence, Kenzie blurted out, "What, though? Just tell us!"

With a sigh of resignation, Sacha finally admitted, "He threatened to kill a girl I was with, a Cuban girl. She helped me when I was on the run. He meant it."

I didn't know what to say, resorted to mumbling some automatic sympathy while internally, I reeled from the shock. "Oh, wow. Is she okay?"

"Yadzia? Yes, she's really good." He seemed pleased that I'd asked. "Aleks put her in a great prep school."

"Who's Aleks?"

"Aleks Rubenovich Atlas. He's the founder of the Atlas Group."

"Any relation to Elena?"

Sacha smiled, a little impressed. "Oh, you know about Elena? Yes, Aleks is her son. Elena and her brother Tovia were among the first two-dubs."

"What do you mean, 'first'?" I asked.

Kenzie nodded along. "Yeah, like, were they manufactured?"

"There was an event in 1908. Something exploded above Tunguska, in Siberia. Elena and Tovia were born nine months later. They're some of the first telepathic humans, part of the Tunguska Generation."

"Like the 'Midwich cuckoos.'"

It was a dumb thing to say, and I regretted it immediately.

TWENTY-ONE

VOLUNTEERS

Atlanta watched me with thinly veiled hostility. "I read about that thing you were talking about last night." Wrapped in a towel, they stood aside, making way for me to use the shower.

I stumbled into the cubicle. It wasn't even six in the morning, and I'd barely slept, but as the hot water woke me up, I focused on what Atlanta had said. They were talking about the 'Midwich cuckoos.' I remembered watching a movie or TV series about them – golden-eyed children with psychic powers born after aliens visited the English town of Midwich.

I called loudly, "I just meant that the first two-dubs were born after a mysterious event in the sky."

Atlanta didn't reply. Later, as I made my way downstairs and took a piece of toast from a stack on the table, I realized that they and Sacha were deep in telepathic chat. For all I knew, maybe at any given time they mostly were, but right now, it was obvious. Both ate in silence, yet occasionally one would give the other a knowing smile, or even giggle. It deserved a snarky response, but I just couldn't. Instead, I decided to be up-front.

"'Jaguar' doesn't hide so much that he thinks you guys are superior. Maybe that's why he's so angry with

Krylov and the Czar. That they presumed to use you, to enslave you, when you're better than us."

"'Gotta make way for *Homo Superior*?'" Sacha asked, wryly. "I don't disagree that it's what Maxim thinks. But not us."

"It's really not different than if you decided to have a conversation in Arabic, right in front of us."

"I don't know Arabic," said Atlanta. "I studied Indonesian languages. Not hugely useful around here."

They'd missed the point, but I wondered if it was intentional. Either way, I wasn't deterred.

"Knowing a lot of languages makes a person more skilled," I said, trying to explain. "Showing that skill off in order to exclude other people who don't have the skill, is both rude and a demonstration of superiority."

Sacha responded quickly, only the slight furrow between his eyebrows indicating any discomfort. "You're right. It was rude. So, I'll tell you why. We were talking about that book you mentioned, *The Midwich Cuckoos*. Powerful, telepathic kids who could force people to do things against their will. Even forcing other people to kill themselves. To be honest with you, Roni, we were… *hurt*. That you would think such a thing about us. Atlanta knows you, cooperated with you. Do you see how that was hurtful? Why we conceivably *would not* want you to hear how it made us feel?"

"I feel like you should discuss all these things openly," interjected Zara as she poured coffee and juice. "You need to trust each other. I'm going to leave you alone to fix this." She flashed Kenzie a telling look and then went back upstairs.

The four of us sat in glum, uncomfortable silence.

After a moment Kenzie said, quietly, "But you *are* superior." He set down his juice, barely touched. "We've seen Maxim do incredible things. Things no…" Abruptly, he stopped, as if swallowing the next words.

"Things no 'human' can do?" said Sacha. "We're human, too."

"The next stage of human evolution, maybe."

"That's getting a little dark. Sounds like you're worried we'll 'replace you.'"

Kenzie's face reddened. His voice trembled a little when he spoke. "Don't lay that racist crap on me."

I glared at Sacha and Atlanta. "Putting words in our mouths is unhelpful. Listen, I'm sorry I mentioned the Midwich cuckoos. I couldn't be sorrier."

"The analogy doesn't even work," Atlanta said, angrily. "The Midwich cuckoos are aliens born to human birth parents. But the first of us were human fetuses altered inside their human moms."

"The last thing we want is a world made up of only telepathic humans," said Sacha.

Atlanta nodded in hearty agreement. "That would suck *so bad*. Do you even know how hard we have to work to keep other two-dubs out of our heads?"

"It was one of the harder parts of living with two-dubs, but it got a lot worse when Maxim, Atlanta and I were in the South Wing." Sacha paused briefly and turned to Atlanta. "Do Roni and Kenzie know about the South Wing?"

Atlanta shook their head a little too quickly, as though they wanted to speed past something embarrassing or maybe even confidential. "Uh, possibly. I…I saw it from the chopper, when we went back to get the others. Nothing much left – the place is in ruins."

Then both were quiet for a couple of seconds. I guessed some silent update was happening. Maybe Atlanta was telling Sacha that he'd spilled the tea about this mysterious 'South Wing,' that it was the first time we'd heard anything about it.

Sacha, on the other hand, seemed happy enough to divulge more information because after their silent conference, he turned to me and admitted, "It was a section of the K-Foundation, where they put kids that tried to escape the main camp. In the South Wing, they blocked our powers with morphorium."

Frowning, I asked, "Wait, I thought they only used morphorium on kids older than sixteen?"

Atlanta scoffed, tossing their head in disdain. "It's used on *everyone* at a low dose. Just that they mix it with an addictive drug on kids over sixteen, the ones who've been sold to a controller."

Sacha said, "Plus, South Wing was a whole different experience, with new rules. When the morpho dose ran out at the end of the day, you'd know it. You'd begin to sense other two-dubs trying to probe your thoughts."

"Then you had to block," Atlanta continued. "Blocking is hard, it's tiring."

"Block other telepaths' thoughts?" I asked. "How do you, even?"

Atlanta shrugged and looked at Sacha for a moment. *Sharing thoughts, again.* Then, speaking in a halting voice, they described it. "You think of a physical object. Imagine it in detail. Really intense detail. Like seeing all the pixels in a digital image, up close. Place your true thoughts inside of it, so all they see is the block."

Sacha took up the thread, and Atlanta listened intently, breaking in now and then with comments like 'uh-huh' and 'facts.' "For instance, to even have a chance to escape the Krylov, I practiced blocking for six hours every day, for six months. All that work to do what comes naturally to you, Roni. You could even try to broadcast your thoughts at me, and I wouldn't hear them."

"Right, because as far as having psi powers goes, I'm as dumb as a rock. But *you* can make us do things," I said, objecting. "Like write on a mirror or fly a helicopter."

"Only if you allow it," Sacha reminded me. "In that book you mentioned, the alien children were cold, ruthless and violent. That is *not* us. But it might be…"

He swallowed the rest of that sentence. Atlanta finished it. "It might be Jaguar."

Kenzie gently reminded us, "Guys, it's ten to seven. We should probably head for the jetty."

We'd been told to bring nothing but ourselves and a rucksack packed with essentials and warm clothes. We'd pretty much figured this meant we were headed north. Kenzie had begun researching pipelines located in the north and given up – there were too many. We'd already guessed that if the Russians wanted to make it appear like a US operation, it'd need to be somewhere close to Russia, like Alaska.

As we drew close to the jetty no more than two hundred yards away, I spotted the speedboat. Its driver had on a sailing jacket sporting the logo of a sea adventure tourism company. *The company is probably a CIA cover*, I thought. He took a register to make sure we were all aboard, then sped off down the estuary towards the open sea. After about twenty minutes we could see our destination – a seaplane. The coastline was no longer visible, which I guessed was the point. No randos would be able to spy on our departure from the land.

We transferred to the seaplane; a DeHavilland DH3-C Otter painted in the livery of the same tourism company as worn by the driver of the speedboat. This time there were two operatives aboard – the pilot and one other, a guy who checked that we'd strapped in properly. The guy was extremely attractive, African American with gorgeous eyes and wore a black windbreaker jacket with multiple pockets over black jeans and sturdy hiking boots. I swear, it was like getting into a plane with Donald Glover.

I smiled, shy and awkward as he handed each of us a headset and ordered us to put it on. The handsome officer didn't smile back. I guess he was used to getting a dumb reaction like mine. Then he took a seat opposite, from where he could see all of us.

Through the headphones I heard him say "Ready for take-off, captain."

The propellers began to spin until a solid wall of sound enveloped us. The plane jerked forward and began to cruise, skimming the water for mere seconds before it floated into the air.

"I'm Programs and Plans Officer Lyle Prince," he announced through the headsets. "You can call me 'Prince.' Your country thanks you for volunteering. I'll be preparing you for Operation Leopard."

Your country thanks you for volunteering. No sarcasm, Prince was serious, as though we'd simply *imagined* Margo Daniels's coercive methods.

I leaned back and craned my neck so I could see Kenzie, sitting behind me. He smiled at me, relaxed and cheerful. Kenzie hadn't actually volunteered, yet I had to admit it, Daniels had been shrewd to select him for the mission, because as it turns out, unlike me, he was totally up for something on those lines.

A pipeline is going down, he'd told his moms. *Good enough for me.*

TWENTY-TWO

OPERATION LEOPARD

So – confession time. When it comes to travel in the USA, I'm a southern girl, haven't travelled more than a hundred miles north from Falls Church, Virginia. Flying to Alaska, especially starting in a seaplane, was a huge thrill. In a *good* way, unlike flying in a stolen helicopter chased by the Cuban military, which is a huge thrill in a *terrifying* way.

The base we were heading to was on St. Paul Island, a remote spot in the Bering Sea. The route from the Maryland coast took us inland to Ohio, where we changed to a private jet. Maybe it belonged to the CIA, who knew? What was clear is that the whole thing had been meticulously organized, as though Daniels had known from the start that we'd agree.

The jet took us north and over Canada's snow-capped mountains to a small airfield in Anchorage, Alaska. Prince, our 'Programs and Plans Officer,' used the flight time to talk us through the operation (he never called it a 'mission'), quizzing us over and over until each one of us could recite the plan in detail. When we were all feeling good about how well we knew it, he announced that it was merely the bones of our work. Then he began to fire questions at us.

"What if one of the other passengers takes an interest in one of you?"

"What if you sense that an enemy agent is on board?"

"What if none of you manage to get on the team to investigate the decoy yacht?"

After an awkward silence Sacha mused, "That's why you have me and Atlanta."

"Too risky to put it all on you," replied Prince, impatient. "That's why I'll train you to use hand signals. We'll prep a solution for these scenarios and any others we think up." He hesitated then, adjusting his mic.

In the pause, I took in the view. Thousands of feet below were glassy lakes, silver and blue as the sunlight stroked across them, nestled in fiercely green meadows dotted with patches of pink and purple and in the shadow of hulking grassy mountains, their upper flanks streaked with snow. Its beauty made my heart tremble a little. This country was a jewel. But this magnificent land and millions of its inhabitants now lived under the threat of pure horror – either from climate change or nuclear war. And now we four, not trained officers of the military or CIA but Kenzie and me, Atlanta and Sacha – we were going to do our bit to prevent that. Instead of living with the itch of an underlying fear, we were taking action. It felt *good*.

Sacha asked, pensively, "Why 'Operation Leopard?'"

"That's classified," replied Prince. After a brief, sullen silence he continued, "A lot of what I know about this operation is classified. Sucks that I can't tell you, but that's life undercover."

We fell into an extended quiet after that, each of us alone with our thoughts. A car was waiting for us in the Anchorage airfield and Prince drove us to a nearby pizza restaurant. He ordered for us without asking –

vegan pizzas all round. Turns out the guy was on a mission to convince everyone to switch to a plant-based diet. We scarfed down pizza, and then he corralled us back into the car and to the airfield. A smaller airplane was now on the tarmac, a Cessna. Prince settled us into the four passenger seats before climbing into the pilot's chair.

"You're a pilot, too? Now you're just being fancy," I said to Prince, intentionally provocative. And yes, flirtatious because the man was *seriously* gorgeous. Prince stayed silent, suppressing a grin. When I looked away, I noticed that Sacha had been watching the exchange and now peered at me, curiously. He knew exactly what was going on. I pouted at him. When he let out a helpless chuckle, I grinned.

Maxim wouldn't have reacted like that. Kenzie and I used to try to make him crack a grin when we were in the wings of the school theater, Maxim waiting to go on to perform something solemn by Schubert or Mozart, Kenzie and I getting bored and up to no good. I'd told myself that I liked his cool, unflappable demeanor, especially when I finally learned that he was telepathic, but watching Sacha creasing up like this made me wonder.

Were the brothers really as diametrically opposite as Sacha had hinted?

It was a relief to arrive at our final destination – St. Paul Island. The weather had turned as we left Anchorage, and the island was shrouded in a thin veil of mist. As we descended, the mossy green sweep of land came into view as well as the town nestling in the curve of a hillside coast, colorful weatherboard homes with gray tiled roofs and in the center, a green-tiled church with its cross cresting a yellow, onion-bulb tower.

I was glad of my warm jacket, when we stepped onto the ladder. Another car was waiting in the car park and rushed us to one of the weather board houses. There were mostly tourists in the streets, people dressed in hiking gear, binoculars hanging from their necks and guidebooks in their hands – classic signifiers of wilderness. No one gave us a second glance.

Entering the house, I let Atlanta and Kenzie take the lead behind Prince, who ushered us to a single bedroom with two double bunks. *No privacy then,* I thought. I couldn't decide whether that was good or bad. On the one hand, it would be difficult for anyone to plot behind the others' backs. On the other, if I wanted to chat discreetly to Sacha and Atlanta, to find out more about them and the ultimate intentions of either Atlas or Maxim, that'd be difficult, too.

"No privacy for anyone," remarked Kenzie. Sacha and Atlanta exchanged a thin smile. It was such an obvious response, but they'd left it unsaid. I wondered then if around normies they intentionally avoided saying 'obvious' things aloud, just in case someone might accuse them of reading minds?

You didn't say it either, dummy, I reminded myself. My eyes instantly went to Sacha. Had he heard that? Or my previous thought?

Why was it so difficult to believe they couldn't read our minds?

Each bed was supplied with a thin pillow and on top of these lay a clear plastic bag containing outfits and equipment for the operation. "Black clothing, ski masks, flashlights and night-vision goggles," Prince told us. "If you don't have room for them in your rucksack, leave something behind." He checked our footwear then, rubber-soled sneakers in every case, and passed all as suitable.

It was almost ten by the time we'd eaten the vegan ham sandwiches that Prince had us make in the kitchen. There was zero talk about the operation, I noticed. Each time anyone even lightly touched on the topic, Prince changed the subject. Later as we lay awake in bed, I mentioned my theory. The other three agreed. Prince had taken control of our lives – decided what we ate, when we went to bed. And when he got us up at five thirty in the morning, I realized that he also controlled when we woke. He was super chill about it, no barking of orders or anything. But during the journey he'd accustomed us to take directions from him.

In the bathroom as we brushed our teeth, I asked Atlanta why.

"Why do I take orders from Prince?" They frowned. "He's the trainer. Which is why you shouldn't flirt with the guy, by the way."

I ignored the quip, which instantly told me that Atlanta and Sacha had discussed this – giant gossips that they apparently were. "I guess I'm asking why you're doing this. Me and Kenzie, they're blackmailing us. What's in it for you, Atlanta?"

But I was curious about a lot more – like, *why do you betray Maxim so easily? Or are you working both sides?* I almost caught my breath on this thought. Working both sides would be the smart move, the move Maxim would make, if it was available to him. Maybe he knew exactly what Atlanta was doing and approved?

Atlanta shrugged, pulling floss through two front teeth. "I do what Atlas asks me to do."

"That's it? Do they pay you, at least?"

For a brief second, I saw Atlanta's shoulders hitch, as though they were considering a different response. Then; "Atlas pays for my prep school and college."

The idea of Atlanta at a prep school took me totally by surprise. I let out a scornful laugh. "Really, prep school?"

"Oh yeah. You should see me in plaid pants and a blazer," they said, settling a calm, superior smile on me. "I'm a killer."

"That's it, then, is it? Atlas is a rent-a-telepath outfit, you're a mind for hire?"

Atlanta's easy smile turned into a sultry pout. "Don't you wish you were hot like me?"

I raised an eyebrow, admiring their saltiness. With a final, reproving look that made it clear this was all they were going to say on the topic, Atlanta pivoted back to the bedroom.

Whatever the Atlas Group did – aside from running a kind of 'underground railroad' for escaping telepaths from the Krylov Foundation – I wasn't going to learn about it from Atlanta.

TWENTY-THREE

CHAIN OF TRUST

It turns out that pancakes made with apple butter instead of eggs are delicious. At around six in the morning, Prince whipped up a batch from scratch and put us all in a good mood. When we were done, he got us to clear up and immediately set about laying the table, like we were about to play one of those tabletop war games.

Drying the dishes, I watched him put down three plastic model boats, a dinghy, a fishing boat and what I guessed was meant to be a cruise liner. Then he opened a plastic box and put down four Playmobil figures.

"I borrowed them from my kid," he said, grinning at my puzzled frown. He handed me the brown-skinned woman wearing a blue evening dress with a slit up the side. "That's you. Pick the others, would you? Save us a fight."

The other three figures were unambiguously male, all with the same bland smile. I set down a figure in green and a frilly collar. "That's Sacha. The doctor is Atlanta, and the construction worker is Kenzie."

Prince gathered the others to the table and began to explain the operation again, this time with props. He didn't even let us leave to go to the bathroom until we could show him exactly where we were expected to be and when. Eventually, he himself had to go to the bathroom. Kenzie and I collectively gasped at the relief. Sacha and Atlanta didn't seem to have the same reaction, but then they hadn't had to hold back their thoughts and questions, being free to conduct non-stop, telepathic gossip.

"I need to get out, get some air," Kenzie said, breathing hard through his mouth. "You think Prince'll mind if I step out?"

"Yes, he will," came a terse reply. Prince was already back. "You'll be leaving soon enough, joining the expedition at four in the afternoon. Until then, spend time practicing anything you think needs work, anything…"

I barged right in, putting myself between them, hands on hips and channeling all my frustration. "Excuse me? Four *this* afternoon, we're on the boat? And the operation is the following day? That's the timescale? *One* lousy day to prepare, that's how the CIA likes to roll?"

Prince arched an eyebrow, then replied with a hint of snark. "Yeah. That's the timescale. You want me to call the Czar, ask him nicely to reschedule the bomb plot to a more convenient time for you?"

There wasn't much I could say to that, at least nothing that'd make things better. "Why wait so long to recruit us? We were sitting home in a cabin in Virginia for three weeks."

Prince picked up a Sharpie pen and began circling areas of the nautical map. "That's what I heard. But we only found out a few days ago that this op was officially green-lit."

I gaped. "And you picked us for this? *Us*?"

He shrugged. "CIA doesn't have a kid's division, there wasn't anyone else suitable who we could get on this expedition. Anyhow, way I heard it, you did a lot bigger in Cuba, with no more training." He waited, watching as I cycled through amazement to bemusement, then demanded, "Are we good, Roni? Because you guys have a lot to get through."

I bowed my head, "Sure, Prince." Kenzie fetched his laptop and did something codey, muttering quietly to himself. Atlanta went into the bedroom to practice some kind of martial art. That just left Sacha and me.

"We should try inclination," I found myself saying. It wasn't something I enjoyed at all, but if I was here because of my ability to do that, it was probably better to be good at it.

Sacha leaned back against the edge of the table, hands in his pockets, watching me. "Maybe we should," he conceded. "But there's something more important than inclination."

He hesitated, as if he expected me to guess. I stayed quiet, although I was silently seething. *Of course* there was more. If Sacha could psychically move *my* limbs, then it made sense his mind could connect to mine in other ways. I felt a tremor in my throat, wondering what else there could be.

"You're a latent," he said.

"Yeah," I replied, flatly. "Maxim pretty much demonstrated that to me."

"Did he tell you what one-dubs can do?"

"One-dubs?"

"Sorry, camp slang, I should have told you. One-way, one-double-u, one-dub."

"Yeah, yeah, got it, I just hadn't heard it before; 'one-dub.' Maxim called me a 'latent.'"

"'One-way' is more descriptive," he said, rubbing the back of his head. He smiled, a little bashful. "I like it better."

I thought for a moment about what he was implying. "Are you saying that I can receive more than just inclination-type signals from a two-dub?"

Sacha hesitated before giving a cautious nod. "Yes. I might be able to broadcast my thoughts at you."

I scoffed. "Nope. Don't think so. Remember, I was surrounded by two-dubs in the K-Foundation camp. Little kids trying to reach me with their thoughts. And nothing. A toddler, not even two years old, had to resort to speaking to me. Yeah, it was pretty obvious that baby couldn't figure out what was wrong with me."

"They were little? Then they were untrained. Broadcasting to a latent is a skill you have to develop. The human brain is not very good at distinguishing thoughts that come from inside and outside of it, so non-telepaths tend to dismiss a broadcast. Instead, they might experience external signals as mental illness, circumstantial confusion, or spirituality. They'll believe that an imaginary being like an alien, or a god might be speaking to them, but the idea that another human could be *sending* those thoughts? That doesn't even make it onto the list."

The hairs on the back of my neck prickled, briefly. I pushed back my chair and got to my feet, beginning to pace the living room. I had the fleeting sense that he'd said something tremendously important just now. Maybe he noticed, or sensed my disquiet, but for some reason he began to speak faster.

"But this is about..." He paused very briefly, now definitely reluctant to go into details. "I was more concerned about other types of one-way signals you might receive."

With a muted groan I asked, "Bad things?"

"Yeah sometimes, afraid so. I can shield you from attacks. The best strategy is that they don't know you are vulnerable. It's not like you have a tattoo on your forehead – *Latent telepath*. But you can help me find other one-dubs. And when we know who they are, I can neutralize them."

"Wait up, I thought being latent was rare?"

"Not on operations," he said, as though it were perfectly obvious. "On intelligence operations, telepaths work with one-dubs. The minimal team is one two-dub, one one-dub, but the ideal team is just like ours – two two-dubs, a one-dub and a normie. The one-dub is a vulnerability but they're essential to the team. So now I gotta ask you something. It might be difficult for you to remember this." He inhaled slowly, watching as I shivered, gathering my arms around myself.

"Do I have a choice?"

Instead of answering, he stepped towards me. His hands reached for mine and they felt suddenly large, clammy, exactly what you'd expect from a slightly gawky fifteen-year-old.

"Do you remember why you went to Mexico?"

I froze, then yanked my hands away from his. Tears sprung to my eyes. *No.* An uncomfortable memory reared – Maxim asking me the same question, Maxim summarizing my final hours in the USA before I discovered that Olga had died. How I hadn't wanted to think too hard about why I'd gone to Mexico in search of a boy I hadn't seen or heard from since I was twelve.

"I don't like Maxim that way," I mumbled, lying even to myself.

"Do you remember a Mexican market? You and Olga in that place, searching for Maxim? Chichi Peralta playing on the stereo somewhere? You find Maxim, and Olga says to you…"

"*Ya chamaca,*" I interrupted. "*Ya lo encontramos.*" I couldn't take my eyes off of him and noticed that I was trembling. Both hands went to the sides of my head, and I pressed hard on my temples, as though that could keep unwelcome thoughts out of my head. "How? How could you know that? Nobody knows that, except me and Olga!"

Sacha spoke a little hesitantly. "It was Olga's idea; Olga created the entire dream. She shared it with me and asked me to incept you. Olga was afraid you'd refuse to help her look for Maxim. She needed you to want to go to Mexico, for you, not for her."

"You actually call it 'inception,'" I said, incredulous. "Like in the movie?"

"'Inception' is a great word for it." He paused, watching me stare at him with goggle-eyes. "Everything okay? You seem shocked."

"I don't know what's more shocking," I admitted shakily, moving away from him. "That I guessed inception was a thing, that it's actually what you call it, or that it wasn't Olga that incepted me, but you!"

Sacha shrugged. "Maxim thought of it – he'd seen the movie when he was living in the USA. I used to think of it as 'dream casting' before he told me about that movie. Because it's not just that we send a dream, we can actually create a desire in the recipient."

There was something that had confused me since Maxim first triggered my memory of the dream. "Why did Olga need you? The whole thing was her idea, wasn't it? Her dream, her mission. So, why?"

"Because that would have been impossible. Olga couldn't do that. I mean, she was literally incapable. It's an ability that only appeared in Generation Six. Olga was Gen Five, same as most two-dubs younger than forty, or possibly a late Gen Four. Only me, Maxim and a couple of the little kids are Gen Six."

"You mean, the number of generations since the original telepaths, the ones born in Siberia?"

Sacha nodded. "That's it, exactly. It's a long story for another time. I just needed to check that incepting you worked. Because if it does, and inclination also worked, then I can almost certainly *broadcast* to you. And we're going to need that."

But I'd stopped listening, was a long way from being done asking questions. "You knew Olga – of course you did, she's your aunt. How could I have forgotten! So why didn't you say anything? I told you all that stuff about Olga and me, when we first met, at the café by the river. You reacted like it was the first time you were hearing anything about her. Why?"

"You forget, I never knew my mother, much less her sister. Maxim was the one who got to have a relationship with Masha. She left with him before I was even born." He'd started out sounding impatient but now his voice softened, sounding tender. "The only mother I know is the woman who gave birth to me, Yoselyn. I didn't reach out – how could I? I didn't even know anyone was out there. It was Olga; she contacted Atlas, asked for me."

"Then Olga knew about you, about your extra, 'Gen Six' abilities?"

"Obviously. There was a third sister, Irina, she was a sentinel. She worked at the Krylov camp. I didn't know she was related to me – we didn't get to know things like that. Irina got messages out to the other two. Irina is how Olga knew that Maxim had escaped the Krylov."

I pressed him a little more. "But Irina knew she was your aunt – she had to."

Sacha inclined his head, a reluctant admission. "Yeah, she had to." I got the sense that it was a painful thing for him to admit, so I didn't ask any more questions about his other aunt.

"You think Olga wanted to meet you, to connect with family?"

He flinched, like it annoyed him that I was missing the point. "Olga was part of the Atlas Group. I already told you, every escaped two-dub joins Atlas, apart from Maxim. *All* two-dubs are like family."

Except for Maxim, I thought. *He was an outcast.* I felt a sudden wave of sympathy for him, the only one living outside the flock. No wonder he'd wanted to rescue the 'unicorns' still trapped in the Krylov camp.

"Why're you here, Sacha? How did Margo Daniels tempt one of the Atlas Group out into the open, after all these years?"

He replied with a bland, if guarded, smile.

I tried to encourage him. "C'mon. We need to trust each other."

"Atlanta trusts me. I trust you. You trust Kenzie. Kenzie trusts you. And Kenzie's a true believer in the cause of climate activism – even if it's a huge Russian self-own, apparently."

"*Gas pipeline is going down,*" I said, mimicking the fierce satisfaction that entered Kenzie's voice whenever he spoke of this. "*Count me in, baby!*"

We burst into laughter. After a minute, Sacha wiped tears of laughter from his cheeks and then immediately sobered up. "We do trust each other. It's a chain of trust, all trusting at least one person in the team."

Shaking my head, I started laughing, again. "You dumbass! That's not what 'trust each other' means."

Sacha closed his eyes, as though he were calming himself. When he opened them, he shot me a wry glance. "We just need each link in the chain to be strong."

"But your chain's missing a link," I pointed out. "Who trusts Atlanta?"

TWENTY-FOUR

BROADCASTER

We assembled on the middle pier of St. Paul's harbor, a short walk from the house where we'd stayed the previous night. The afternoon air was heavy with moisture and carried a salty tang of the surrounding blue sea that mixed with the subtle scent of boat oil. It was like being hit in the face with an intoxicating maritime aroma. Mist enveloped the bay, and the sky above was a blend of muted grays and ethereal whites. The sea itself was a little bit choppy at the top, surface wind that whipped up plenty of white caps, but only small waves. The weather overall seemed calm.

Seven vessels lay in the harbor, all but one were tourist boats, their hulls bright with blue or red, weather-wrecked paint. Only one, a traditional fishing boat, stood as a testament to the island's seafaring history. There were even a couple of fisherman-type guys on its deck who had on heavy sweaters with high collars, their hair unruly with salt – extreme beach waves.

Flashiest of the tourist boats was the sixty-eight feet long Nordhavn 68 expedition yacht named '*Perseus*,' which in that company was like the embodiment of nautical refinement. Its gleaming, steel-gray form and smooth lines wove seamlessly into the mood of the

Alaskan island scene, suggesting adventure with a *soupçon* of elegance.

Members of the Alaska Youth Marine Expedition rolled up in dribs and drabs, all of them with their parents or carers. Superficially they were a lot like us, kids aged between fourteen and eighteen and dressed in off-brand windcheaters, jeans, hiking boots and beanies.

Prince instructed us to blend in from the start. "Now get into character, team. You're all extremely privileged, kids of parents that pay for expensive hobbies, especially if they get you into the outdoors. You've been *longing* for this experience. I want you meeting and greeting like you just got out of a Covid lockdown."

Kenzie, Atlanta and I surged forward. I counted a total of twelve teenagers and two expedition leaders, a trim, athletic looking pair: a white man with a chunky beard and a woman of Asian descent in matching black wetsuits bearing the turquoise 'Whale Adventure' logo. The guy seemed to know Prince, hugged him hello and chatted quietly, just out of earshot.

I positioned myself on the edge of one cluster of burgeoning friendships, smiled and said, "Hi how's it going?" like I meant it, but I didn't. Meet-and-greets aren't my thing, not a bit.

Sacha swerved between two groups, making his way over to me. Speaking close to my ear he whispered, urgently, "We can try it now. I'll head over to Prince and his new friend. And I'll broadcast what they say." He looked into my eyes to check I'd understood. "Well?" When I backed away, he asked again, "Will you?"

"What're you waiting for?" I growled. Last night I'd refused Sacha's request to attempt to 'broadcast' his thoughts at me, but now my curiosity was strong. Partly to learn whether the expedition leader was maybe another CIA person and partly to see if I could act as a psychic receiver. The second of these shouldn't have been a giant surprise but it was. I'd already been inclined and incepted by him – obviously Sacha would be able to broadcast, too. Hearing his voice in my head, however, was a whole other thing.

Another minute later he was back at my side, eager to find out if it'd worked. It occurred to me to lie – would he know? Maybe I should have – it'd have saved me some trouble later. But the logic of it seemed so straightforward: if I could be inclined and incepted, then surely I could receive a broadcast. Maybe he'd suspect something, if I lied? We were trying to build trust and that wasn't a trustworthy thing to do. One weak link in the chain of trust was already too many.

"Repeat what I broadcast to you," he said. "As accurately as you can."

"Lemme think. Okay, they said: *They're reasonably well-prepared. The Cassiopeia layout, especially. And if a Chekist attacks them? The cover ought to hold. Why should it, you think the TRE doesn't use teenagers?*" I paused, enjoying his astonished reaction. "Weird how I hear it in *your* voice, now I think about it."

"It happens like that if you know the broadcaster – the brain fills in, gives the thought a voice. But Roni, that's great," he breathed, delighted. "*You're* great!"

"Glad you're happy. What about the whole getting-attacked-by-Chekist, thing? Seems like we should maybe worry about that."

He seemed skeptical. "Too late now." Then curiously, he added, "How did Maxim talk you into everything you did in Cuba?"

"Why d'you ask?"

"You did some wild stuff on that operation, by all accounts. Way more dangerous than removing fake evidence from a boat. But now, on this op, you're anxious. So – how did he do it, get you to liberate the Krylov camp?"

I didn't want to answer that question. In a helpless funk, I watched first Sacha, then the other kids on the pier, then turned my attention towards the *Perseus*, whose crew were now lowering a boarding ladder. Finally, I turned my face up to the sky. My mind felt equally blank and misty. "Honestly? I don't even know."

Sacha studied me for a few seconds and then nodded, thoughtfully, as though he'd seen enough to understand. But if he had, he didn't share his conclusions.

"They're boarding," I said, waving at the boat.

He rested his hand on my shoulder and squeezed. "It's going to be fine. Trust me like you trusted Maxim."

How could I? Maxim and I went way back, a friendship rooted in the time of my life when I was happiest. Sacha was a cute boy, intriguing even, intelligent, quick-witted, powerful yet refreshingly sincere. We could be friends, sure. But it just wasn't the same.

TWENTY-FIVE

CONFESSIONS

During late summer in the great state of Alaska, temperatures flirt with the dizzy high of seventy degrees. Paradise for sailors, hikers and lovers of a light-weight jacket. For fans of marine wildlife, the Bering Sea, a body of water that connects east and west, is the destination of choice.

Last June, along with another eleven teenagers, I boarded a Nordhavn 68 expedition yacht going by the name 'Perseus.'

Our mission? To locate, follow, observe and photograph a pod of beluga whales. Our real mission? To observe and track the Third Russian Empire's decoy, a fifty-foot yacht known as Cassiopeia, registration redacted. The remote-operated underwater drone carrying the bomb would be launched and controlled from another, smaller boat nearby, but shade would be thrown onto Cassiopeia.

The CIA received leaked documents that outlined a 'false flag' plot to destroy a gas compressor station belonging to Gazmak, located at – coordinates redacted – and plant evidence that the perpetrator of the gas pipeline destruction was the CIA. These leaked plans would reveal exactly when the plotters would abandon *the Cassiopeia, leaving us a forty-minute window to remove all evidence planted to implicate the CIA.*

Kenzie eventually managed to drag his attention away from his phone and cast an eye over the first draft of my script.

"Yeah – no. The CIA will hunt you forever if you make *that* podcast. D'you forget the non-disclosure agreement we signed?" He watched me pout unhappily and slump into one of the four bunk beds in our cabin. "Maybe you could change the names and locations, switch the perps?"

"That'd be fiction," I said, morosely. "My pod is a true crime show. Gah! What a waste of perfectly good material."

Kenzie was mute, his throat bulging with tension until eventually he swallowed hard and maneuvered himself in front of me. "Is that why you're doing this, Padi? For *material?*"

"Obviously not! Jeez, d'you think so little of me?"

"Then, why?"

For a moment we stared at each other. I forced myself to stay calm. How could I confess what I suspected to be my true reason for being here? If Kenzie thought I had put myself in danger for him, he could become angry, resentful.

"You didn't have to do this," he said, accusingly. "Even Margo Daniels told you that."

Biting my lip, I tried clearly to recall why. Kenzie was angry about something; I could see that. But now, I wondered if I was mistaken. Perhaps he wasn't raging at the idea that I joined the operation to be with him, but with Sacha.

"It's Maxim, isn't it?" He dripped bitterness. "You're obsessed with him. So much that you'd even latch onto his kid brother, if it gives you a chance to get close to him again."

My cheeks flared up, burning with shock and indignation. If I told Kenzie now that I'd done all of this so that I could help him, he would surely blow up at me. However, turns out that staying silent was a bad decision. It seemed to confirm his fears.

Kenzie's face crumpled; angry tears sprung to his eyes. "God, I'm right, aren't I? It's Maxim, it's always been Maxim. You should talk to Atlanta about him. Seriously! He's not the guy we knew all those years ago."

I reached out, gripped Kenzie's arms. "I know. I know he's problematic."

He pulled away, laughing bitterly as roughly, he wiped tears away with the sleeve of one arm. "*Problematic*? 'Problematic' is a guy who hassles you for a date. Jaguar is way beyond that. Ask Atlanta how he used to treat the kids in the Krylov camp. Maxim – *the Jaguar* – isn't interested in girls, he's interested in building an empire."

Who even knows what I would have said next. Things had escalated, gotten away from me. I wasn't certain that Kenzie was wholly wrong. Fair to say that I'd gone in search of Maxim, and then to Cuba to help him stop child telepaths being taken by the Czar. But surely *this* mission had nothing to do with Maxim?

There was no chance to reply, however, because at that moment Sacha and Atlanta joined us in the quarters. They'd been on deck or whatever and had finally descended to check out the berth that would house all four of us. This, I assumed, had been at the request of Prince, arranged, presumably, by his buddy on the expedition team.

"Ooh, the tension in this cabin," grinned Atlanta. They smirked at us, then playfully punched Kenzie's shoulder. "I'd say 'get a room' except you did and we seem to have interrupted you."

Kenzie didn't take this well. He scowled and turned away, sitting on his bunk. My heart raced and I felt light-headed. My feelings were knotted, I couldn't untangle them. Somewhere in the mix was something close to panic at the thought of hurting Kenzie. Confused and defenseless, I contemplated his back. Should I approach him, hug him? The intensity of his outburst and its unexpectedness had shaken me. Now only seconds later I was beginning to fear the fracturing of our friendship, could sense the possibility of a terrifying chasm.

Sacha and Atlanta may not have been able to read our thoughts but something in the energy of the room had clearly reached them. Despite my tunneling vision, I noticed them exchanging concerned looks. And where there were looks, there was inevitably telepathic communication. After another minute it seemed they'd decided on a plan.

Sacha said dryly, "I'm getting the impression that you two need some space. We'll go check out the food arrangements."

Then they were gone. Kenzie had calmed enough to turn a little on his bunk, not entirely showing me his back. Hesitantly, I approached, still unsure what I would do or say. When he saw me getting close, he moved aside a little, making room for me to perch on the bunk next to him. We were inches apart. Close enough to kiss and I was getting the impression that he maybe wanted that. Trembling a little, I picked up his left hand in both of mine and held it tight.

I began, speaking hesitantly at first. "I'm not in love with Maxim. Maybe I was, for a while, I'm not sure. If I was, it isn't because anything happened or even that I really felt anything. I had this dream about him, before we went to Mexico. That dream made me think I liked him, maybe more than liked. But I know now that dream wasn't mine. Sacha incepted me to dream it, so that I'd want to find Maxim. So that I'd go to Mexico. Those thoughts I had about Maxim, about seeing him again, about wanting to see him again, Sacha did that. They weren't my thoughts; they weren't my feelings."

As I described to him how Sacha had incepted me, Kenzie's expression morphed from disbelief to revulsion. He pulled away completely, jumped to his feet and began to pace around the edge of the quarters, next to the portholes.

"He manipulated you!"

"No. I don't think it works like that. Inclination only works if you want to cooperate with the incliner. Pretty sure inception works that way, too. You know that I wanted to find Maxim. Going to Mexico wasn't such a big extra. That dream just intensified my desire to find him. Going to Cuba, that was because we wanted to stop the two-dubs getting taken to Russia. You came along for the same reason, didn't you? And nobody manipulated you."

Kenzie looked devastated. "I didn't need to be manipulated, Padi. All you had to do was ask. Not even that. Where you go, I go."

I knew he meant well. Even so, I overreacted, because the sudden enormity of my responsibility was unbearable. "I didn't ask you to come with me. That was all you."

And there it was – with that careless, flimsy and *entirely* untrue comment from me, the chasm opened.

TWENTY-SIX

DARK EFFECT

I stormed out of the cabin and up the staircase until I found myself on the middle deck. Two or three others from the group were out, two on the top deck and another on the middle, each one alone, deep in contemplation of the sea. I found my own vantage point and gripped the metal railing that went around the deck's edge. Adapting to its swaying motion, I let myself be soothed by the waves, until my confusion and anger dissipated, and I saw only the roll of the sea. The sky had cleared a little, and patches of blue appeared, occasionally glinting in the sun.

"*Hola*," said Atlanta. I hadn't heard them approach and turned to my right where – at a respectful distance – Atlanta leaned forward on both elbows and smiled. Speaking in accented Spanish, they told me that Kenzie had sent them.

"Ah," I replied, and turned back to face the waves. "How come you have an accent speaking Spanish? Maxim doesn't."

With an eye roll they said, "Kenzie's right. You've got it bad. 'Maxim, Maxim, Maxim.'"

I flared up again, zero to sixty. "Oh really? In Mexico, you were the one hanging on his every word…" I snapped my mouth shut. An embarrassing thought had just occurred to me. Did Atlanta remember that I'd asked Maxim if the two of them were a couple?

God, I hope not.

They smiled again, friendly and empathetic. "In Mexico, I was on an op for the Atlas Group. They rescued me too; didn't I tell you that? Fifteen days after they got Sacha out of Cuba. Which is why I don't speak Spanish as good as Maxim – he was in Havana for over a year, long enough to learn properly. We didn't learn Spanish in the camp – didn't even know it existed. It's harder to escape if you can't."

I turned to face Atlanta, copying their casual lean against the side of the boat. "He didn't see through you?"

A head shake and then: "Jaguar is not very empathic, not like his brother. And I'm really good at blocking. I genuinely wanted to help him get the others out of the Krylov." A victorious grin spread across their face. "I guess that helped me to play the part."

"Wow. You sure fooled us." It was true for me and Kenzie, although I wasn't as convinced Atlanta had also tricked Maxim.

"Hey." They prodded my shoulder, gently. "You have a thing for Maxim, yes?"

There was no way to control my blush, so I tried to change the subject. "You said you're an empath. Can you sense the feelings of people who aren't telepaths?"

"Not if they're total mundanes."

I froze for a moment, on the verge of objecting, then peeked up at the sky to cover my irritation. Maxim's word for non-telepaths had been 'mundanes.' I'd asked him to call us 'normies,' and only now reflected on the fact that Sacha had used the term 'normies,' right from the start. To hear Atlanta using the word made me a little more suspicious that they were still, despite all protests, on Maxim's team.

"But you're *not* a mundane," continued Atlanta, sounding thoughtful. "You're a one-dub. To answer your question, I can sense your feelings. Quite well. Enough to know you're pissed at me, right now. And that you sure have the hots for Maxim. Also, a little bit, Sacha, am I right?"

It took me a few seconds to be able to reply. The anger I'd felt a moment ago was now replaced by some incomprehensible emotional charge, a desperate need for release.

"Let it go," Atlanta said, softly encouraging. "It'll be good for you."

The tears began to flow. Within a minute I was quietly sobbing, putting all my effort into keeping the volume down.

"It's just feelings," said Atlanta, with a blithe shrug. "Everyone has them. Yours are pretty contained, relatively speaking. And nobody blames you for wanting the Jaguar. That's his M.O. People fall for him. Girls, boys, non-binary, doesn't matter. He uses them, then he throws them aside."

I faced Atlanta, blank with disbelief. Turns out, I didn't even need to express it.

"Don't get me wrong, he's not a slut or anything." They gave a sarcastic laugh. "I mean, he probably was for a little while, just to survive, when he was alone in Havana. Surviving on your own is not pretty, at any age. You do what you gotta do, right? But other than that, and I'm only guessing about that, then nothing. A few people who maybe thought they had something with him..."

"Like me?" I tried hard to keep the resentment out of my voice, but it wasn't easy. If there was nothing, nothing at all between me and Maxim then how come he'd been able to incline me over such a huge distance?

Atlanta didn't reply right away. I guessed they were taking a moment to consider what they detected in my feelings. Then they took my hand in theirs. "I know it hurts. I know people who went through the same thing. Everyone thinks they're different, that they're the one who really 'got' him."

I withdrew my hand. A cold, brittle anger descended. "You came here to talk about my idiotic crush on Maxim? Fine, mission accomplished. It's not the huge issue you seem to think but, whatever. Are we done?"

Atlanta shook their head. "No. There's something you need to understand about him."

I turned to them with a sad, resigned smile. "Oh. I get it. He's power mad, is that what you're trying to tell me? I should stop thinking about him, cos he'd never be interested in someone like me?"

The problem with petulance is that it can backfire. Atlanta had seemed up until that moment to be eager to let me down gently, but after a second or two they simply nodded.

"Yep. That's it. Exactly."

"Oh my God!" I exploded. "'Power mad,' are you even serious?"

"Oh yeah, very much serious. Jaguar has a plan and it's something bigger than you, me, Kenzie, old friendships, temporary loyalty, and a lot bigger than anything you believe happened between you and him."

I won't lie, 'anything you believe happened' rankled.

"Padi, don't misunderstand, I'm not judging. It'd be great if we only liked the people who were right for us. Wouldn't it?"

"What happened?" I asked, my teeth chattering a little. "In Cuba, after you dropped off Kenzie and me at that beach?"

The question seemed to take Atlanta by surprise. After a moment they answered, haltingly. "He had that contact, remember?"

"Narcojunior's family?" I asked, using our nickname for the youthful *narcotraficante* whose Mexican hacienda Maxim had been house-sitting, while the guy was in prison.

Atlanta nodded. "Yeah. One of the Havana Carillos. Jaguar had it all set up, a safe house in the country. We dropped off the helicopter and walked there."

"You walked? How far?"

"It was a few hours," Atlanta admitted. "But buses and taxis aren't safe if you're on the run. In Cuba, there are informers everywhere. So, we split up into groups and hiked, separately."

I thought for a moment, imagining twenty-odd, recently liberated kids and teenagers who'd had no sleep, walking through Cuba for hours, Maxim and Atlanta taking care of them all.

"Seems like he's watching out for them," I said. "Not really getting the 'power mad' vibe."

"A general needs an army."

"Did he say that?"

Atlanta bent their neck, smiling slightly. "No. But it sums up his aims, I'd say."

"What does he want? Cuba?"

They laughed. "Not even close. *The earth has become small, and on it hops the last man, who makes everything small.'* That's what Jaguar believes. It's from Nietzsche." She hesitated, then added, as if for dark effect, "Adolf Hitler's favorite philosopher."

"And Maxim, he's the 'last man'?"

Atlanta shrugged. "Who else?"

Breathing in, I managed to say, "And you, Atlanta? You said you were trying to save Coati from the camp, but Coati stayed behind."

"Because of Jaguar. Coati knows him, won't trust him."

"But you knew that already, right? Why'd you even try?"

Atlanta glanced up then and I followed their eyes. A dark gray cloud was now directly above, and drizzle had begun to fall. "Jaguar needed to believe it," they said in a voice tinged with shame. "He might have doubted me, if I didn't have a really solid reason."

My chest felt hard, my facial muscles taut as drums. I decided to say nothing more, a smart choice, because I wouldn't have been able to stay calm. Atlanta and the others wanted me to believe Maxim was a bad guy? Okay, cool.

Show me something convincing.

TWENTY-SEVEN

WHALE WATCHERS

"First night, you acclimatize. Take a walk or three. Get to know the boat – the *Perseus*. You've had a chance to study plans for the *Cassiopeia*, where the Russians have planted the fake evidence. May as well get familiar with your initial surroundings, too. Eat a good meal, lots of plants, then meet up somewhere private to go over the plan one last time. Set your alarms, get some sleep. You start bright and early. Should be back in time for breakfast."

Prince's final words to us had stayed with me, had presumably stayed with all four of us, because after a while I saw Sacha and Kenzie were also strolling about the boat, spending several minutes on each deck. Getting 'familiar with their initial surroundings,' I guessed.

The first scheduled expedition activity began after a lunch of toasted, roast vegetable and mozzarella paninis. We put on the waterproofs they'd provided and assembled on the middle deck, using binoculars to observe the subtle signs of two distant right whales. The expedition leaders, who were also crewing the boat, were unashamedly excited, calling out and giggling with sheer delight. This type of right whale, apparently, was super-rare. Their joy was infectious and within minutes the other teenagers were caught up in the excitement of pursuit, clicking away with fancy cameras and long lenses. It's lucky they were all so thrilled, because the fact that unlike them, the four of us had no amazing cameras, nor were we all that stoked to see the whales, might easily have been noticed.

On the deck a bunch of teens clung to the rails and after a few minutes, swiftly crossed it as one of the crew turned the *Perseus* for a better view. I caught Sacha's eye, then Kenzie's. Atlanta, I realized, already had eyes on me, as well as a coolly appraising gaze.

We need to act a lot more enthusiastic.

The thought was broadcast from Sacha, and made me jolt, until after a second or two, I recognized the voice in my head as his. He was close enough to Kenzie to speak into his ear. In the next minute, we began to mimic the others, jumping, squealing with joy and taking photos of what were basically some big, but distant fins.

"North Pacific right whales!" announced the expedition leader, an Asian American woman in her early thirties named Dr. Susie Jang. "This pair were last seen in the Bay of Alaska – it's a mother and her cub. We're going to get in a little closer, but not so much that we chase them off. Oh my goodness! This is incredible, you guys!"

"Will we also see beluga whales?" said one of the kids, a young teen boy. "I kind of came for that."

"We'll see belugas," Dr. Jang replied, not taking her eyes from her binoculars. "A lot of belugas. Rare to see a North Pacific right whale as far north as here. This is a story you'll tell your grandkids – they're endangered!"

I grabbed Kenzie by the arm and tugged him to a relatively empty section of the deck, out of earshot of the animated whale watchers.

"What does this mean for the plan?" I demanded. He seemed confused, so I followed up. "This course we're on feels kind of spontaneous, doesn't it?"

Still puzzled, he nodded, then his face lit up with comprehension. "The rendezvous! We're screwed!"

I pursed my lips together, tightly. "Then, you agree," I said, deflated.

"I mean, maybe they'll get back on course after this."

I nodded. It felt like grasping at a straw but at least it was hope. "Or we could sail to the rendezvous. Maybe?"

"Sail... this boat?" Kenzie was aghast.

Now flustered, I nodded. "Yep. Why not? How hard could it be?"

His eyes widened but after a few seconds, he shrugged his shoulders. "Well, maybe. You flew that helo."

"Not really, Maxim did. I'm guessing a boat is simpler."

Kenzie blinked and looked out to sea, still doubtful. "I think we have to trust the plan. Prince would have given us coordinates, if he thought there was any chance we'd end up in the wrong place. He'd have trained us to sail the boat."

"He does have a buddy on the crew," I admitted, and quickly filled him in with what Sacha and I had observed when Prince greeted the bearded white guy, who'd since introduced himself as Gary Killarney.

"Cool, cool," Kenzie said. He sounded reassured. "Then it's under control. Doctor Jang will course-correct, and we'll cross paths with the *Cassiopeia* the way they planned."

It was a lot to take on trust but at the time I was persuaded. The alternative plan entailed one of us steering the boat. Maybe we could but also, maybe not.

The North Pacific right whales detained us for several hours, the *Perseus* meandering about fifty yards behind the pair the whole time. Sacha and Atlanta were worried, too. We did our best to play along with the main group, pretending to be as rapt as them at our proximity to the whales.

I couldn't help glancing rather too often in the direction of Gary Killarney. If he was, as I suspected, a silent partner of Prince's, possibly undercover for the CIA or at least an asset, then maybe he'd give us some hint or reassurance. We needed to know for sure that this boat, now wildly off-course, would be returning to the original route. I swear, I gave that man every chance to communicate something to me on the downlow. But no.

The whale-chasing ended around eleven at night, as the light was beginning to go, with sunset due at eleven-twenty-one, yes, you read that correctly. Out of the window went our plans for an early night. I've never lived anywhere that didn't get dark by eight at night, so the extra-long day was something of a surprise. Prince had warned us, but it's a different thing to experience midnight sun. Prince had also warned us that sunrise was due around five-twenty next morning, which was why we had to be within reach of the *Cassiopeia* before then, to board it while there was still some darkness.

As things turned out, by the end of that long, long day, Kenzie and I were so stressed from thinking about where our random sailing had taken us, we didn't even bother to take selfies of ourselves on the deck, bathed in the golden light of perhaps the most spectacular sunset I've ever seen. The other kids didn't seem to notice, too absorbed in enjoying the dying moments of what might have been the best day of their lives.

"I'm actually jealous," murmured Kenzie as we leaned on the rails, staring out at the horizon, into which the shimmering, red sliver of sun was sinking. "How cool would it be, to be on an expedition like this for real?"

"We can relax and enjoy it from tomorrow," I reminded him. "The op will last an hour, max. Then it's back to the *Perseus* for waffles."

Kenzie didn't reply, but leaned both elbows into the railing balancing there, ringlets of red hair flopping across his forehead and his expression unreadable. Seconds later, Sacha and Atlanta joined us, flanking us on either side. Next to me, Atlanta broadcast their thoughts.

He's in love with you, do you realize?

I didn't want to encourage this, so I scowled and didn't reply.

But Atlanta continued. *Kenzie loves you. He followed you to Mexico even though he didn't really want you to find Maxim.*

I glared at Atlanta in disbelief.

He always suspected that you liked Maxim. But...

"Gotta hit the 'head,'" I announced, and left. This time I'd had enough. Had Kenzie asked Atlanta to say all of this or were they, basically, a whiny gossip telling tales out of school? It would be a major dick move from Kenzie, if he'd done that. Yet, I doubted it. Kenzie was intensely private about his feelings. I didn't doubt that what Atlanta had told me was true. The way he'd blown up at me made it seem likely he was jealous of Maxim. But the idea of Kenzie admitting this to a relative stranger like Atlanta? That, I doubted. And when? We'd barely had ten minutes to ourselves in Mexico, or Cuba.

The only other explanation was that Atlanta had used their empathy to read his emotions. They'd said, clear as day, that it wasn't possible to read a normie like Kenzie.

Was Kenzie really a normie?

In the ship's 'head' I sprinkled cold water on my face and then washed my hands. Watching myself in the mirror, I noticed how tired I looked, bags under my eyes, like I was twenty-five years old. At six tomorrow I had to be up and preparing to get across to a nearby yacht, climb aboard and remove the fake evidence that would make the pipeline bombing appear to be a CIA job.

Most definitely, it was time to sleep.

TWENTY-EIGHT

DARK WATER

On the surface it seemed like a small ask. Paddle across to a nearby, deserted yacht. Climb aboard, document all discoveries of fake evidence, and then remove them. We knew the layout of the *Cassiopeia* inside out and had taken virtual walks around the yacht blueprints with our eyes closed for two hours after lunch.

The 'HUMINT' – human intelligence – came from a document leaked by a 'highly-placed source with a solid track record.' That's all Prince would tell us about the source of information that for us could be the difference between life or death. Although, not according to Prince, who'd commented, "You won't be killed. Kids, like you? Nah. Ilyin will trade you in a juicy prisoner swap."

"Not all of us," Atlanta had said, sharply. "He'll keep me and Sacha."

"Only if he figures out how very special you both are," Prince had replied.

It came across as patronizing, at the very least. How could Prince know what Cheka knew about Sacha? There was a good chance the Chekist who'd dropped by our hotel room in Tapachula could now recognize Maxim, and maybe Atlanta, too.

"Anyhow," he'd continued, oblivious to the effect of his dismissive attitude. "You won't get caught. Because you'll watch them leave. They no leave, you no go. Capeesh?"

Well, the time had come. It was four-thirty in the morning, about an hour before sunrise. Kenzie, Sacha, Atlanta and I were out on deck, in the dark and dressed in the all-black combat pants and fleeces provided by Prince. I pulled a black knitted ski mask over my face and made sure the eyehole was wide enough that I could use the night-vision goggles. As the most physically strong, Kenzie carried a backpack containing an inflatable dinghy that we'd use to paddle over to the *Cassiopeia*. He and I were on the port side, the others were starboard, all four of us peering through the goggles.

"There's nothing," I whispered to Kenzie. With the help of the starlight, I could distinguish midnight blue sea from a slightly lighter sky, but in terms of any craft anywhere nearby? *Nada.*

Footsteps on the stairs coming from the lower deck had us instantly pressed up against the inside walls of the hull, crouching in the shadows. From our shady recess, I turned to see Dr. Jang amble out of the lower deck staircase and head for the next deck up, which contained the saloon and pilot house. She didn't seem to have spotted us and was covering her yawn with one hand.

"No frickin' way…" murmured Kenzie.

Jang is checking there are no other vessels near the horizon. You have to do that at sea, you have to check for new boats every half hour, day and night. Or else something huge might run you down while you sleep.

Sacha's voice, calm and assured, was in my head, again. I was mesmerized, wondering how my brain managed so well to capture his tone. Was that just my interpretation, was the Sacha of my imagination always so cool and confident?

We held our positions in silence for three minutes, which was how long Dr. Jang's sleepy horizon-check lasted. We waited a few more seconds after the sound of her footsteps had faded away as she returned to her berth. Then we got to our feet and turned back to the sea. After a few seconds Sacha and Atlanta joined us on the port side.

"Guys," I whispered, gathering them close. "Face it, the *Cassiopeia* isn't here. Which means our boat missed the rendezvous. Doctor Jang had a chance every half hour to change course, but she hasn't. I think the op is blown."

Three silhouetted heads nodded in agreement.

"We should wait a little longer," Kenzie suggested.

Atlanta turned at once to Sacha, who after a moment shook his head.

"No. The *Cassiopeia* crew were scheduled to vacate between three and three-thirty in the morning. Wherever it is now, we can't reach them in time. Even if we could sail this boat."

Sometimes, after all that's happened, it can be hard to recall how startling it was at the time, to see a guy who looked as young as Sacha speaking with such authority.

Kenzie groaned loudly with frustration.

"Are you trying to get caught?" I hissed and immediately envied Sacha his ability to stay silent in stressful moments, to be controlled enough to speak only minimally, yet with such resonance.

This time Kenzie sighed. "Caught? By who? Susie Jang? Yeah, that's scary."

"Quiet, both of you," I said. Commands weren't my style, so the others seemed a little taken aback. To my surprise, they obeyed. I was facing the water and staring into it almost directly below, close to the hull. For a long moment I didn't move until Kenzie spoke up.

"What is it, Padi?"

"I saw something. In the water."

A strip of LED lights ran along the outwards-facing railing of the yacht, creating an outline of the vessel that could be viewed from across the sea. The faint glow they cast lit up a narrow section of sea around the yacht. We all watched the sea closely, now. This time I saw nothing, just the faint movements of the motor keeping the boat in position.

Kenzie tried again. "What kind of a 'something'?"

I hesitated, then said, "Something dark, slick-looking and slow."

"Did you see a right whale?" Kenzie asked, mockingly.

Atlanta asked, "Where did it go?"

There was a pause. I spotted Sacha glancing at Atlanta before I answered, conferring again, probably.

"Along the side."

"So, a nosy right whale," Kenzie concluded.

I paused. That solution hadn't actually occurred to me, but he had a point. "Yeah. Maybe."

Then we felt it. On the port side, something hit the hull. The yacht immediately listed, rocking towards the starboard side.

Kenzie was aghast. "It's messing with us!"

"But there was nothing there!" Atlanta said, astonished. She had a point. Nothing had come close to the port side of *Perseus* in the last ten seconds.

After a few tense minutes, the yacht seemed to settle. We scrutinized the surrounding sea awhile. Sacha shrugged. "No *Cassiopeia* to be seen. I guess we're off the hook from the CIA."

"Awesome," grinned Kenzie. "Screw 'em."

Beneath my feet, however, I sensed something strange. It was difficult to be sure, with the horizon fully dark. But I had the weird sensation that I was tilting to the left. I licked my index finger and held it in the air. A light breeze from the east, nothing that'd be making waves. I gripped the rail and stared down into the sea. The same gentle waves that had surrounded us all day, lapped at the hull.

Then Sacha's voice was in my head. *What's wrong?*

We're leaning to the left, said a second voice, Atlanta's. *Great*, I thought. *Now they're having a conversation in my mind.*

"Atlanta is right," I said.

"Right about what?" Kenzie asked, bewildered. In a voice tinged with dismay he asked, "Padi, can you do psychic stuff with them, too?"

"We can broadcast our thoughts to her," Sacha said super-casually, as if he were telling us his favorite pizza topping.

Kenzie's bitter, disappointed "Oh!" in that moment was, to me, worse than anything gross he could have said in reply. Then he added, flatly, "Has anyone noticed that the yacht is listing, it's tilting?"

I thought hard, furiously trying to figure out what was happening. Listing presumably happened when a boat took on water.

Atlanta said, "Could that thing have rammed us hard enough to cause a leak?"

"Rammed? Roni said it was moving slowly. So, I'm guessing not." I couldn't see his face but, in his voice, I heard it clearly: Sacha was scared. "Kenzie," he commanded, "Inflate the dinghy."

Kenzie didn't budge. "Inflate the dinghy, oh sure, why not, let's paddle a couple hundred miles to Siberia or wherever."

"The boat is sinking," I said, breathing hard. "We have to tell the others. Jeez, you think this yacht has a life raft?"

"None that I've seen," replied Sacha.

"Nor me," Atlanta said.

"Now you mention it…" added Kenzie, glumly. "Prince told us to check this yacht out. Guess I wasn't paying enough attention."

I refused to let their negativity get to me. "Maybe not to this boat, but we studied the plans for the decoy boat pretty good. *Cassiopeia* had a life raft. It was in a plastic cylinder, on the starboard side deck. Seems likely this yacht would have something similar."

Somewhere in the hull, metal groaned, and the *Perseus* lurched a few more degrees to the left.

"I'm going to wake Doctor Jang and Killarney," I announced. I pocketed the night-vision goggles and pulled off the ski mask. "The rest of you, get everyone else."

The dark water that surrounded us no longer appeared welcoming to our expedition. In its opaque blackness hid creatures that might tear us apart. Without the safety of our metal cocoon, what would protect us from the elemental forces of the depths?

TWENTY-NINE

LISTING

I didn't need to wake her because Dr. Susie Jang was already scurrying up to the middle deck. Loitering at the top of the stairs, in the dim light from the cabin below, I could see her puzzled expression, which grew mildly suspicious as she scanned first me in my all-black outfit, then the others.

"You… you guys are already out?"

"Yes," I said. "What happened?"

"I'm not sure. Maybe we hit an iceberg. Anyway, we're taking on water. Going to capsize, probably. Need to wake everyone up, get them onto this deck and into a life vest."

I balked. Hearing how bleak the situation was from one of the crew made it terrifyingly real. At least the four of us had prepared to sleep only a few hours, but the expedition kids hadn't. "You think we can survive in the sea?"

"In *this* sea? You'd be useless within five minutes. Unconscious after maybe a half hour. Dead after two. But no worries, there's a life raft. It inflates when the boat capsizes."

Dr. Jang stepped up onto the final step and gripped my shoulders. Her expression was remarkably composed, given our situation, but fear lurked just beneath the surface, rigidity in her hands and jaw. "Stay calm. You got out quick, that's a great start. The four of you stay here, counterbalance the tilt, who knows, maybe we'll last a little longer." She turned to leave.

"Wait, let me help!"

She paused. "The other kids are already getting ready to evacuate. I'm going to look for Gary."

The other expedition leader was missing? This sounded bad. "I can do that; I was about to…" I insisted.

"No," she said, extremely firm. She continued on down the stairs. I called out "Back in a bit!" to the others and then followed Dr. Jang.

The doors to the other two berths were open and I could see the other teenagers, pulling clothes from the closets, getting hurriedly dressed in silence apart from the occasionally exasperated gasp. The lights of the corridor flickered. I guessed the water hadn't yet reached the fuse box. It was only a matter of time. Jang checked on everyone, then returned to the staircase.

"I told you to wait up on deck."

I stepped aside to let her pass. "Maybe you can repair the damage?"

Ignoring me, she disappeared behind the door to the lower deck and I guessed, the engine room. And then, it struck me.

Iceberg? Could there even be an iceberg in June?

I stood on the threshold of the berths, watching the rest of the expedition group dressing, urging them to be quick and counting them out. They hurried through the corridor until they reached the stairs. When they'd all gotten out, I turned to go, but instead of climbing to the outer deck I went further down into the boat, toward the engines. There'd been no sign of Gary Killarney in the berths, nor up top. There was nowhere else he could be but downstairs. When I reached the lower deck, I turned the wheel to open the door to the engine room. Water instantly flowed out, soaking me up to my calves.

The engine room was flooded.

For about three seconds I was peering into the white, bright engine room full of gleaming machines and orderly pipes. There was just time to glimpse Dr. Jang and Gary Killarney crouching in one corner of the room. Then the entire boat went dark as simultaneously, the lights popped out. Cries of shock and fear rang out all over the yacht and then, silence. Other than the sounds of the two expedition leaders sloshing through waist-high water as they exited the engine room, all I could hear was the slap-slap of waves against the hull and a soft breeze.

"Get back upstairs!" shouted Dr. Jang, when she noticed me hovering by the entrance to the engine room. She appeared to be supporting her colleague. He wasn't saying much and seemed to be injured. I backed up, nearing the stairs. But the two expedition leaders paused, obviously waiting for me to go first.

As I reached the back of the lowest deck, a band of pink light materialized at the eastern horizon, low clouds lighting up as the sun's first touch reached us. One crucial sound had been subtracted from the soundscape. It took me a few seconds to understand what had happened.

The engines had stopped.

I kept climbing. When I reached the middle deck, I saw that the angle of tilt had increased a fair bit – from maybe ten degrees to twenty. Eleven teens had clustered together on the starboard side, toward the yacht's bow, which is at the front. Some wrapped arms around each other, huddling in the brisk, early morning breeze.

When Sacha saw how Susie Jang struggled to support Gary, who was a foot taller than the petite marine biologist, he rushed forward and took Gary's other arm. A pained cry escaped Gary, and he staggered.

"His arm is badly broken," explained Dr. Jang.

"Why is this happening?" wailed one of the older teenage boys, who no one was hugging.

Sacha knelt down on the deck supporting Gary, who winced sharply every time Dr. Jang touched his right arm.

"It's the forearm," she was saying. "Seems to be broken in two places. We'll use the first aid kit to make a sling and get you something for the pain, all right?"

But Gary couldn't seem to take his eyes off the kids on deck. Through gritted teeth our wounded expedition leader said, "Some of these kids are still in their pajamas, what the hell?"

Over his shoulder, Susie Jang shot me a look of pure fury. "You had one job – make sure they got ready to be on deck."

Her criticism stung. I wanted to clap back, defend myself, but she was right. What was I thinking, letting them leave their rooms in pjs?

"I thought we were going to watch the sunrise," complained the boy who'd asked why this was happening. "Nobody told us the boat was sinking."

"The boat is sinking?" shouted a young girl and then a panicky chorus joined in.

"Hey, hey, the sea's calm," said Kenzie, raising his voice above the din. "There's still time to dress warmly."

"How long will it take to sink?" I asked.

Dr. Jang replied, "A couple hours, maybe. Depends on the size of the hole. Could be as little as one hour."

I called out, "Sacha, come help me get more warm clothes for the kids."

But he and Atlanta were already teaming up and on their way.

Better if it's me and Atlanta, Roni. We can update each other through walls.

"Roni, go find me the first aid kit. It's in a storage unit under the sofa on the aft deck." Dr. Jang pointed to the deck above.

"We should all go up," groaned Gary. "To the pilot house, past the seating area upstairs. Then the flybridge, if necessary. Get everyone as high as possible. And the life raft, someone needs to engage that, someone should…"

In a soothing voice Dr. Jang reassured him, "Gary, let me take care of that. Let's get your arm in a sling first."

Then the questions started.

"Doctor Jang, how come the boat is sinking?"

"Did we hit something?"

"Did someone attack us?"

They came thick and fast, but the final question snagged my attention and clung on, like a plant's burr.

Did someone attack us?

What if the slick, black object that I'd spotted moving slowly along the side of the boat had been some kind of attack? Could it be that the Cheka somehow got wind of our plan to foil their 'false flag' plot? My mind reeled at the implications.

Dr. Jang's voice cut through my stupor. "Roni don't be afraid. We have drinking water. We have life vests. We have a life raft. Someone will rescue us in time. We can do this. Please, just bring me the first aid kit."

Just then, dazzling pink light burst across the sea, touching all our faces and making our skin glow. The water turned dark midnight blue dappled with rose gold. The starboard side of the boat now lined up facing east. The sunrise, however, was confined to a shiny band of light that ran along the horizon. Towering above was a tall bank of dark clouds that reached as far as I could see.

A gust suddenly blew across the deck, a stiff blast of cold air that made me wish I'd brought gloves and a hat. Dr. Jang was still urging me to get the supplies, so I hurried to the deck above. Higher up, the tilt of the yacht felt ominous. I forced myself not to focus on the angle, which could easily become forty-five degrees in the next twenty minutes, based on how things had been going so far. I began tossing sofa cushions aside, looking for the storage space beneath. When I found it, I hoisted the first aid kit, which was the size of a school bag. Next to it, I noticed, were extra food supplies – two boxes of Twinkies. I took both and placed them on the picnic table. We'd all be on this deck soon enough. Might as well grab some food before we abandoned ship.

From behind me I heard Sacha call out, "Don't."
I turned to face him.
He pointed at the boxes of Twinkies in my hands. "There's no time. The water level is rising. It'll drag down the back of the boat. We'll have to climb. So, leave the Twinkies, because you're going to need your hands free."

THIRTY

STORM

Standing a little ahead of me on the aft deck, Sacha's brow creased, as though turning something over in his mind.

I pointed towards the stairs. "Gotta take the first aid kit."

He gave a brisk nod, only half-listening. "Yeah, go." He sighed then and shut his eyes tightly. "Wait."

"What?"

Sacha shifted uncomfortably, a small, helpless shrug. "I have to tell someone."

I stilled. A stiff breeze hit me in the face, sent a rush of air through me. I asked Sacha, "What?"

"There's supposed to be a storm today." He waited, watching this information sink in. If it hadn't been for the sudden gust we'd just experienced, I would have laughed at him. Literally five or at most ten minutes ago, the sea had been calm. Now it seemed more agitated, if only on the surface.

"A storm? Who says?"

"They were talking about it yesterday. Doctor Jang and Killarney. They were planning to sail to Saint Matthew Island, anchor there until it passed." He paused. "I think it's coming earlier than expected."

Another wild gust stung my eyes. Panic was finding its place within me, but I refused to notice. The operation we had been blackmailed into assisting, well, it had failed. Now the USA would successfully be framed for blowing up a Russian gas pipeline. They would use it as a premise to attack Alaska. Who knows, maybe World War Three would start as a result. If it didn't, would the CIA really count this failed mission and let us off the hook for any others? Or would they push us into something else?

All of which was assuming we'd even get out of this situation. Our boat was going down. I didn't want to think too closely about how that had happened or why. Fine; ignore that, for now. We would get into the life raft, get rescued. Except, would we? If this storm hit while we were in the life raft, what would happen to us?

Pushing past Sacha, I headed back to Dr. Jang. Fixing Gary Killarney was the priority now. Dr. Jang needed someone else to help her, someone who understood the boat. The rest of us didn't even know how to find or activate the life raft.

Getting Killarney's broken arm into a sling was a haphazard affair that entailed a lot of pain. I handed scissors, bandages and tape to Dr. Jang as she fixed him up, meantime keeping a wary eye on the sea.

By the time she'd finished the job, the wind was steady and strong, not just savage pulses of air but a sustained gale. The tower of storm cloud that had been on the horizon now filled most of the sky and turned it as dark as it had been before dawn. The air cracked suddenly with a distant boom and close to the horizon, bolts of blue-white lightning burst from the clouds, electrifying the sea. A beautiful, terrible sight that I never want to see again. As Killarney rose unsteadily to his feet, the rain began.

The angle of the yacht's tilt was easily twenty degrees and had happened in a fraction of the time I thought it'd take. Waves were buffeting the craft, one in five washing over the deck. While I finished helping Dr. Jang with Killarney, Sacha was in the aft section of the yacht, monitoring the moment when the lowest deck, directly below, went underwater. Meantime, Kenzie and Atlanta found life vests and handed them out. The other teens sat in a huddle on the soaking deck, arms interlocked in a chain that tethered them to the heavy steel of the anchor chain. They were surprisingly calm, probably because neither expedition leader had told them the truth of our predicament – even the truth as far as I understood it at the time, which was far from the full picture.

By the time Sacha noticed the lower deck slip below the surface of the water, his yells wouldn't have reached me – the wind noise was way too intense. But he had another option.

That's it, said his voice, in my mind. *Tell Doctor Jang to get everyone up onto the next deck.*

The climb to the aft deck was already treacherous, with the yacht already half-tipped into the sea. I wondered; how long would it take for the *Perseus* to be fully on its side? Or was Sacha right that it would start to sink from the back, some time before we had a chance to see the boat get to ninety degrees? We clung to rails, edges of steps, anything that we could to stop ourselves tumbling onto the deck below.

The waves were choppy now, battering the hull and buffeting the boat so badly that seasickness hit and most of us let go at least a bit of vomit. We'd all taken Dramamine the day before, but it'd worn off and it was too late to take more. Eating was out of the question, even if the boxes of Twinkies I'd saved for us hadn't slipped right off the table and onto the lower deck.

Dr. Jang called for our attention. She had to shout above the howl of the gale, and it was difficult to pay attention, when most of us were busy trying to hold onto something fixed. The boat shifted, a sickening lurch backwards. I found myself sliding towards the edge of the deck, stopped when one of the older girls caught me. She grabbed my left hand and guided it to the railing. I fumbled between the girl and her neighbor on the railing, finding the rail with my right hand until I, like everyone else, was clinging on for my life.

"On my mark, you all need to get into the saloon," yelled Dr. Jang.

The door to the saloon was no more than six yards away, but there was nothing secure to hold onto on the way, other than the metal pole that went through the dining table, holding up the ceiling. I figured that if I could get to that pole and wrap one arm around it, I could function as a fixed point and help others to walk along a human chain. The next time the stern of the boat lifted with the swell, I used gravity to throw myself at the pole. As I collided with it, I hooked my right arm around it and stretched as far as I could, extending my left hand.

"Grab on!"

Sacha saw what I was doing, and he released his grip on the railing, letting himself fall towards me with his right hand outstretched. We linked arms for a firmer hold. Another wave smashed over the aft deck, hitting me in the face. Both my hands were occupied, I couldn't wipe away the seawater, so I kept them screwed shut. Dr. Jang caught onto our plan at once, scrambled into position and used her body as the final link between me, the metal pole and the saloon door, which was open, but which kept wafting shut with the violent motions of the boat. Jang began to bellow instructions, ordering the kids by name to begin their journey to the pilot house, climbing along the chain of Sacha, me, and Dr. Jang, until they'd reached it. Sacha went next, then me and then we were all inside.

Dr. Jang battened down the hatch, a firm seal. The floor of the saloon was wet but otherwise relatively free of seawater.

"It's nice in here," one of the older teenagers said. (I later learned that his name was Sandro.) "Why can't we stay until we're rescued?"

"Because we'll drown," answered Dr. Jang curtly, not even looking at him. "Once a boat has taken on ten percent water, it's just a matter of time before it sinks." She turned to the boy who had asked the question. "If we stay in here, we'll go straight to the bottom of the sea. Not the tomb I had in mind, Sandro. Now, keep going! Up the stairs and inside, down to the wheelhouse."

Huddling through the saloon and then the galley, we found the narrow stairway up to the pilot house and crowded into it. The bridge, all sophisticated screens and fancy knobs, was totally dead. We lined the windows on the port side, kneeling on the sofa-chairs of a cozy booth behind the deck controls, peering outside. Less than fifteen yards below, the waves frothed in turbulent rage. Nobody spoke. The yacht lurched again, twisted, and then slipped backwards, sinking a little deeper into the sea.

It felt like every one of us stopped breathing for a few seconds, cringing as we waited to see – would this be the lurch that sent the boat to the bottom of the ocean? Would it go slow-slow-quick? Or would we drown gradually, by degrees?

I turned back down the stairs and into the galley, surveyed the scene through to the end of the saloon. The door we'd come through just moments ago was now below the surface, deep blue water was all I could see beyond it.

The panic that had lain dormant inside me now stirred. A thought I'd tried to block out seemed to scream, a deafening blare inside my head.

We're all going into that water. Am I going to drown?

THIRTY-ONE

VERTICAL

When I'd clambered my way back to the pilot house, Dr. Jang was struggling to keep a lid on the kids' mounting terror. It was infectious, like watching someone vomit. I was glad of the chance to focus instead on helping everyone to get out. It was the first time it occurred to me that maybe there's no such thing as heroism, just the determination to stay busy and distract the mind, when the crazy is getting scarily real.

"Stay calm!" urged Jang. "Get to the stairway and up to the flybridge. Gary will go first."

Protecting his broken arm in its sling, Gary climbed awkwardly up the leaning staircase and toward the ceiling. Following close behind, Sandro opened the hatch. The wind flung it open, whistling across the opening like a flute to create a blood-curdling howl. They made slow progress, pausing every few seconds to brace themselves as the yacht moved, all of us tensing as we watched, just waiting for it to be over and the boat to plunge, dragging us to a blue hell.

It was a simmering tension that bubbled beneath a veneer of calm as some of us tried to act like this was no big deal, the kind of thing you do at the weekend and then comment on nonchalantly at school; 'Oh yeah, we went out in the boat and it almost took a dive. What did *you* get up to?'

Eventually, Gary managed to squirm through the hatch, protecting his broken arm by leaning his back towards the open hatch. Seconds later, Sandro followed him through the ceiling, and after a moment stuck his head in the opening and shouted down, "Okay, we're out."

Dr. Jang had jammed herself into one of the pilot seats, chocked her heels between it and the huge metal steering wheel so that she hung in midair, her torso supported by the seat-back. The bridge was the highest point of the pilot house now, so she seemed to lean out as if to conduct a choir of petrified teenagers in life-vests, all of them hanging from whatever solid fixture they could grab onto, around the edge of the saloon.

"Listen to me, everyone," she instructed, waving towards the stairway to the flybridge. "Get up there. Kenzie and Roni, you come help me with the life raft."

I glanced at Sacha in disbelief. As its stern sank below the waves, the yacht's tilt was becoming almost vertical. Nobody that wasn't already close to the stairway had a chance of reaching it, there were almost no handholds.

I yelled, "Are there ropes?"

"In the closet under the stairway," Jang shouted back.

The kid nearest to the stairway hurled himself across the pilot house and landed with his hands on the floor near the lowest step. Before he began to slide back down the sloping floor, he grabbed ahold of one of the steps and dragged himself up the floor and onto the stairway. Then he was climbing up to the flybridge. Sacha followed him, using the same technique. When he was able to perch on the lower step, he leaned forward, opened the closet under the stairway and pulled out a loop of rope. Before Dr. Jang could give him instructions, he'd tied one end of the rope to the metal railing at the side of the yacht that led to the lower deck and our accommodation. Then Sacha threw the other end at me.

Together we fixed the guide rope, a lifeline that ran from one end of the pilot house to the other. One by one we clawed our way to the stairway close to the deck controls, which led to the lower deck. Beside it was a door to the side deck. The door itself was getting close to being horizontal, as the tilt of the yacht steepened. Meanwhile the yacht rocked and twisted, helpless to resist the power of the storm.

When it was our turn, Jang told us to wait on the stairway, which was at least easy to stand on. Her position was well chosen, the steering wheel a fixed vantage point from which to see everything and also from which to issue orders. Yet I couldn't help but feel she'd reacted too slowly, at first, even if she now seemed to be in control.

"The life raft is on the side deck," she said, unhooking her feet from behind the steering wheel. She pointed through the door next to the lower stairway, the railing of which was one anchor point for the rope. "It's out there. On a thing, next to the boarding platform. It's in a white cylinder, a capsule. There's a release. It's like… You have to…you have to…"

She sounded flustered, distracted by the brutal slap of waves against the front of the pilot house window. Even worse, water now flowed through the lower stairway from the deck below, noisily sloshing against its walls.

I asked, "Do you need help to do it?" Because I really did not want to go out there. If you lost your handhold, it was basically a vertical drop into a fearsome, frothing ocean.

Dr. Jang swung her legs over the bridge and launched herself at the guide rope, wrapping arms and legs around it until she could stand upright with her feet braced against the lowest step. The floor of the pilot house was now a wall behind her back and the external door had become a horizontal window.

"We're going out there. And yes, Roni, I need your help. Because if I don't make it, you're up."

Then she pulled on the external door handle and stepped outside, into the storm. I moved to follow but Sacha held me back. The door to the side deck slammed shut and then a moment later, flew open. Dr. Jang hadn't managed to close it properly.

"We need to go after her," I said.

Give her a minute.

I turned to face him. Sacha was impassive, calm.

"We have to," I insisted, and pulled away. "What's wrong with you?" Water splashed over my toes and began to flow over them, into the stairwell to the lower decks. "Oh no. The water's coming in."

Holding open the door/window to the side deck, which was now vertical, I leaned out and peered along the yacht. Dr. Jang was there, hanging from the platform that held the white cylinder she'd described, the container for the life raft. With her free hand she was trying to unlock it. I hesitated. There was no other hand hold; the side deck was almost vertical.

A few seconds later, Sacha wedged himself into the external doorway, balancing on the threshold. In tense silence we watched Dr. Jang struggle with the life raft's release, until suddenly the cylinder rocked sideways on its platform. Then it toppled over and fell straight down towards the end of the side-deck, instead of going over the gunnel. The cylinder's weight dragged Jang and she hurtled down behind it, until both bounced over the end of the side deck and crashed into the foaming water below.

I watched as she rolled onto the cylinder that contained our one, slim hope of escape. Between the waves I caught a glimpse of her face. Jang wore an expression of absolute despair, mouth wide, eyes scrunched shut, her wails almost inaudible amongst the billowing winds.

She can't open the life raft, Sacha told me.

I glared at him, wondering why he resorted to telepathy when I was right next to him. Then I leaned out a little father and looked across towards the flybridge. It too was now vertical. I had no idea how eleven people were managing to hang on there – they had to be packed like sardines in a can. I couldn't see if Kenzie was there, could only hope. I tried to remember where he'd been when I last saw him. On his way to the flybridge? Or, where? But I couldn't think straight, couldn't think backwards at all, actually. My mind refused to go anywhere except the immediate future, the next few minutes and everything I needed to do in that time, to stay alive.

Soon it wouldn't matter much, anyway. Dr. Jang was in the ocean, nothing but a plastic cylinder to hang onto. Soon we'd all be in the water. In fact, I reasoned, there was probably an optimal time to leap free of a sinking yacht. The suction might take us down, if we didn't get away.

But the sea, I thought. It looked utterly terrifying, dark and fierce and hungry for our souls.

"She needs our help to open that thing," I told Sacha, making my voice sound firm and full of a conviction that I didn't truly feel. "We have to jump. Now."

For the first time, I saw Sacha's fear. Wrapped around the edge of the door, his knuckles were white. He pulled his head back inside and shut his eyes.

Jump. You have to jump, now. Please.

I didn't recognize the voice in my head. *Atlanta?* I straightened up, let the door to the side deck close gently and with one hand, wiped the sea spray from my eyes. A quick glance down confirmed my worst fears – the water level was climbing, was flowing steadily to the stern end of the pilot house and filling the room up. We were sinking fast.

Sacha grabbed my arm. "Who said that?"

I shook my head, clueless. So, not Atlanta, apparently.

He frowned. "Maybe it's long-range telepathy? Could someone else be out there?"

The voice interrupted. This time a slow realization began. I knew that voice. It couldn't be, could it?

Please. Sacha, Atlanta, I need your help.

Our eyes locked. Hesitantly, I said, "I think that might be… Could it be Doctor Jang?"

Sacha began forcing the door open wider, making space for me. Heavy gusts drove it back and we both had to lean heavily against the door to the side deck until we tumbled out. It wasn't how I'd planned to leave the yacht, but before I could do much about it, I was sliding down the vertical side deck and into the sea.

Sacha landed a second later, as a wave lifted me out of his way.

Resurfacing, I opened my mouth to breathe and couldn't. My throat spasmed, I thrashed around for several seconds until finally my throat unlocked and I gasped. Then my body registered the cold, every inch of my flesh stung as though hundreds of ice needles were pricking my skin.

Perhaps twenty more seconds passed before I was able to take in my surroundings: Dr. Jang struggling to sit astride the life raft capsule, carried a little further away with each wave, Sacha motionless in the water, maybe five yards from me.

Once I was able to move, I swam over to him and saw that Sacha's eyes were closed. I shook him, slapped his cheek and shouted at him to wake up, before my mouth filled with water as a wave washed over us. As I was dunked, I managed to grab his foot. We had to stay together, at all costs. When I surfaced, I pulled myself alongside Sacha.

After a few seconds, his eyelids fluttered open, and he gazed at me in momentary confusion. *Where's Jang?*

From the corner of my eye, I noticed a shadow fall across us. I heard a loud splash. Someone went into the water a few yards away. I guessed they'd jumped from the flybridge.

It's Atlanta, said Sacha in my head. I could sense his relief. *Jang can't open the capsule. We need to help her.*

Seconds later, Atlanta swam up to us. Her lips trembled; she looked too shocked by the cold to speak.

In my head the voice spoke again. *The raft came off its mooring. I'm going to throw a rope. Loop it around the railing of the yacht. When it sinks, the capsule will open.*

This time I definitely recognized the voice as Dr. Jang's. At that time, it didn't seem super strange that she was able to broadcast her thoughts – survival had become this all-consuming issue that thrust everything else into the background. It was more like, 'cool, she's telepathic, too.'

The end of a rope hit me in the face. I snatched it up and began to swim back to the yacht. A wave threw me backwards. The cold had stopped stinging now but instead had begun to seep into my bones, a deep ache, a pain like I'd never known. My movements were already becoming slow and dull. How long had Jang said until we passed out? Maybe thirty minutes? Now that I was in the water, it seemed incredible to me that it'd take even that long. I had to move now and as fast as I could. I took a deep breath and then plunged into an oncoming wave. After some flailing, I found the railing of the side deck.

That's it! You got it! Now tie it real tight!

Several seconds after I'd tied the raft capsule's mooring rope, about fifteen yards away, the white cylindrical casing of the life raft opened, like an egg hatching. The contents gently unfolded, inflating rapidly to form a large orange-and-black raft with a cone-shaped cover, at the top of which a light began to blink.

When the raft was still nearing full inflation, Dr. Jang was already shinnying nimbly up its edge and sliding over the rim, into the raft. By that time, Sacha had made it halfway to the raft. A moment later Dr. Jang leaned out through an opening in the tent-like covering. She stretched out one hand to him, helping him to climb inside.

Watching them, I couldn't feel my hands or my toes. I understood suddenly that if I didn't reach the raft and climb in soon, I never would. As I got closer to the raft, Sacha anchored his feet on a rope inside the raft and leaned out with his whole body, offering both arms to me. I wouldn't have made it inside without his and Dr. Jang's help. To my chilled muscles, which by now moved slower than slow motion, the side of the raft seemed impossibly high.

One by one, people on the flybridge began to drop into the sea. Joining hands, they assembled in a floating cluster close to the yacht, of which only the top quarter remained above water. One by one, they filed towards the raft and painstakingly battled the waves to reach it. If they reached the raft, we dragged them in.

Not everyone did. But I didn't think about that at the time, I just could not.

The sky rumbled, deeply enraged. Another, dazzling bolt of lightning ripped through the sky and into the sea, now only halfway between us and the horizon.

At least the worst is over, I thought.

I was wrong.

THIRTY-TWO

HALEY STOKES

"Nine, ten, eleven." Dr. Jang frowned.

"Who's missing?" asked one of the kids.

Jang didn't answer. She seemed anxious. "Call out your names, going clockwise starting from you, Sacha."

We began yelling our names loudly enough that we could be heard above the piercing gale. Even sitting in a tight circle around the inside perimeter, the life raft was barely large enough for all the teenage passengers and two expedition leaders. In other situations, my claustrophobia might have kicked in, but in the dire cold, I suddenly felt the benefit of having people pressed against me on either side.

At Jang's suggestion, a few of us had tethered ourselves to fabric handholds around the edge and then interlocked arms, so that when a wave lifted the raft we wouldn't tumble around inside, like kids in a bouncy castle.

Sitting between Kenzie and Sacha, I was close enough to talk to Atlanta, who was next to him. But other than shouting the occasional warning or instruction, no one talked. It was the first time I really understood that for a group of people to chat there needs to be a level of comfort that cannot be achieved, when everyone is terrified for their life.

Despite the almost-silence, I guessed that Sacha and Atlanta were communicating telepathically. Back then, I didn't understand that this was almost as tiring as physical speech. I managed to ask Sacha one time and very quietly, whether he'd known that Dr. Jang was telepathic. He only blinked at me, once, then shook his head, eyes widening with wonder.

Gary, whose arm had been broken in the engine room, could only offer one arm so he and Jang were each the terminal points of our chain. There was, I was starting to suspect, more wrong with him than a broken arm. Since the incident in the engine room, he'd been extremely quiet, contributing almost nothing to the evacuation effort. He obeyed Jang's instructions, but with his right arm broken he wasn't able to do a lot more than move himself around.

After the cycle of names was completed, Dr. Jang was silent for a moment. Then; "I didn't hear Haley Stokes." An instant later, a huge wave swelled below and lifted the raft. Everyone groaned as we felt the raft cresting at the top, then screamed as the wave dumped us and the raft plummeted. My heart seemed to have sunk into my belly. I tightened both arms, Kenzie on one side and Sacha on the other.

For the next five hours the storm tossed the raft around and spun it so many times that by the time it eased off, I had no idea what direction we were facing – Alaska or Siberia? The raft had filled with six inches of water, and we spent the next half hour bailing it out with our shoes.

In all that time, nobody said anything about the missing girl, Haley.

The kids who'd been on the flybridge had been with Gary. Had Haley fallen off when the yacht tilted?

For them, it would have been like hanging from a wall by their fingertips, while the water gradually but surely numbed their flesh to the bone. Had someone been holding her hand, and let go? In the whole trip, I couldn't remember saying even one word to Haley Stokes, couldn't picture her face. I spent a few minutes with that, wondering how I had become the type that ignores other people, who'd managed to spend the entire day with all those other kids and never even ask for their names. The shame sat uncomfortably within me. What had happened to me? How had I allowed my relationship with the telepathic kids to take over my life?

Even though we had scooped out most of the water from inside the raft, every one of us was soaked to the skin and shivering. Dr. Jang asked everyone to search their pockets for any food. We came up with three candy bars and one cereal bar – enough for one bite for each person. I thought back to the boxes of Twinkies and dreamed that I'd been able to hold on to even one. I'd be a hero right now, instead of what I was, which was at best a survivor.

"When is the rescue coming?" asked one of the kids. I'm ashamed even now that I don't remember their name. Prince had firmly advised us not to bond with the others until we'd finished the operation. To this day I am disappointed at how easily I was able to obey that particular instruction.

Dr. Jang hesitated for an uncomfortable minute before replying. "I managed to send a mayday call before I got you all out on deck. In this storm they won't be able to send anyone."

"But the storm has stopped," murmured several of the kids.

Dr. Jang's eyes were downcast, and she shook her head, unable to face the kids she'd dragged into this situation.

"It's the eye," I said, looking straight at her. "The eye of the storm. Am I right?"

For a few seconds, Jang faced me with a quizzical tilt of her head. "Yes," she replied, flatly. "The storm wasn't due until later today. We were going to head for Saint Matthew Island, until it passed."

Sandro asked, "Why don't you have a radio or satellite phone?"

Jang carefully avoided answering the question. "Stay awake and focused, all of you. We'll get out of this. They will send rescue. We managed to get into the life raft, so that's a big start. We just have to hang tight here for a few more hours, at the most."

A chorus of questions followed. "But how will they even find us?" "The yacht went down!" "We don't even know where it is or was!"

Yet the voice we heard over all of them was Gary's saying bitterly, "No. We didn't all make it into the life raft. Haley is gone. Haley Stokes. Thirteen years old. From Little Rock, Arkansas. She had never been out of state. This was the first time. Haley was obsessed with whales. They were the great love of her life. Now she's gone. And it's my fault." He broke down then, bending his head forward and sniffing hard before the sobs began.

I saw what happened, Atlanta's voice said in my head. *And he is totally right. Haley started to slide off the flybridge. She reached for his hand. It was the broken one of course because he was using the other one to hold on. And that idiot snatched his hand away. That's why she fell. What a loser.*

One by one, I looked at the faces of the other kids in the life raft. It was obvious they were worn out and doleful. Only two would even meet my eye. There were no heroes among us, just shocked, exhausted teenagers that were still reeling from the speed of the turn of events. They'd gone from enjoying the adventure of a lifetime to wondering how much lifetime they had left.

And I was not very much different. A girl had died, a girl that maybe I could have helped, a girl whose name I didn't even bother to learn. Searching the expressions of the teenagers alongside me, I hoped with all my heart that at least one of them had gotten to know Haley even a little and would be able to tell her story. Deep down though, I knew it was unlikely. After all, nobody had even noticed she was missing, until Dr. Jang took a roll call.

In those moments I had time, the luxury to feel sorry for myself. Conversation was out of the question, we were also cold and spent, a deep penetrating chill that was sinking relentlessly into our bones, a dull pain that made it difficult to think of anything else.

I imagined being in the horrible, freezing cold life raft for a little longer and then being rescued, although I didn't go so far as to conjure up that particular scenario. I couldn't sustain it for very long, because after a few minutes as I was staring through one of the gaps in the tented ceiling, I saw a sudden brilliant white flash.

Before I could even explain why I had gasped so sharply, a thunderclap sounded, a single boom that seemed to come across the sea and not from the sky. I whipped around to stare back through the opening and in the distance saw a huge fireball that seemed to be sitting on the horizon. A colossal plume of black smoke bloomed in the sky.

"They did it," breathed Kenzie next to me, awestruck. "They really fucking did it."

THIRTY-THREE

PULL

Sacha, Atlanta, Kenzie and I knew at once, what had exploded. I think Dr. Jang knew, too. To everyone else it was a total unknown and obviously, they assumed the very worst – a nuclear strike on Alaska.

Czar Ilyin and his Kremlin minions had been rattling the nuclear saber for the past few years, threatening to nuke London or Paris or Berlin, pretty much every time they got particularly irked that something wasn't going their way. Oftentimes, they issued dark but more veiled threats against the USA. Ilyin had been grumbling that as well as half of Europe, by rights, Alaska also belonged to Russia, and that no one should be surprised if one day soon, they exerted their God-given right to reclaim it.

The panic that broke out a second after the blast was like an electric shock that rippled through the tightly-packed life raft. Even if I hadn't jumped to that conclusion, I experienced the power of its jolt – the power of a terrifying idea.

"It's not a nuke!" I shouted above people's distressed wails. "It's… it's a regular explosion." Any conviction I'd started out with soon fizzled out, when I realized that I'd need a good reason for how I knew as a fact it was a gas pipeline explosion, not a distant nuke.

"No mushroom cloud," added Kenzie.

A couple of kids objected. "It's a little mushroomey."

"No blinding flash of light," I said.

I could see they weren't convinced, because there had indeed been a flash, even if it hadn't been all that blinding. Jang said nothing at all, but she gave me a thoughtful look.

Her being a telepath was still a surprise without explanation, but I pretty soon figured out a theory to make sense of Jang's telepathy, how come we'd missed our rendezvous with the *Cassiopeia*, and the explosion of the gas compressor station, just over the horizon.

There was no time to mention any of this though, no more than a few minutes during which everyone else reacted to the shock of the explosion. Obviously, I wasn't going to offer up information that'd make it clear I had inside knowledge. I acted as stunned as everyone else and to be honest, maybe that wasn't an act.

There was no time, because as soon as we'd adjusted to the reality of the explosion, we felt a pulse of power beneath the raft. A wave was approaching from the horizon, a wave so enormous that some of us saw it from far away. The others in the raft heard our sudden intakes of breath. Fear like that cannot be masked. There was just time to shout a warning 'hold on' and then it hit us.

The next thing I knew, I was in the water. The wave had capsized us, and I was floating in the air bubble underneath the capsized raft. Hurriedly, I wiped my eyes and looked around frantically for Kenzie. He wasn't there. As I spun around, I spotted Sacha and then Atlanta. They surfaced just behind him and threw both arms around him, gasping with relief.

"Kenzie's not here," I told them.

Sacha nodded but didn't stop counting heads. "Four people are missing," he said in a hollowed-out voice. "Kenzie, Gary, Sandro. And Susie Jang."

A violent shudder went through me. Being immersed in cold water made me understand that we hadn't been all that chilly in the raft, even if our legs were soaked. But now we were about to learn the meaning of *cold*.

"Thirty minutes," I sputtered. "That's how long before you pass out, in this water. That's what Susie said." From the appearances of the survivors of the capsizing, it was obvious; I was now the oldest. They knew it too and were eyeing me with something like expectation. I swallowed and tried to push down the surge of raw terror that was rising inside me.

No leaders. No radio. Thirty minutes until I'm helpless. Two hours until we die.

What if there was no rescue coming?

Some kids had started to cry. I paddled over to the closest, a girl of about fourteen, and asked her name. "Delilah," she managed to whisper, between trembling sobs. "Are we going to die here?"

Close to despair, I sensed myself on the verge of hyperventilating. Which absolutely, I could not succumb to. I had to do something, say something that would give them hope. "I'm going to look outside, see where the others are."

Before anyone could reply, I ducked under the rim of the life raft, surfaced outside of it and began scanning the waves for our missing friends. I spotted Kenzie at once. He was about ten yards away, floating on his back. I hesitated before letting go of the raft. Was I even strong enough to bring him back? It wasn't very far, but the sea was choppy, and I was already tired and shivering. In water that cold, it's really hard to make yourself move even a little bit. Your body just shuts down, it only wants to shiver itself warm.

Someone tapped my shoulder. Behind me appeared a face that gave me such overwhelming relief, my voice cracked. "Oh, Doctor Jang, it's you!"

Dr. Jang couldn't bring herself to smile. She was visibly shaking. Despite everything she managed to seem confident, at least more confident than me.

"Your friend will die if we don't bring him in."

"I don't think I can swim there and back."

"No," she said. "We need help to get him."

"Where's Gary?" I asked, suddenly. "And Sandro?"

She didn't answer but instead ducked under the raft and called Sacha, Atlanta and Delilah to join us at the outside perimeter of the raft.

"Is there any way to flip the raft?" I asked. I assumed not, because it was super heavy. But I couldn't see a way out of this, if we didn't get back into it.

"Maybe. We can try. But if we don't do it quickly, we have to give up. Most important, we cannot afford to waste our energy."

I nodded. "Can we get Kenzie first?"

Sacha, Atlanta and Delilah were outside now. Dr. Jang instructed us to make a human chain from the raft to Kenzie. Sacha was on the outside and grabbed hold of Kenzie's life vest, then we towed him in as though he were a stray dinghy.

I held him by the life vest while Dr. Jang began to resuscitate him. Kenzie quickly recovered, and didn't seem to have swallowed much water. Dazed, he looked at me in bewilderment. I threw my arms around his neck and hugged him tight.

"Yeah, keep doing that, feels good," Kenzie murmured against my cheek. In that all-encompassing, bitter cold, the heat of his breath felt incredible. The tiny scrap of his warmth felt like the full heat of the sun on a summer's day.

Jang had already moved on to survey the survivors, asking them how much they weighed and if they worked out. She hadn't answered my question about Sandro or Gary, and I was already concluding the worst about them. The wave must have picked up the life raft and hurtled it some horrible distance. The fact that we couldn't even see the others chilled my blood another couple of degrees.

"Kenzie, you're one of the biggest here. Can we count on you for some heavy lifting?"

Kenzie grinned the grin of someone who has cheated death. "Yes ma'am."

Thirty minutes until we're unconscious. Two hours to death.

I couldn't stop thinking about what Jang had said earlier. If we didn't right that life raft, we would soon be dead.

Jang had decided that a fifteen-year-old boy called Nathan and Kenzie were probably the strongest of us. Began to talk them through how to right the capsized raft. She had them both brace their feet on one point on the edge, each grabbing hold of the looped rope that was connected to the opposite side of the raft. "Now pull," she urged. "Lean back as hard as you can and pull!"

She let three pairs of us try for one minute each to flip the raft. None of us could do better than lift the opposite edge a yard or two above the water. I was stunned at how heavy it was and how little we were able to move it, but Dr. Jang didn't seem surprised.

"Get on top," she ordered. "Out of the water, now!"

Minutes later, we'd all managed to scramble up the sides and onto the bottom of the raft, which now served as its deck. The weight of nine people made a shallow dip in the surface, but not enough to keep anyone out of the water that wasn't clinging onto either the ropes that traversed the raft's diameter, or onto someone that was.

We huddled close to the person on either side of us and clamped our fingers tightly around anything that'd help us survive. We took it in turns to watch each other for five minutes at a time, making sure they didn't come loose from our huddle and slide off the edge of the raft. That way, we all had a chance to close our eyes at least briefly.

I felt tired like I didn't know was possible, felt the slick damp of my clothes slowly drain all my energy, but still I clung on. There was no more talking.

THIRTY-FOUR

To Sleep, To Dream

"Again," Maxim said and then grinned, allowing a hint of pride into his eyes. "You've gotten so good at the drums!"

I paused then, silencing the high hat between a finger and thumb.

"Where do you practice? At home? I bet that goes down great with your parents."

For some reason, I didn't correct him or wonder why he was acting like he'd forgotten that my own parents were in prison. That was the first sign I ignored. The second one should have been how freaking *amazingly* I was playing the drums. I'm talking about rolling with a rhythm that flowed from one arm to the other, from one leg to the other, my entire body pulsing in time and energy exploding as my kicks and sticks hit the drums.

But it was a dream, and, in a dream, I can easily believe I play drums like a goddess of beat.

Maxim was more beautiful than I'd ever seen him. The truth is it was the first time I admitted it to myself: he was beautiful. He was as I saw him last in a relaxed context, in the kitchen of Hacienda Narcojunior, making sandwiches. His dark blonde hair was tousled and slightly sweaty, strands of hair clinging to the back of his neck. There was a hint of stubble to his cheeks and as he buttered slices of bread, his gaze would occasionally land on me, an easy smile, pleasure in my company. His arms were tanned, sun-bleached hairs swept in the same direction on his forearms, veins visible on the back of his hand and light musculature evident in his biceps.

Then for no readily apparent reason, those arms were around me and my face was sinking against his shoulder, my arms sliding around his waist and squeezing until we were pressed close.

"It would be bad if anything happened to you, Padi. I have big plans, and you are part of them. Tell me you know that."

Yes, it should have been extremely obvious by then and maybe I knew. But can you blame me for wanting an experience like this to continue?

"What plans?" I asked. "I've heard some weird stuff about your plans."

"Oh really?" He pulled away a little so that he could look into my eyes with that reassuring grin he so often used. "What 'weird stuff'?"

"Well, maybe you should just tell me about them, and we'll decide afterward if they're weird."

His grin shifted just a tad and became quizzical, enough to take off its reassuring edge and become almost brittle, as if one negative comment or even a thought might shatter it.

"There is a lot wrong with this world, I'm pretty sure you would agree," he said, not really asking a question. "And to quote Spider-Man, 'With great power comes great responsibility.' You agree with that, right?"

Who could argue with that? I don't remember what he said next because a few seconds later I was blinking my eyes open to the wide blue sky above us, my back against the damp raft, both arms at my sides, my hand in Kenzie's. Sea spray splashed occasionally over the edge of the raft and drizzled over us. Then the sensation of cold hit me. Not an inch of my skin was dry and inside soaking wet sneakers, my toes were totally numb. Pain was a dull, constant presence.

"You, okay?" Kenzie murmured, touching my face gently with one finger.

I can't have been asleep for more than two or three minutes. But even those minutes were such a welcome escape, I didn't question why I was dreaming that way about Maxim.

Struggling to sit up, I forced myself to smile at Kenzie. "Yeah. Thank you, I'm good, that helped a lot." With numb fingers I gave his hand a feeble squeeze. "You should take a turn."

I didn't have to ask him twice, Kenzie shut his eyes and relaxed. He snuggled his head against my thigh and closed a hand around mine. I longed to return to that warm, stirring dream, but it was my turn to watch Kenzie.

"How long d'you think we've been in this?" I mumbled, half to myself.

"In the sea? Nine hours," Sacha murmured in reply. "Maybe ten?" His head was close to mine, his body pointing the opposite direction. Then he spoke directly to my mind; *Do you often dream about Maxim?*

I was so shocked, I couldn't answer.

Don't worry, he said, and I even heard a lazy smile in his telepathic voice. *I didn't construct the entire dream. I just incepted you to dream something good about my brother. Tell me what happened? Did it work out nicely?*

Now furious, I could only seethe in silence. Why was he wasting his time making me dream about Maxim? It struck me as hugely manipulative.

"Why don't you do something useful?" I snapped. "Like, can't you contact your relatives? I know some of them are in Siberia – we traced them to Perm. Why don't you get them to come and rescue us?"

To my mild astonishment, Sacha took a few moments to reply and then very meekly said aloud, "That's not such a bad idea. I'm an idiot. Long range telepathy! I'm sorry, I should have thought of that."

"What are you chuckleheads talking about?" asked Nathan. "How can he contact his relatives? Gary and Susie Jang lost the radio, didn't they? You really think we'd be freezing our asses off in the middle of the ocean, if there was any chance of a rescue?"

I shuffled into a more upright position, keeping one hand wrapped around Kenzie's. Dr. Jang lay on the opposite side of the upturned raft and from where I was sitting, she appeared to be asleep. Two young teens sat on either side of her, each one holding one of her hands. My mind had not slowed down as much as my body, yet I still struggled to make sense of what we had observed of Dr. Susie Jang.

I whispered to Sacha, "We need to talk." But he didn't answer. His eyes widened, staring at a point in the sky. I got the immediate sense that he was using his telepathy, and that it was costing every ounce of energy and attention he could summon.

Casting my eyes over the survivors of the *Perseus*, I saw Atlanta, Sacha, Kenzie, Delilah, Nathan, four other kids and Dr. Susie Jang. They lay like discarded matchsticks, barely clinging to the top of the raft. Gary Killarney, Sandro and Haley Stokes were already lost to the sea. If the storm brewed up again, the rest of us would be tossed into the water. If that happened, few of us would survive.

I couldn't stop thinking about how unsurprised Dr. Jang had seemed through the entire series of unfortunate events.

How had we ended up here? A change of plans that brought us to a part of the sea far from the *Cassiopeia* yacht, with which we were supposed to rendezvous. A storm that hit us hours before expected. And finally, a mysterious collision that had put a deadly hole in the hull of the *Perseus*.

What if none of this was an accident?

What if Susie Jang had diverted the *Perseus* from its original route, taking it elsewhere, where some explosive device or even a remote-operated underwater drone, could on very direct and *specific* orders sink the *Perseus*?

Just hours ago, something similar had blown up the gas compressor station, after all. The Kremlin's plan was to plant evidence that a military 'remote-operated underwater vehicle' or 'ROUV' had been operated from the *Cassiopeia*, loaded with explosives and sent to blow up the Russian gas pipeline.

What if a smaller ROUV, the sleek, black object I had glimpsed just underneath the surface of the sea near the *Perseus*, had been sent with a smaller payload, just enough to punch a hole through our yacht and sink us, slowly?

I rolled onto my side and stared across the waves, trying to blot out the sky. My heart was racing, and a pleasant burst of adrenaline washed through me. Was it possible I was on the right track? I could almost smell the solution, as if I were a hunting dog with the rusty tang of blood in my nostrils. But it wasn't hanging together – not yet.

Why would anyone try to sink the *Perseus*? It couldn't be that they wanted us dead, because we had a life raft. If it hadn't been for the storm and the mini tidal wave from the gas compressor station explosion, the chances of our survival would have been good. But then I remembered Dr. Jang's wary avoidance, when Sandro had asked about the satellite phone. Without that phone, we had no way to call for rescue. It made what was happening seem more by design than accident. No rescue was coming; Dr. Jang hadn't called them.

It didn't make sense – for one thing, it would mean that Dr. Jang was prepared to die out there, with us. Why would she ever agree to die for this? Why would she agree to put thirteen other people at risk of the same fate?

After not much longer, I finally recognized that I was too physically and emotionally drained to logic my way through the mystery. Unless I could get some food and warm up a bit, I'd need help to pull together all these strands.

I rolled onto my other side, now facing into the center of the raft. Kenzie lay close by, mouth squashed against the raft, eyes quivering beneath closed lids as he weathered his own dreams. He needed to sleep, for sure. A few more minutes, then. After that, I'd wake up my puzzle-solving buddy and despite the bitter cold, the encroaching darkness and our blurred mental processes, together we'd figure something out.

Because we had to. It was that or, like it says in the poem, to 'go gently into the dark night.' And that's what I will *not*, cannot do.

THIRTY-FIVE

ENEMY GAINS

Five minutes later, Kenzie still appeared to be deep in sleep. I knew Dr. Jang might wake up, any second. If we wanted to communicate without any chance of being overheard by her, it had to be now. I shoved him gently at the shoulder, then again more forcefully, until he woke with a groan.

"We have to talk," I said in a low voice, close to his ear. "I need you. I mean your mind. I need your mind."

For a few seconds he looked steadily into my eyes, as if daring me to continue. Then, sadly, he nodded. "Gee, always wanted to be wanted for my mind. But then I guess your heart belongs elsewhere."

I blinked rapidly, then hissed, "You really want to talk about this, now? Seriously Kenzie, we've got a real problem here!"

Something about my tone must have gotten through to him because he flicked his head from side to side, as if trying to shake off a bad dream. He sat up, wincing from the stiffness of a cold, damp body roused from the slow process of freezing solid. "Yeah, sure. Ow. Sorry. You know I don't mean anything by that, right?"

I didn't know that at all, so I didn't answer. Instead, I said, "I've been trying to figure out why Doctor Jang is a telepath."

Kenzie looked at me, momentarily confused and then stunned. With a sickening sensation, I realized that no one had told him. Very quickly, I followed up with, "Well you know, she's been listening most of the time since we found out, we couldn't say anything openly and you can't..."

"I can't receive telepathic messages. Oh yeah, remind me a few more times about that, I love to hear it."

Over the next couple minutes, I caught Kenzie up with my theories to this point.

He was quiet, thoughtful. "But why wouldn't she at least call a rescue? If we don't get rescued, she's gonna die, too."

"Exactly. Which doesn't make sense at all, does it?"

He shrugged. "Not unless she called someone else."

"Who else?"

"See, if she's a telepath, then she's either with the Atlas guys, or she's part of some intelligence agency. Remember the Vault 7 leak?"

Kenzie made a great point. One of the first things we had uncovered about the K-Foundation kids was that they were sold off to a variety of international security agencies. Later, Maxim had told us that they were auctioned off around age sixteen, and sent away at eighteen, when they had completed their training.

"And... They bred them," Kenzie said, hesitantly. "Didn't like to say at the time, but did you notice? The 'unicorns' we rescued. There were white kids like

Maxim and Sacha, but also brown kids, black kids and at least two Asians."

I grimaced, thinking of 'Puma,' Atlanta's crush. A beautiful girl with what I'd taken to be far eastern, Asian features. "The TRE is a huge empire. There are parts where people are brown, parts where they're Asian. And they're in Africa now, too."

"Custom-designed telepathic spies, then," Kenzie agreed.

"They don't sell to the West. CIA don't have any telepaths," I breathed, mind reeling at the implications. "Which means Jang cannot be CIA. But she *could* be a mole, working for someone else."

"Like who?"

I took a breath. In my mind it had sounded far-fetched, at first. "Like North Korea."

His reaction struck me as akin to sober alarm. Maybe my theory wasn't so out there, after all?

Warming to the theme, I continued. "North Korea's leader, the 'Kim,' hates the USA, maybe even more than the Czar does. The Kim would be stoked to help the Czar throw shade at us."

Kenzie nodded. "Could be that's why Jang changed the route – so we'd wind up a long way from the *Cassiopeia*."

"Right. Far enough to stop us getting onto the yacht to remove any of the false evidence they'd planted."

"In which case, looks like 'mission accomplished,'" he said, tilting his head in the direction of the recent explosion that had sent a tidal wave our way.

"But it's even worse," I said, staggered at what I'd finally understood. "It'd mean that North Korea has penetrated the CIA. Otherwise, how would they know to plant an agent on the *Perseus*?"

"You think Gary Killarney was in on it?" Kenzie whispered. "He was Prince's contact."

"Could be. But I'm guessing Killarney is dead. Maybe it was no accident that broke his arm?"

It was horrifying how much trouble we were in if our theory was right. And yet, there was something pretty thrilling about figuring it out with Kenzie, as we lay shivering cold, on a capsized life raft under the Alaskan sky.

When I spoke again, my teeth chattered. "And… would… also explain why Jang… doesn't want us to be rescued by Americans. We have cargo. Valuable cargo."

"What cargo? We left everything on the boat."

I raised a trembling finger and pointed toward Atlanta and Sacha, on the other side of the raft. They sat back-to-back, in silence, Atlanta facing us, Sacha out to sea.

"Oh crap," Kenzie whispered, with a sharp inhale. "It's them!"

"People still want to '*Find unicorns*,'" I murmured.

You should lower your voices, said Sacha, speaking directly into my mind. *Jang is a light sleeper.*

Kenzie intuited at once that I was receiving something from Sacha. With undisguised sarcasm he said, "Why don't you come over here and join our private conversation, my dude?"

"Quiet!" I hissed.

Sacha didn't move a muscle. Instead, he continued the one-way conversation with me.

I managed to reach someone in Siberia. I never tried long range telepathy without enhancement. It's a kind of tech we use to train with, at the Krylov. Without it, best I can do is about five

241

hundred miles. The man I reached; his name is Artem. I think he's pretty old.

"What's he saying?" whispered Kenzie. I quietly repeated what Sacha had told me and then expectantly, we both turned to Sacha.

Sacha shrugged. *That's it, that's everything I have. Can't do more. There's nobody else in range. We're lucky I found even one person within five hundred miles; cos Siberia is huge. Whoever it is, they must be living in the boonies, hundreds of miles from any major settlement. I told Artem that we're drifting somewhere west of the gas compressor station that just exploded.*

The precarious nature of our situation threatened to overwhelm my thoughts. Yet, hearing Sacha say out loud that we were drifting somewhere off the coast of Siberia, and that our only hope of rescue was some old guy who lived miles from civilization, suddenly brought home to me, just how desperate we were. I could see it in his face, too, he was trying to look hopeful, but behind his eyes and in the tenor of his thoughts, I sensed rising panic.

We heard what you said about Doctor Jang, he added. There was a sense of resignation in those words. *It makes sense. We really let our guard down. Atlanta and I never received the full training in espionage that the Krylov gives to kids over sixteen. I wanted no part of that. I left as soon as I could. But truthfully, it might have helped us to identify her earlier as a threat. I'm sorry. We let you down, too.*

Even that small effort of mental communication was exhausting. Without discussing or agreeing on anything, we fell silent for a long time. Well, I can only speak for myself and Kenzie. Who knows – perhaps Sacha and Atlanta kept each other company the entire time. But at the time, I had the impression that they, too, were drained of all energy, even whatever it took to send and receive telepathic messages.

I shuffled closer to Kenzie and after an unspoken moment of acquiescence, we each put one arm around the other and held each other close. For the first minute or two, our muscles were tense. Then, we relaxed into each other's embrace. What did it matter, if he got the wrong idea? Maybe it was the right idea, now. Tomorrow, we might be dead. Nothing mattered anymore except honesty. Kenzie was my best friend in the world, as close as a brother. If I could change my feelings for him, to look at him the way he looked at me, I'd do it in a heartbeat.

We'd been in the sea or the raft for what seemed like a whole day, most of it thunderously dark, but thankfully, the daylight persisted. I wasn't sure I'd survive the terror of being lost at sea through the night.

Dr. Jang sat up around that time, looked around and took in the bleakness of our situation. She didn't bother to hide her despair. Whatever she had in mind, it apparently hadn't panned out. I wondered if she took any responsibility for the deaths she'd caused.

As the empty hours dragged on, the despair I'd seen in Dr. Jang's face seemed to have spread to all of us. We were chilled to the bone by then, exhausted from managing to stay on the upturned raft, dehydrated to the point of cracked throats and lips, especially those of us who, retching from motion sickness, had vomited over the side of the raft until only green slime came out. We didn't even have enough water in our bodies to cry tears, but every now and then some kids continued to heave with desperate sobs.

"So much for his lousy Siberian connections." Kenzie huffed a bone-dry chuckle, embracing me tightly as he pressed his face against my hair. Then his tone turned dark. "We're going to die. Eh, screw it, might as well tell you the truth. I love you, Padi, always have. I love you, really. And if dying here with you means you never end up with Maxim, I'm good with that."

I couldn't bear to face him, rigid and unable to reply. *My best friend would rather I died than ended up with Maxim.* But then, overhead, I heard something. With Kenzie's arms still wrapped around me, I turned my head towards the faint, very distant but unmistakable sound of clattering helicopter rotor blades.

For the first, excruciatingly long, minute, we remained utterly silent, disbelieving. Dr. Jang was the first to react. She leapt to her feet but faltered immediately, unsteady until Delilah struggled onto both feet and stabilized her.

"They're here," cried Dr. Susie Jang, sounding almost delirious. "They're here, they're here!"

THIRTY-SIX

CHOPPER

"Flare gun! Where's the flare gun?" Dr. Jang was beside herself, rifling through her own pockets and then clutching at Nathan. "Do you have it? Did I give it to you? Did Gary?"

Nathan startled, pulling away from her desperate hands. Dr. Jang seemed to take a turn for the worse. With both hands, she grabbed at the sides of her face, hands in her hair, tearing, pulling as her voice became more deranged.

"The backpack! There was a backpack. I had a backpack ready, had everything inside. Where is it? Did you have it, Nathan? Delilah? Sandro?"

"Sandro is gone," Nathan reminded her, his anger close to the surface. "He's lost, probably already dead. And even if you packed for a situation like this, then too bad, cos it's gone."

"They can see us from the helicopter, surely?" I said to Kenzie. It was the first thing I'd said to him, since his declaration of love. Any fears I had that he was still clinging to five minutes ago, swiftly disappeared. His arms slid from around my waist to take both of my hands in his, gripping tightly, not with affection but rather, in full survival mode.

"They must be here for us," he said, sounding less certain than his words. Although we could see the silhouette of the helicopter against a lighter sky, we were just a shadowy dot in a murky sea. A flare gun would have been a giant comfort. As it was, all we could do was wave and scream, as loud as our sawdust throats would permit.

The helicopter was soon close enough that the roar of its rotor blades made even our shouting, redundant. Over a loudspeaker, a voice began to bark instructions. Instantly, my stomach lurched. I didn't understand the language, but it sounded like Russian.

Dr. Jang, however, did. "Get ready," she yelled at us, "Get ready, they are sending a ladder. Sacha and Atlanta, you two go first."

I heard a couple of the kids asking, "Are they speaking Russian?" and "Why are we being rescued by Russians?"

A bright yellow beam suddenly flooded down from the helicopter, lighting up a descending rope ladder and about half of the raft.

Behind me I felt a hand on my shoulder. Then in my mind I heard Sacha say, *Artem Atlas is with these guys. Don't say anything, though. If Jang is sending me and Atlanta first, then maybe you are right about us being the cargo. Which means she thinks these are her people. But she might still figure it out and try something.*

Someone needed to answer the kids' questions. "Because we've drifted near to Russia," I told them. If I managed to keep my voice calm, it was by sheer effort of will. "I guess it's their version of the Coast Guard."

The boy who had first asked the question was skinny and short. I felt a pang of sorrow when I remembered the face of the young girl who usually paired with him, right until both were anxiously waiting their turn to climb onto the flybridge. *Must have been*

Haley Stokes, I thought. Had they come to the expedition together, only for him to watch her drown?

I bent down and spoke close to his ear. "What's your name?"

"Jai."

"Jai, don't worry. We won't stay long."

Don't act so confident, Sacha warned. The thought felt urgent. *We can't let Jang find out what's happening. Not yet.*

I longed to ask him whether he or Atlanta had communicated telepathically with Dr. Jang. Had they learned anything? But I managed to keep any snark to myself. It was impossible not to feel some resentment at the difference between me and the three two-dubs; they could talk with their minds and I couldn't, yet they insisted on doing it right in front of me and also, other people who were blissfully unaware.

"Voices in your head again?" Kenzie murmured into my ear. "Something going on that I should know about?"

I turned to face him and held his gaze for several seconds, directing my thoughts at him. *You must have a sixth sense, cause you're usually spot-on with these intuitions.*

It was useless of course. We were both, basically, 'mundanes,' and had no ability to share telepathic thoughts. Kenzie merely regarded me with a kind of mellow astonishment. I pulled away from him and turned my attention to the rope ladder that now dangled tantalizingly close to the opposite side of the raft.

Seeing it, Dr. Jang pushed her way past both Jai and Atlanta, positioning herself as close as possible. It was no use; she couldn't reach the end of the rope ladder. Between Atlanta, Delilah and Nathan, Dr. Jang was the shortest. Realizing this, she grabbed Nathan's hands and insisted that he lift her up onto his shoulders.

But Atlanta grabbed Jai at once and within seconds he was sitting on their shoulders, arms wrapped tightly around his legs. Nathan and Sacha grabbed hold of Atlanta to stabilize them. After a minute I heard Jai cry out "Got it!"

"Good job, Jai," declared Dr. Jang. "Hand the ladder over to me. It's best if I go up first, so I can explain to them what we need."

But once again, Jang's demand was ignored. After a brief struggle, I heard Sacha in my head. *I'm going first. Follow my lead, all right? I'll play along with Jang's plan, let her think our rescuers are on her side. Make sure everyone gets into the helicopter.*

Over the next few minutes, thick gray clouds rolled across the sky. It began to rain. Within seconds the driving downpour made it impossible to look up without getting an eyeful of water. Dr. Jang couldn't prevent Atlanta from climbing up the rope ladder after Sacha, but as Jai grabbed the ladder to go next, she snatched it from him and made her way up to the helicopter.

Jai seemed understandably dejected. I went over to him, right away. "You're next. Promise."

Jai went next, then Nathan, Delilah, then the three younger kids, whose names I hadn't yet learned. Hope is a powerful drug, because over the next few minutes I became infused with levels of energy that had not existed until we'd heard that helicopter. It struck me then, how crappy it was that I'd gotten to the point of almost-death alongside kids whose names I didn't yet know. I made a point to ask each one their name as I helped them onto the rope ladder.

Oliver, Maddie and Ashtyn.

Kenzie and I were the last two left on the raft. By now, we were once again soaked to the bone. Despite the hope I felt, the cold eating its way into me and turning my bones to ice, had become impossible to ignore. Moreover, I'd been too preoccupied with the job of getting everyone onto the ladder to notice that the waves were now strong enough to make staying on the raft into a serious challenge.

We tucked the toes of our boots beneath taut ropes, which crisscrossed the raft's base. Somewhat immobilized there, it took us a while to catch the end of the rope ladder – the violent motion of the raft made it seem like it was swinging like a pendulum.

What's going on asked Sacha in my head. I tried to ignore him. One-way communication is seriously annoying, especially when you can't ask them to shut up.

"You go next," shouted Kenzie.

"No. I promised I'd watch everyone get on the ladder."

Kenzie gazed at me, bewildered and hurt, water streaming down his face like tears. "Promised *who*?" he asked, head shaking, his eyes full of betrayal. "It's never going to be me, is it?" Firmly, he placed the end of the rope ladder into my hands. "Couldn't live with myself if I left you down here. Can you give me that, at least?"

After one final reluctant nod at Kenzie, I pulled on the ladder. Eyes closed, I began to climb, afraid to look down, the one glimpse I caught of the foaming black waves more than enough to put me off looking again. When I was about halfway up, I became aware of voices above me, screaming their alarm. Instinctively I froze, clinging to every inch of the ladder that I could grip onto.

It's Kenzie, said Sacha's voice in my head. *The waves just flipped the raft again. I'm so sorry, Padi. He's lost. But you aren't. Please, just focus on climbing the rest of the way.*

I couldn't move, could only look down in terror as the raft slowly righted itself. Slightly more than halfway over, it seemed to pause, as if the weight of the water inside the raft was dragging it down. The sight was paralyzing, my mind struggled to deal with what I was seeing. If Kenzie's feet were still tucked into the ropes on the base, he'd drown.

This could not be the end of Kenzie. I would never smile again if that happened. Part of me would remain in this moment, forever lost with him in the sea's black maw.

Climb, climb! insisted Sacha. Atlanta's telepathic voice joined in. I ignored them, instead concentrating on the shimmer of a new idea that was occurring to me.

If Kenzie was still tethered to the base of the raft, he could hold his breath long enough to free himself, and then use the ropes as a guideline to climb out from underneath. The raft might still sink, but it'd take on a lot of water, first. Every minute would extend our time to save him.

That tiny scrap of hope was enough to unfreeze my muscles. Climbing once again, I surveyed the water below for any sign of Kenzie. By now, a minute had passed. There was no time to waste. I lifted my right foot free of the ladder and prepared the left foot to float away, too. Then I let go of the ropes and plummeted.

THIRTY-SEVEN

RESCUE

A second later, I plunged yet again into frothing, shockingly cold sea water. I'd fallen almost twenty feet and sunk deep enough that when I surfaced, I couldn't catch my breath.

Luckily, by the time I resurfaced, Kenzie had swum close enough that I could hear him shouting, "It's just the cold-water shock, Padi, it's just cold. Easy, easy, you can breathe."

When my lungs began to work again, I clutched at him. "I found you," I repeated over and over against his face. "Not going without you."

He pulled away. "They were going without me?"

"Thought you were trapped… underneath the raft."

"Yeah, I *was*, didn't like the idea of dying though…" he began. The helicopter's spotlight caught us, briefly. For a moment, I saw the way Kenzie looked at me, with a tender reverence I'd never seen from anyone else. A wave lifted us both and we clung to each other. The light beam drifted away from us and towards the raft, which was about ten yards away. Then it tracked back to us, as if to show us the path we had to take.

Kenzie brushed a soaking wet lock of hair out of my eyes. "Did you come back for me?" he asked, wonderingly.

I glanced in the direction of the raft. Maybe it was my imagination, but it seemed to be drifting further away. Between gasps for breath, I replied, "Of course I came back for you, dummy."

And I thought, *I got you into all of this madness. I'm responsible.*

Another wave tugged at us, almost dragging us apart. Struggling to keep our heads above water, we interlaced fingers, so we'd stay connected.

"I'd follow you anywhere," he told me.

"Then follow me back into the raft."

From above, we heard the shouted encouragements of the survivors of our group, yelling at us, urging us to reach the raft, and then to climb in. Kenzie let me brace both feet against his shoulders to help me scramble over the high edge of the now upturned raft. Once I was inside, I offered him both arms, heaved until he slithered onto the raft, landing him as if he were an exhausted tuna.

The very last thing I wanted to do then was to climb up a rope ladder and into the belly of a hovering helicopter. Yet somehow, we found the strength, urged on by yells of encouragement from our expedition companions in the helicopter and in my head, unbroken reassurance from Sacha.

By the time we both collapsed on the floor of the chopper, I was done. No more energy. All I could manage was to listen.

Dr. Jang was speaking fluently, Russian, I guessed. She asked something of an elderly Russian man seated inside the passenger section, where Kenzie and I now lay, exhausted, on the floor. When the elderly Russian replied in English, I began quietly to smile. If I'd had the energy, I would have rolled onto my side, for a chance to watch Dr. Jang's reaction to his spoken English. It must have been her first clue that these were not the Russians she was looking for.

"We are taking you back to Saint Paul Island," he announced. I guessed that introductions had been made minutes ago, probably while Kenzie and I had been struggling in the sea. Sacha was strapped into a seat next to the window and I was facing away from him, yet he kept up the steady background of thoughts.

Ooh, I can literally see Jang figuring it out in real time. No, she is not happy, not a bit.

Then my mind was blasted by a thought that was filled with pure rage.

This changes nothing.

I didn't realize this was from Jang, until Sacha followed up in my mind.

Oh wow. Jang is one angry two-dub.

Then Atlanta chimed in. *This changes nothing. Sure, lady.*

Another voice was in my head next, someone I'd never heard from before.

Veronica? I'm so glad to meet you. You did a very brave thing there, going back for your friend.

I heaved myself around, groaning as I turned to look. Was the man whose telepathic voice I'd just heard, the guy who was sitting behind me? He was crouching over me, on the floor of the passenger section of the helicopter, one hand reaching tentatively to touch the side of my face. I saw him clearly then – a man with thin white hair cropped in a military style. His face was wreathed in lines, tanned skin and heavy-lidded eyes that stared at me with a mixture of curiosity and delight.

You are able to hear me, yes? Nod if you can, my dear.

I took a breath and nodded twice. "I'm so tired," I managed to say.

The elderly man chuckled. He must have been fit for his age because he was apparently pretty comfortable in a squatting position. *My name is Artem*, he told me. *And you are not only very courageous, my dear, but fortunate. I have never known a telepath whose thoughts could reach so far as young Sacha.*

Thanks, Uncle, I heard Sacha say in my head. *But pretty soon, it'll be all the rage. Any Generation Six telepath can do it.*

How many are you? he questioned. *Generation Six, I mean.*

Maxim, me, Nikita and Ellya. Nik and Ely are only six years old. They're with Maxim.

This was news to me. Maxim hadn't mentioned that any of the little kids were also 'Gen 6.' Now that I thought about it, it seemed obvious. I should have guessed that the list of things Maxim had yet to tell me, was likely to keep growing.

I've been honest enough in this account for you to understand that I couldn't easily struggle against my feelings for Maxim. The same logic surely applied to Kenzie, however. He should have walked away from me, the minute I told him I was getting on a plane to Mexico without telling his moms, the two people who'd taken care of me since my parents had gone away.

But just like me with Maxim, poor Kenzie was all in.

THIRTY-EIGHT

ROUV

I must have passed out, because I don't remember anything more, until the rescue helicopter landed. After being roused gently from my sleep by Sacha, I was the last to leave the chopper. They took me to a room in the tiny airport, where a variety of warm clothing had been laid out on a bench. I changed out of the all-black clothing we'd worn for our aborted mission, and which was still damp after so many hours in cold water, selecting soft blue jeans and thermal socks, a thermal undershirt and fleece.

My entire body ached, but other than that I was fine. They gave me Advil for the aches and something to make me sleep, which I did for a solid ten hours. I woke up with a banging head, popped two more Advil and got to my feet, searching for the others.

Sacha and Atlanta had changed while I was still asleep, they had on warm-looking thermal jackets, trousers and sneakers. I asked after Kenzie. He'd been taken to a hypothermia unit to be checked over. Atlanta thought he'd probably be all right – he'd only been in the water a few minutes longer than me, but he'd shown signs of shock, so they wanted to be certain. I asked after the other kids.

"All taken to the hospital. They called all the parents and guardians. People are coming to collect them."

My throat felt dry, raspy. *Not Haley's. Not Sandro's.* I didn't even want to imagine what it must have been like, to make those phone calls or to receive them.

When I felt awake enough, the three of us stepped out of the airport building that was little more than a hut, and onto the asphalt. Thirty yards away, two police cars were parked, one with blue light still flashing. Beside them, three armed police were leading Dr. Jang away.

"You were right," I commented to Sacha. "She was a traitor. Or a spy. One of those."

Sacha shot me a curious look. "You mean *you* were right. You're the one who first suspected her."

I couldn't really remember. "Anyhow, it felt like a team effort. So… What happens now? Where are we?"

"Back on Saint Paul," Sacha said. "Artem Atlas arranged it all. Called Aleks and they figured it out. Called the cops, everything."

Nodding, I tried to think of anything I'd forgotten. "Lyle Prince?"

Atlanta shook their head. They were quieter than usual, noticeably subdued. At the time, I didn't think much about it. "No sign of him. He wasn't expecting us back today, though."

"Figures," I said, sourly. "You think he's another mole, like Susie Jang?"

Sacha replied with a helpless shrug. "Could be. Or maybe he's just lousy at taking care of his assets."

"What about the gas explosion? Are they blaming that on the USA? Has it led to war, or whatever?"

His expression became tight, grim. "I don't know the latest details. But, yeah, not very optimistic."

"Then we really failed," I said dolefully, with a glance at Atlanta, who returned my glum look. "I feel like... There must be something we can do. I mean, we were there, we saw the thing that put a hole in the *Perseus.*"

Sacha put his head on one side. "Really?"

"You saying you don't believe me?"

"No, no," he said, suddenly unsure.

"It's not that," Atlanta added. They both seemed eager to reassure me.

I took a slow, deep breath and forced it into my chest, where I held it for several seconds, trying to calm the rage that was threatening to overtake me. I wanted to speak but feared I'd sound incoherent.

"This..." I began. I shook my head, and a despairing chuckle escaped me. "You think it can end this way? No. No," I repeated, louder. "That CIA woman," I stumbled, barely able to remember her name. Nothing that happened before the *Perseus* went down seemed to matter anymore. "Margo Daniels," I said after a few seconds. "Daniels will not let this be the end. Not for me, not for Kenzie and definitely not for the two of you. You... *We* sold ourselves to that woman, to the CIA. We owe them a completed operation, if we don't give them that, they will never leave us alone. They own us now; don't you get that?"

Sacha watched me for a moment, seemingly shocked by my outburst. But then he blinked a couple of times and gave a smile so inscrutable, it reminded me of his brother.

"Let's say you're right. What did you have in mind?"

I recoiled, surprised at his abrupt question. To be honest, I'd expected some pushback on everything else I'd said. But really, I had no concrete plan. When did that ever stop me?

"There has to be something," I repeated, stalling for time.

Sacha continued to watch me, now with a calm yet non-threatening silence. He didn't doubt me, I realized. He was simply waiting.

"I saw a goddamn underwater drone, ROUV thingy, okay?" I insisted. "It came right up to the *Perseus* and planted something on its hull. That's the only explanation for what happened. Because we weren't torpedoed, were we? We would have felt that I'm pretty sure."

Sacha and Atlanta agreed that we almost certainly had not been torpedoed. "All right let's say it was another ROUV," Atlanta suggested. "Then, what?"

"It's a decent enough theory," Sacha admitted.

I sniffed in derision. "It's better than that. Anything operated remotely has to have some sort of range, right? So presumably, whoever is controlling it has to be within a certain distance?"

As I spoke, a car drove up and parked close. The passenger door opened, and Kenzie stepped out. He looked a tad fragile but otherwise, well. A thick, blue fleece blanket was draped over his shoulders and swaddling his arms. I rushed over and hugged him tightly.

Kenzie smiled, a little bashful, struggling uselessly to move his arms beneath the blanket so that he could return my hug. "I'm good, I'm fine. Catch me up, where are we?"

Sacha brought him up to speed. Kenzie liked my theory. "You thought of that, Padi? Or should I say 'Pad-awan?' I'm loving my influence, for you."

I punched his arm. "Ha, very humorous. Funny, funny guy."

He beamed. "Yeah, I am. And you know what? You're right about the ROUV having a range, because they are usually operated via a tether cable. But we can look it up. Do you remember how big it was? The color? Any distinguishing features?"

I narrowed my eyes briefly, trying to recall the fleeting image of the sleek vessel I'd briefly glimpsed alongside the *Perseus*, to remember every detail, including the shiver that seeing it had sent through me. "It was maybe three yards long? No more than that. And it was black."

Sacha whipped out his phone and began searching. Then he showed me a picture of a remote-operated underwater drone. The craft was labeled BlueROV2. "Did it look like that?"

I squinted again. "Maybe. Yeah, basically."

Kenzie shucked off the blanket enough to release his right hand, which he opened. "Gimme your phone, Sacha." Sacha obliged and Kenzie scrolled the screen awhile, reading several seconds until he crowed, "I'm right! The range is less than a thousand feet."

"If we can calculate where the *Perseus* was when it went down," I reasoned, "then we can create a search range for the yacht, we can narrow down where the person was, who remote-operated any underwater drone."

Atlanta seemed to be confused. "How can we find out where the boat was when it went down?

There's no black box and even if there is, it's at the bottom of the ocean."

"We can find out where it went down," I pointed out. "Doctor Jang sent out a mayday message, before we abandoned ship."

"But she probably sent that to Russians, or North Koreans. Not to anyone in Saint Paul, or to any person we can easily reach," Kenzie said, his mood suddenly low. "Think about it, if she'd made that call to anyone in Saint Paul, we'd have been rescued sooner. We're screwed."

Adamantly, I shook my head. "There has to be a way. Satellite data, something. Or just the position where they found our raft – that has to be close enough. It's not like that wave moved us so very far. Also, we know which direction the wave came from, so we can guess which side of it we were on."

All three were briefly silent until, impressed, Sacha admitted, "That makes sense, Padi. It should be possible to find out where the *Perseus* went down."

"Even so," Atlanta said, "that leaves a search area of, let's see, *pi* times a radius of a thousand feet squared. That's still a pretty large chunk of ocean to search."

Kenzie thought for a second and then slowly, a smile spread across his face. "But the Bering Sea is hardly a busy shipping area. We should be able to find data on what boats were registered in the area."

"What do you mean, 'registered'?" asked Sacha. "You think someone who is planning on taking out a yacht and then blowing up a gas compressor station, is likely to register their travel plans with the local mayor's office?"

"Okay then," snapped Kenzie. "Satellite data cross-referenced with local registered boats."

Sacha replied with a challenging thrust of his chin. "And what will you do? Hack into the databases?"

"Probably could," Kenzie acknowledged, all fake modesty. "But in this case, I don't think we'll need to." He grinned. "My dudes, Padi said it: we work for the CIA! We can get into those kinds of databases, no problemo."

THIRTY-NINE

RESISTANCE

People on boats in the vicinity of St. George Island heard an explosion at the gas compressor station. Bizarrely (to me at least), this happened at 11:31, only three hours before we'd been rescued. Prior to the explosion, we'd been in the raft for at least five hours. Before that, two hours trying to stay dry in the sinking *Perseus*. Altogether, it put our total time struggling to survive at sea at around ten hours.

It was now the following day, around one-thirty in the morning, but my body clock was messed up. Someone could have told me it was pretty much any time they chose, and I couldn't have corrected them.

Artem Atlas's priority was obviously Sacha and Atlanta. He wanted to get them to safety and thoroughly checked over, so that any hypothermia could be treated. But after Sacha introduced him to me, something shifted.

Artem beamed and patted me once on the shoulder. "A one-way telepath, really? How fascinating to meet you, Veronica."

"I prefer Roni."

In an excitable gesture, he clapped a palm to his cheek. "Oh yes! Then 'Roni' it is! You know, you one-ways are so very valuable to us. You make us feel...

connected. Yes, that's the word. Connected to the normal world." Abruptly, his manner switched, became brisk, business-like. "Now; it is time you rested. All of you. Hot soup, chocolate and more sleep." A broad grin appeared on his leathery, clean-shaven face. "Yes?"

"No," I countered. "We need to act fast, while there's still some evidence."

He seemed bummed that I would reject such an enticing offer. "*No?*"

"I mean, no for me and Sacha and Kenzie... and Atlanta. But the kids, yeah, they should definitely do all of that."

He folded both arms across his chest, rocking back and forth on the balls of his feet as he assessed me. "I see. And what's so important that warmth and sustenance can wait?"

"We had a mission," I tell him, standing up straight and tall, my face just a few inches from his. "The Czar wants my country blamed for blowing up that gas compressor station."

"Well, it is rather serious," he said. "An environmental crime. Millions of tons of carbon released into the atmosphere, just like that."

Out of the corner of my eye, I saw Kenzie scowling. What Artem said was true, but I'm not sure that Kenzie had ever really thought about that side of pipeline destruction.

"That's bad," I agreed, nodding. "But it's not the point, is it?"

Artem seemed to be humoring me. "And what *is* the point?"

Exasperated, I shrugged my shoulders. "We were supposed to prevent the whole thing, the 'false flag' plot. Thanks to Doctor Jang, our whole mission was a bust. But there might still be time to find out what *really* happened. Then maybe..." I took a deep breath and sighed. "I don't know if we can do it, but there's a plan. We have to resist the Chekists! Why should they get to spread a lie? We came to *stop* them from doing that. While there's still a chance we can do it, we totally should."

For a few seconds Artem regarded me with skepticism, as if he half-suspected I was joking. Then he clapped a heavy palm onto my shoulder and with an expression as grave as any I'd seen from him, he said, "I am going to remember you, Roni Padilla. There aren't too many people in this world that will refuse to give up."

I caught his tone and looked from Sacha to Kenzie to Atlanta. "It's not just me who wants to complete the operation," I told him, gesturing with a nod at my friends. "Ask any one of them."

I guessed any reply he got from Sacha and Atlanta was telepathic because they said nothing. On the other hand, Kenzie nodded firmly, moving to stand at my side in solidarity.

"Padi has it right," he said. "We can do this. We already sent the information, got the CIA to run searches on the shipping databases, so we have a pretty good idea where to find whoever pulled this stunt. And yeah, fair to say that I'm generally the first one to blame the CIA for fuckery like this. But in this case, we can be pretty sure it was Chekists, or their allies, probably the North Koreans, with Doctor Jang being involved."

"Even without the geopolitics, we'd do it for Haley Stokes, for Sandro and Gary Killarney," I added, stubbornly. "Someone has to take responsibility for their deaths."

Artem didn't need any more persuasion. He found us the equipment we'd asked for – one small flashlight apiece and black plastic trash can liners that we'd use to bag any evidence we collected. Then he led us to a rigid inflatable boat – he referred to it as a 'RIB' – that was moored a little farther along the pier from where the *Perseus* had picked us up.

We piled in, put on the life vests that were on the floor of the boat, and sat back as he steered the boat out of the harbor. The sky had dramatically cleared and from low in the sky, an almost-full moon was rising. The sun wouldn't rise for another two hours, but thanks to the moonlight and the powerful headlamps of the RIB, visibility ahead was good.

Steering by coordinates Lyle Prince's contact at the CIA had returned to Kenzie as the location from where the ROUV had been controlled, the boat headed back towards the coast of Siberia, almost parallel with St. George Island. As we approached the target, he cut the headlights, cut the engine and our RIB floated under its own momentum, making only light splashes as it sidled up to a completely silhouetted yacht, slightly longer than the *Perseus*.

It had to be the *Cassiopeia*.

There was no sound or light coming from the yacht. The silence was infectious. As I sensed Sacha's thoughts reaching out to me, I stretched my hand to touch Kenzie so that he wouldn't feel isolated. I'd finally noticed that he was usually aware when a telepathic conversation was going on around him. I knew how badly it sucked to sense that happening around you, and I didn't like to see him uncomfortable.

They haven't left! There's someone on the yacht. Two people. Both telepaths, Sacha said inside my mind. There was just enough moonlight by which to notice that Atlanta and Artem nodded in agreement. *Definitely, two.*

"What are they still doing there? They were supposed to have gone by now," I gasped, aloud. "What can we do? There's no way we can complete the operation."

"Hey, what's going on?" Kenzie demanded. "D'you mean, there are people on board the *Cassiopeia*? What the hell?"

A one-dub and a two-dub, Sacha broadcast. For a long moment there were no more thoughts, just five people peering at each other in the darkness. Then he seemed to stand a little taller, his right hand raised slightly, the fist clenched. *I can take them out.*

"Tell me! What's going on?" whispered Kenzie.

Sacha, Atlanta and Artem turned to him with glances of poorly disguised derision. My fists clenched; sympathy for Kenzie, anger at their arrogance and inability to hide it.

In a very low voice, Sacha said, "There's a two-dub inside, broadcasting to their partner. I can deal with them," he breathed, quiet but confident. He glanced at me briefly, a wary look in his eye. "They don't know we're here – yet. But I should probably still stay close to Roni, so I can block any psi interference."

I frowned. "Interference? Like, what, what could they do? Is this what you meant when you talked about 'bad things'?"

Sacha gave a terse nod and looked away now, unable to meet my eye as he murmured, "I won't let them harm you."

My throat tightened. "Harm me, how?"

Alarm sounded in Kenzie's voice, too. "Exactly *what* are you going to do?"

But Sacha didn't answer either question. Instead, he closed his eyes and sank slowly to the floor of the RIB, until he was sitting cross-legged there, arms outstretched, one hand resting lightly on the inflated edge.

Kenzie's voice rose ever so slightly. "Seriously. Is *anyone* gonna tell me what's happening?"

Mystified, but with gradually increasing anxiety, I watched Sacha for several long minutes, saw how he seemed to slow down time by regulating his breathing, saw how his chest rose and fell as the breaths deepened. Then deliberately, almost fearfully, he opened his eyes and nodded, once. "It's done."

And then from somewhere deep inside the *Cassiopeia's* accommodation cabin, the screaming began.

At the sound of this, a look of panic crossed Sacha's face. Then, gazing high into the sky his features suddenly relaxed, as though he'd been injected with powerful meds during some major pain episode.

I looked up too, watched ghostly waves of soft greenish light slowly ripple across the sky. Not as bright or colorful as photos you see, but moving smoothly, surreal and magical, like the sky was alive and breathing. It felt unreal, totally mesmerizing.

"The Northern Lights," Sacha said, sounding exhausted, practically gasping the words out. "Finally, I get to see them."

FORTY

One-dub, Two-dub

Like so many others that terrible day last year, I ended up watching multiple videos of the assassination of two front-runners in a special election for the United States Senate.

'You loved to see it,' the murderers boasted on social media, in posts they'd chillingly enough, scheduled in the hours before the attack. *We came, we saw, we conquered.'*

Until that day – as naïve as it might seem now – I truly believed that most regular people hated violence. But no. That day, the violence was the point. It erupted in a bloodbath, under the glare of a hundred cameras.

'This is what commitment looks like.'

All six killers were shot to death by cops, of course, one firing off bullets until the last. So, we never found out what motivated them. Most assume it was money – had the Czar transferred millions to secret bank accounts set up for their families? If so, those folk would never get near the money – not under a fierce glare of the FBI.

The other suggestion was that they'd been brainwashed. *Mind-hacked.* The Czar's greatest triumph so far in the 'Mind Game' – a psyop that turned six apparently random, regular US citizens into an armed unit with one, highly determined aim: to shift the balance of power in the House. The next candidate in line was rumored to be a Kremlin puppet, and after the front-runners were gotten rid of, would have given control of the House to the pro-Ilyin faction of the US Senate.

I've seen even more videos since then, and photos of the dreadful aftermath. The crowds of the injured. Blood on nearby walls, despair and panic.

I had wondered often about what it'd been like for the cops and emergency workers that day. Did the scenes I'd watched on screen tell the whole story? But imagination alone cannot take you to places like that, as I discovered, when Sacha, Atlanta, Kenzie and I boarded the *Cassiopeia*.

When you witness the aftermath of violence with the benefit of all five senses, there's another level to the experience. The anguished sound of survivors sobbing, desperate and heartbroken, begging to be moved, to be helped, crying about the pain. Slinking aboard the *Cassiopeia*, I caught a tang of iron in the air. I stepped onto the deck and felt something slick and sticky underfoot, a pool of blood. That's when my thoughts returned to the day when we'd all watched the group of assassins known as the 'Hand of Peter' put into action one of the deadliest plots ever hatched against our nation.

The screams we'd heard while still on the RIB, had died down by the time we'd boarded the *Cassiopeia*. In all, they'd lasted less than a minute. Panicked, low screams, a roar of anger then anguish, pain. Now it was silent, again. I'd already heard enough to be filled with dread as we took our first steps onto the deck of the 'decoy' yacht.

We moved stealthily toward the aft deck, until we arrived at the saloon. Its door slid open easily, unlocked. No sign of anyone there, nor in the galley. Taking the lead into the pilothouse, I paused before the stairway that led to the lower deck. "Down? Or not?"

Beside me, Sacha grabbed my arm.

I whispered, "What?"

He didn't answer, just paused, his hand on my arm suddenly tense, his whole body alert, as if listening. A chilling expression settled onto his face. "We shouldn't go down."

There was something oddly final about his statement. It was more than a suggestion.

"But we have to," Kenzie said, simply. He switched on his flashlight and turned it onto Sacha, for a moment observing him with almost dispassionate curiosity.

So far, we'd managed to find our way with only starlight and the neon green lick of Northern Lights. The lower deck, however, was a gaping maw into darkness. I felt inside my jacket for the mini flashlight. Kenzie was right; we had to go downstairs. Why else were we here?

Kenzie advanced down the staircase. I made to follow, but Sacha and Atlanta held back. To my astonishment, abruptly, Sacha swayed. 'Swooned' might even be more accurate. He caught himself on the edge of the deck controls, one hand grabbed the steering wheel and managed a controlled fall onto the deck. He crouched there, both arms wrapped around his head.

"What's wrong?" I demanded. Sacha didn't reply, instead tightened fingers against his scalp, interlacing them. I faced Atlanta. "Is he having a panic attack?"

Atlanta couldn't seem to answer. Their eyes moved rapidly, as if staving off a panic attack of their own.

Kenzie and I stalled; all our momentum lost. I repeated, "What's wrong, what happened?"

Atlanta didn't budge, made no movement toward Sacha, almost as if he were suddenly contagious. "Don't go down there," they instructed me and Kenzie. "You won't like it."

"What the heck is going on with you two?" Kenzie raged. "We can't leave without removing the evidence!" He barged past me on the narrow stairway and disappeared into the cabin below.

Atlanta called after him, "Remember, I warned you."

We exchanged a brief look then, Atlanta and I. Throwing back my shoulders, I glared at Sacha. "What did you do?"

Even then, I sensed that Sacha was responsible. A wave of *déjà-vu* hit me as I recalled the sight of those helicopters in Cuba suddenly crashing into each other. Jaguar had 'clouded' the pilot's mind and seconds later, they and their passengers were roasted in metal cabins when they plunged to the forest floor.

Jaguar – Maxim – had killed those people. I'd known it at the time, thought about it since, but always rationalized it. Because a telepath couldn't make anyone do anything they didn't deep down want to do, right? But I'd never asked what happened to people when their minds were 'clouded.' I didn't want to know.

Firing a defiant stare at Atlanta, I ran downstairs. The door to the main bedroom had been thrown wide open. That's when the stink hit me. The deadly trio, markers of a violent death, blood, pee and shit.

One of the people lay across the bed, her head lolling over the edge, eyes like black-and-white marble and very dead. For a moment, I couldn't see what had killed her, until I saw that the bed cover wasn't bright red – it was white, at least, it was white on the half of the bed that hadn't been soaked with the woman's blood. Draped across her chest, her left hand still held a long kitchen knife.

From behind the double bed, next to the window I heard a long, drawn-out groan from a second person. I could only see the legs of the survivor, jean-clad and barely moving, while the rest of him lay out of view, behind the bed.

Two people in the cabin; one was dead, one still clung to life. Turning my head slightly, I saw Kenzie standing a little way back, beside the open door to an en-suite. He appeared stricken, paralyzed by the sight of the dead woman lying on the bed, in a pool of her own blood.

"Suicide…?" Kenzie murmured, his voice echoing with disbelief.

I closed my eyes then, willed it all to vanish. All of it, everything. Except Kenzie and me.

We could have been happy. We had a good life, back before I started asking so many difficult questions. Before my curiosity shattered our peace. We could still be blind, blissfully ignorant of daunting forces that swirled in the geopolitical undercurrents of our world.

Yet I'd made my choice. Kenzie and I had walked into this with eyes open. After all, nothing that wasn't fundamentally dreadful could lurk behind a child-trafficking operation such as the international exchange of 'unicorns.' Maybe we didn't know back then, the degree of awfulness, but we knew it'd be grim. In Cuba,

I'd seen it clearly in the explosion of those colliding helicopters, yet I'd shielded myself from the reality.

I forced myself to approach the man who lay groaning on the floor. When I was almost within range of any kick he might suddenly attempt, I said loudly, "What can we do to help?"

Don't approach the two-dub. Atlanta's voice was suddenly in my mind. *They could be dangerous.*

I took a step back.

"Why," groaned the man on the floor. He began to kick the wall repeatedly and with increasing desperation. "Why, why, why, why, why, why?"

Kenzie handed me a plastic bag. "Get everything." He sounded flat, disconnected. "All the tech, all the paperwork. Not just stuff written in English, get it all."

I took the bag. "You go," I told him, gently. "I'll do this room."

The light from Kenzie's flashlight dazzled and I couldn't see his face, but in his reply, I heard fierce anger and resolve. "No. We should make *him* do it. Sacha." His voice shook. "He did this to them, didn't he?" He slapped the wall, and his voice cracked. "Make him do it!"

FORTY-ONE

BLOWBACK

On our return to St. Paul, we brought Artem Atlas to the nearby house, which Prince had rented for our operation prep. Finding it locked, he'd broken in using an old school method of crowbarring open a window. He'd gone directly to the kitchen, raided the fridge looking for something to fry for breakfast, cooked up apple fritters and whipped cream with berries.

To avoid any listening devices that Prince might have set up inside the house, Artem had us carry the bowls of fritters and cream outside to a nearby picnic area that looked out onto the sea. The place was deserted. We assembled around a wooden table, our last time as a team, taking turns to dip our fritters in the bowl of cream.

As the sun climbed higher above the remote Alaskan island, a gentle haze hung over the picnic area, occasionally clearing to reveal glimpses of the vast Bering Sea. Beyond, the sky had begun to clear, casting a serene ambiance over the nearby harbor. Now that nature's quiet majesty had returned, the violence of last night seemed like a bad dream.

Artem stood to one side as the four of us enjoyed the breakfast he'd served up.

"Apple pancakes and sweet cream," Artem said, sighing blissfully. "I ate this every day through the winters of my childhood, in Yakutia." Then he waited, arms folded as we prepared to say goodbye to Sacha and Atlanta. After a glance at Sacha, who hadn't said a word since the *Cassiopeia*, his mood seemed to shift abruptly. He leaned across the table, took another fritter, dipped it in cream and stepped back. "Now, I will leave you for a moment. Make a nice farewell, you have achieved something important today. Be proud!"

As he took off, strolling away into the cool, early morning breeze, I looked at Atlanta.

"Farewell?"

Atlanta took a fritter, eyes downcast. "Sacha and I are going with Artem. Back to the Atlas Group."

I stared in confusion. "Can't we all go back together, with Lyle Prince? He'll be here in, like, an hour."

"They're not going back to the US," Kenzie said, evenly. He looked Atlanta in the eye. "That tracks, doesn't it? And you can't tell us where you're going, either. Because we might tell the CIA."

Neither Sacha nor Atlanta said anything, but their silence pretty much confirmed it. I couldn't tell you if they felt good about this, just that they'd become guarded around the whole subject. Disappearing back into the ether, probably.

"Well," I said, with a humorless smirk at both, "I guess it was nice knowing you."

Sacha refused to look at me. Whatever distress he'd experienced on board the *Cassiopeia*, the acute stage seemed to have passed. Now, it was as though he'd gone into a lengthy reboot. I wondered where he'd land when it was over.

"At least tell us what you did to them," I said, my voice weary. "You owe us that, at least."

"We don't owe you anything," Atlanta said, sounding brittle. "Like you kept reminding us, you did all of this because CIA basically blackmailed you and Kenzie."

"Why did *you* do it, then?" I blurted. "Because Artem Atlas ordered it?"

To my surprise, Sacha finally spoke up. "Not Artem; Aleks Rubenovich Atlas. Artem had no part of this, until I found him with my long-range broadcast."

"Huh – welcome back, my dude!" Kenzie said, grinning. "And – didn't you tell us Aleks is his son?"

"Rubenovich means 'son of Ruben,'" Sacha said, softly. "So no, I didn't. I said he's Elena's son. Elena Atlas, who owned the house in Perm, Siberia."

I asked, "Who is Artem, then? I heard you call him 'Uncle.' Is he Aleks's brother?"

Sacha lifted his eyes to me and nodded. "He is. We didn't even know Artem was still alive. I think he's kind of a recluse. Anyway. You don't have to like that we did something for Aleks Rubenovich, it's really nothing to do with you. Atlanta and I owe our freedom to the Atlas Group."

I fixed my gaze on him then, refusing to let go. "What did you do to the people on that boat."

"They were Chekists," Sacha began, defensively. "Just look at the pistols we found on the boat. Pya – that's a standard Chekist gun. They weren't supposed to be there."

"Pya?" muttered Kenzie. "Never heard of it."

"Pistolet Yarygina – P-Ya. Also known as MP433 Grach. They were – are – Chekists."

Kenzie stared into the cream bowl and in a low voice said, "The woman who cut her own throat, she's not a Chekist. She's not anything, now. What did you do to the other one, the man? Sounded like he'd totally lost his marbles."

"Did you enjoy ruining CIA's plan, Kenzie?" Sacha said, his eyes shiny and hard, his tone dripping with accusation.

"What are you even talking about?" I turned to look at Kenzie, whose eyes had become secretive. "We did what they wanted – we removed the evidence."

Atlanta gave a stubborn shake of their head. "You removed *all* the evidence. Not just the evidence those Chekists planted to implicate the US."

Now I was even more confused. "They didn't tell us to leave evidence."

Firmly, Sacha shook his head. "Kenzie was supposed to replace the software on the laptop that controlled the drone. Remember? He was supposed to upload a hack that would have been full of Russian-originated code. False flags of CIA's making this time. Then, when investigators reached the *Cassiopeia*, they'd conclude that Chekists blew up the pipeline. Which would have exposed the Kremlin's 'false flag' plot against America. Why'd you do it, Kenzie? Why did you disobey?"

Kenzie had become calm, detached and expressionless as he returned Sacha's gaze. "Why didn't you stop me?"

Incensed, I ground the toe of my foot into the gravel. "And why didn't anyone tell me?"

Kenzie put a hand on mine. "I wanted to, believe me. But I also wanted to keep you out of trouble. When Daniels blows her stack – and she will – you can simply tell the truth – that we were so shocked by what we found in that cabin, we weren't thinking straight. We wanted out of there as fast as possible, so we just grabbed everything that wasn't nailed down."

The 'everything' now lay in neat, categorized piles on the bed in Prince's room. The laptop computer that'd controlled the bomb-laden ROUV, all the printed materials, identity documents (Russian and USA), cash (US dollars), and the two Pya pistols. While Kenzie and I had gathered the evidence for Lyle Prince, Sacha and Atlanta had dealt with the horror show in the master bedroom. They'd wrapped the dead body in the blood-soaked bed linens and left Artem to move it onto the RIB, as well as the traumatized two-dub. What he planned to do with both was at this point, anyone's guess.

"We did the right thing," Atlanta said. They sounded confident. "This way, no one will know for sure who blew up the pipeline. And that's the safest outcome. No premise for either side to start a war."

But Kenzie had a point – Margo Daniels would be ticked off, to put it mildly. She might even refuse to count the operation as completed and continue to hold over us, the threat of 'legal consequences' for our actions in Cuba, not to mention Kenzie's dalliance with climate vandalism.

"Daniels should worry more about her own organization," I commented. "The *Cassiopeia* was supposed to be deserted. That was part of the 'solid,' 'reliable' human intelligence she told us about. Which turned out to be junk. How come?"

Slowly, Sacha shook his head. "Things rarely go to plan."

I looked him in the eye. "Did you plan to kill someone today?"

He answered aloud, "I didn't." Then switched to telepathy as he implored, *No, Roni, please believe me. It was my first time doing that. I didn't know it would be so powerful.*

"It's called 'derangement,'" Atlanta said, speaking carefully. She seemed to check with Sacha before going on. "And 'somatization.' Only Gen Six telepaths can do it."

I swallowed. "*Derangement?* You drove them insane?!"

"The one-dub," he said, with a grim nod. "She didn't have defenses, unlike the two-dub. Him, I somatized. Made him feel sick, very sick. It's just psychosomatic pain, he'll be over it soon. I didn't know she'd kill herself, though. I had no idea it'd be that bad. Just meant to knock them off their game, so we could handle them, so they wouldn't be able to harm us."

I blinked a few times, trying to see some way out of this for us, some way that we hadn't been responsible for a death. His statement, '*So they wouldn't be able to harm us,*' was doing a lot of the work. After a moment, I said, "Then it was an accident? Just…" I gave a helpless, sad shrug. "Just *blowback?*"

The other three agreed at once, it had been a totally unintended consequence of Sacha's use of two abilities he'd never tested in a genuinely life-threatening situation. I nodded along with them, we finished our breakfast and then we hugged Sacha and Atlanta goodbye.

As I held him to me, I whispered in Sacha's ear, "I know this was rough on you. If you ever want to talk about it…?"

Still hugging me, Sacha replied. *Maybe one day. If I ever do, I'll leave a comment on your first podcast, the one about Rich Wonders. By the way, is Jaguar 'The Dream Thief'?*

Startled, I pulled away. "Is Jaguar... What?!"

With a rueful smile Sacha replied, *Better check your podcast comments, 'Chica Curiosa.' Someone else wants to talk.*

FORTY-TWO

WAITING FOR PRINCE

Sacha was right about Maxim's comment on my podcast. After he and Atlanta had left with Artem Atlas, Kenzie and I returned to the house to wait inside for Lyle Prince. Finding my phone in the bedroom the four of us had shared, I deleted the brief comment a few seconds after reading it.

This looks interesting. I may have something for you. The Dream Thief.

Perhaps Maxim could believe his comment appeared innocuous, just one more clueless person on the '*What Happened to the Santiagos?*' podcast. I couldn't, though. Now that I knew the CIA had been monitoring me for a while, everything looked sus to me. Sacha had guessed who 'Dream Thief' was, maybe Margo Daniels had, too.

Moreover, Maxim and I agreed to communicate via Telegram. So, what even *was* this podcast comment? If Maxim genuinely was trying to reach me, we'd need to find a new way to communicate.

For now, Kenzie and I had to assume that while we remained inside any property owned by the CIA, our words, actions and phones were all being monitored. The few phrases we'd managed to develop in our own private sign language, plus the hand signals Lyle Prince had taught us, were a start. Until we found time to develop it further, however, we could only communicate using pen and paper.

Prince had cleared out any paper we'd written on, in fact he'd removed pretty much all documents and equipment from the St. Paul house, including the blank sheets of paper, but I found a couple that had slipped under the nearby sofa, and a stray ballpoint pen in a kitchen drawer.

Kenzie and I managed to have what we hoped was a convincing, albeit fake, light-hearted conversation about ways to kill time until Prince arrived.

"How long do you think until Prince gets back?"

"Could be now, could be a while. Who knows?"

"What do you want to do until then?"

"We could make some more food."

"What do you wanna make?"

Meantime, our real conversation was conducted by scribbling in increasingly small writing on the two sheets of paper I'd managed to rescue from Prince's purge. We agreed to stick together in the event that Targeting Officer Daniels forced us to do another operation for the CIA. Our position would obviously be to consider it, given the not-so-veiled threats she'd made.

Compromise? Or coercion? I thought bitterly. There had to be better ways to get people to work for the CIA, but I had to admit it; we'd handed Margo Daniels one peach of an approach.

I told myself that we'd only accept a mission that we believed in, and hoped that Kenzie would agree, if it ever came to making that decision.

Not that they're likely to trust us with anything again, I wrote. *You literally put the kibosh on their plan, while blowing up a pipeline, which you wanted to do all along.*

Kenzie was pretty chill about the outcome, all told. There was room to argue that we'd held up our end of the deal, after all. If Prince hadn't been around to pick us up right away after the rescue and had therefore missed out on Sacha and Atlanta, that was on him.

"Tell me the truth," I mused, aloud, "Would you do another mission for Daniels?"

"Maybe," he replied, nodding. "Maybe I would, at that."

For myself, I don't know why I was even contemplating it. The adrenaline rush was a major high, for sure. I'd never tried extreme sports, never been drawn to that kind of thing. So, I really didn't know what it was like to have your life on the line, to know that you might be minutes or hours away from a painful, terrifying death. What we'd done in Cuba had been an absolute thrill, compared to what had happened to us here in Alaska. And yet both experiences had left me with a deep-seated hunger for more.

Finally, I admitted to myself that I wasn't just eager for information, not merely curious to solve a mystery. I had some other kind of risk-seeking pathology; the kind that makes you join the police or military or intelligence services. Even if the idea had occasionally crossed my mind, because of my parents' crimes and their connections to a range of hinky characters, I'd assumed this was off limits for me, that I'd never pass the background checks.

It hadn't occurred to me that their crimes might be the very reason I'd find the motivation to do it.

Thirty minutes passed and Prince still hadn't returned, although he'd texted both our phones to say he was on his way. We taped an empty cereal box over the broken window and left the house open, carrying our phones with us as we set off for a stroll. We figured Prince and his CIA buddies were tracking us anyway, so at least we could help them to find us.

Partway to the harbor, and without preamble or drama, Kenzie took my hand. It felt natural and comforting and as he gently squeezed it, I turned to him.

"I wish *we* were telepathic."

He smiled and squeezed back. "That'd be so frickin' awesome."

We didn't talk about what Sacha did to the Chekists on the boat – not yet. We didn't talk about Maxim, and I didn't tell Kenzie what Sacha had told me telepathically about the 'Dream Thief' message. I wasn't ready to talk about any of that.

We *did* talk about the beauty of St. Paul, the deep blue of the sea, the powder blue of the sky as it emptied of clouds, while the sun arced higher, and about the offshore wind farm whose turbines we spied, clustered like a horde of distant, sword-waving marauders approaching from the horizon.

"That's the future, right there," Kenzie told me, his face lit up with pride as he pointed them out. "Floating wind turbines. Renewables, baby."

I fell silent and gazed out to sea, which was now becalmed, like a vast blue lake. It was cool to think we'd maybe helped the world to take a step closer to a future without fossil fuels, without the influence of malign actors who wanted only power and riches.

Yet I was starting to get a sense of the depth of the struggle, to understand that what we'd achieved was a small victory, one battle in the vast and spreading 'Mind Game.'

A Message From The Author

Hello and thank you so much for reading the second book in *The Mind Game: Volume One*.

I hope you have enjoyed following Roni Padilla's journey into the world of spies, telepaths and watching her and Kenzie grapple with the wider issues at stake in their not-so-different fictional universe.

If you have enjoyed *False Flag*, please do post a review on Amazon and anywhere else you find your favorite reads, telling other readers what you liked about it. The best way for me to reach more readers is via word of mouth and happy readers!

And please sign up to my email newsletter to be the first to find out when new titles will be released, and to hear about special discounts and giveaways – go to **TheMGHarris.com** and click on **Newsletter**.

In the next installment, *Cyber Warrior*, Maxim Santiago reaches out to Roni once again. Max has a favor to ask – can she help an old buddy escape his North Korean handler? It doesn't sound all that dangerous, but of course, Roni suspects right away that there's more to it than meets the eye.

And when Margo Daniels of the CIA reaches out for another 'favor,' Roni is in a bit of a quandary. Dare she venture once again into the perilous 'Mind Game'?

About M.G. Harris

Born in Mexico, Maria Guadalupe "MG" Harris grew up in Manchester, England. She's been a massive *Doctor Who* and *Blake's 7* fan since childhood.

Her writing addiction began with B7 fanfic. Before being published she was a molecular biologist followed by a stint as an Internet entrepreneur.

MG has authored three book series for young readers. *The Joshua Files* (Scholastic Children's Books UK), which was translated into 17 foreign languages, *Gemini Force One* (Orion Children's Books) and a young adult crime trilogy, *Emancipated* (Harper Teen, as M.G. Reyes), as well as a novel for the Doctor Who universe – *Doctor Who - Doom's Day: Extraction Point* (Penguin RH).